I0618466

THE KINSMEN

BETWEEN GODS AND MORTALS

Pete Cruickshank

Pete Cruickshank

First published in the UK in 2013 by Pete Cruickshank

ISBN 978-0-9927964-0-2

Copyright © Pete Cruickshank, 2013

www.thekinsmen.co.uk

For Mum and Dad

Acknowledgements

To Rob for believing in me and the book

To my copyeditor Claire Rushbrook for showing me the many ways I was going wrong, and for the kind and informative advice.

To my proofreaders: Sarah Herman, Catherine Cruickshank, Rob Kingsnorth, Ed Pulis, Linda Coombs and Steff Madawi, for helping me turn a tsunami of ideas into a coherent narrative.

To my wonderful wife, Catherine and my two beautiful girls, Jessica and Heather, for all their love and support.

And finally to Adam for the website and putting up with me going on and on about my ideas for the Kinsmen, sorry dude.

Prelude

I do not know who or what may be reading these words. It is my distinct hope that if the worst should come to pass in the dark days ahead, there should be some record of what truly happened during those final days – that not everything or everyone is who or what they appear to be – to serve as a valuable lesson about the past and more importantly to help us survive what is to come.

It may interest you to know that this is no ordinary book. It may seem so and yet, in many ways, it is so much more. There are many copies and yet there is only truly one. Destroy it and it will appear again at some point, at some place in space and time. Within these pages is an account of my involvement in what is known as the Nacuerian-Galacien War – a war, despite what some may like to think, Is still happening to this day. It may seem, to some, that that is all. However to a few selective beings, there is the capability of unlocking a more intimate knowledge of these and subsequent events.

There are three distinct levels of translation within this account. Firstly, my own. I am writing this in the language I have adopted, not my first language and certainly not my last. Nonetheless it is the language I use now. My recollections of other languages include those of ancient Aramaic or standard Galacien. I have encountered many other languages in my time, but all these words are in my adopted tongue.

The second level of translation is more for the purpose of deception. It will become quite clear why such deception is necessary. I have taken great pains to ensure that only those I wish to can read these words – 'they' will see the real words I have written down here. Anyone else? Well they will see something quite different. From what they would like to believe I have written, to nothing more than blank pages. How is this possible? If you knew, then it wouldn't be a very a clever idea on my part, would it?

The third and final level of translation is for the benefit of the observer, for there is something quite unusual about the words on these pages and about the pages themselves. If you are capable of the same 'technique', then you already know of that which I speak. If not, let me enlighten you. Look closer and see what lies beyond the words. If indeed you can read this, you will see this text in that of your own language, whether Elamite, Yan, or English. However this is merely an illusion – a very functional one, but an illusion nonetheless. Languages are all different and though it may seem that the world and, therefore, truth is shaped by our words, they only scratch at the surface of true reality, of what most of us can perceive. However everyone, whatever their destiny, has a name.

Mine is Jonas.

PART 1. Chapter 1. Origins

I was born in Assyria on Earth around what would become known as the year 300 BC. I do not know the exact date for I lived in a remote area on a farm, where only the seasons are important, and the dates on any such calendar were unknown to me.

From an early age we all knew I was different. Work on a farm is long and hard yet my strength was always equal to the task, and I never seemed to tire. I was also unnaturally fast, and my senses could perceive far more than any normal human. As I grew into early manhood these abilities became more pronounced. I took on more work at the farm as my parents grew older, and as time passed, my parents continually pestered me to find a woman with whom to bear and raise children of my own. This was no easy request, for not only was it my extraordinary physical abilities that separated me from the rest of humanity, but also my perception of the rest of humankind. With the exception of a few, such as my loving parents, I found humanity in general to be despicable and a constant source of frustration. On those occasions we ventured to the nearest town to trade, my keen senses would see that which others could not: lies and deceit. I could feel their greed, envy, and jealousy, like rotting food that I was being forced to eat. The ugliness of human nature was everywhere and I was a grim spectator whose senses were overwhelmed. I found it hard to look upon any girls who secretly lusted after me, their thoughts hidden from their fathers, yet not from me. Some considered me backward due to my lack of response and I had to keep my anger in check for fear of shouting across town that it was they who were backward and I could barely stand the torment of it.

I commented on the things I saw to my father who replied that I should not involve myself in the business of others, as I might end up regretting it. I could see that he spoke from experience and heeded his advice as best I could. I was always glad to be away from the crowds and eventually return to the peace and quiet of our home.

We lived alone in the valley and the new king's soldiers rarely patrolled the area. A few times a year groups of mercenaries or bandits would pass through our farm en route to some unsavoury business, and would take it upon themselves to consume our food and drink with no payment of any kind in return. Due to my unnaturally keen senses I was always the first to know when they were coming. My mother was hidden on such occasions, for my father feared, if seen, they would take her as willingly as they did everything else. Thus, those that passed through saw only my father and I. From an early age I was taught that they were only interested in fresh supplies and travelling light, and that it would be best not to interfere. We were farmers not fighters, and we were alone.

Early one morning I awoke uneasily. Moving quietly past my sleeping parents and outside to find that the sheep had gone during the night. I quickly dressed and set off to collect the wandering animals. I examined the gate on my way and saw it was, indeed open, yet nothing was broken or disturbed. Listening intently I was soon able to deduce their location and, after a few hours, I managed to herd them together and set off back in the direction of the farm. As I came closer, I began to feel a great sense of foreboding which grew stronger with each step, until eventually I knew for sure there was something wrong. I broke into a sprint, hearing the screams of my mother before I reached the crest of the final hill. I took in the sight of what had happened in an instant.

This time, when some unsavoury characters had arrived at the farm, I, who usually acted as an early warning system, had not been there. My family had not realised they were coming until it was too late. I saw before me nine men, eight of them were pushing and beating my father as he tried to stop the ninth from dragging my screaming mother into our home, his intentions obvious. The anger I had held under control for so long in my life rose and burst forth through every fibre of my being as I bore myself down the hill as fast as a stallion towards the fiends.

The men were oblivious to my rapid approach, due to the sounds of my mother's screams and the shouts of protest from my father. Before I could reach them, my father managed a well-aimed punch to a man he grappled with, lifting him off his feet. In response, his comrade drew out his sword and, in a quick movement, slashed my father's side. I ran into armed man with a force far greater than any chariot, barging with the full momentum from my long sprint. He flew into the air and hit the wall of our house with a sickening crunch, falling to the ground like a broken doll. The others, though shocked, responded quickly, having been trained to live a life where fighting is a common occurrence. I was only able to steal a quick glance at my father on the ground clutching at the bloody wound in his side, when one of the men attacked me, thrusting with his sword. Although I had no fighting experience, I was fast, my reaction like lightning; the man's attack though quick in its own right seemed slow to me. I managed to sidestep his thrust, turn into him, grab him, and bring him to his knees. I quickly broke his arm like a twig and mercilessly finished him with his own sword. As his comrades took another step towards me I unsheathed his dagger and in a flash of movement it was in another man's throat.

A mounted man, perhaps the leader, ordered the others to rush me at once. Again my speed and agility seemed boosted to a degree where it appeared as if my opponents were moving in a viscous liquid. I was able to dodge their attacks and turn their own weapons against them. After a few seconds though, their swords began to make contact with me. I did not notice it at first but at some point I realised that their swords were simply glancing off my body with no effect, as if I were made of polished bronze. This unlikely revelation was confirmed when, after managing to kill another two men, my exposed chest was struck hard with a dagger. The dagger broke and the man who had tried to run it home with such force, grasped his crippled hand in agony. The point at which he had struck me remained unmarked and, before he could recover himself, I knocked him to the ground. I somehow sensed that two arrows had been let loose from their bowstrings and were about to strike me. I moved with unnatural speed and managed to grasp one in mid-air while the other simply ricocheted off my neck.

The two bowmen exchanged a disbelieving look before running quickly for the hills. I turned on the last man, who stood before the doorway to our home, holding a knife to my mother's throat. Having seen me kill most of his comrades without any initial weapons of my own, he was naturally scared and desperate. The rage was still coursing through my body and it took some amount of will to just stand there and talk calmly to him. I assured him that if he let my mother go, then he would come to no harm. He told me to get him a horse and then step back. My father was lying quietly near me in a puddle of his own blood and I had no choice but to do as he wanted. I looked at the bandit waiting for him to move. The frightened man looked at me, and then glanced at the horse. I could tell he was unsure as to whether he would be able to make it out alive. Then something changed in his eyes and I knew in that terrible moment what he was going to do. As I shouted in protest, he cut my mother's throat and pushed her away. I reached her in moments and clasped my hand to her throat in a desperate attempt to stop the blood, but it was no good. I did not know what to do. I sat there with her in my arms, water streaming from my eyes blurring my vision as I felt my beloved mother's blood pouring down my arm. I could feel her slowly losing strength, slipping away, terrified in her final moments.

The rest of the day I tried to keep my father alive, again to no avail. I buried them both the next day. With each shovel of earth heaped upon their graves, I died a little bit more. The noblest parts of me were buried in those graves that day, and all that was left was mistrust and hatred. Those small flecks of decency left on the stinking hide of humanity had been killed by the sickening whole and I wanted nothing more to do with them. I mourned my parents' deaths and was torn between avenging them, or staying to tend the farm they had built and loved so much. Despite my almost irresistible urge to seek vengeance, I managed to see clearly that the best way to honour them both would be to not let that which they had worked so hard to build and maintain, fall to ruin.

Through the rest of the season I tended the farm in a melancholy and unbreakable routine.

Chapter 2. Soldiers

The air was fresh and the sun low in the morning sky, casting long shadows on the dry land, when I sensed over sixty men on horseback approaching from the east, twenty of whom were suspiciously left hidden behind the last hill. I walked up to meet them. They were the new king's soldiers, not the Persians from whom they had so recently taken this land. They fell into line, their horses snorting restlessly, as their captain approached me.

"We've heard reports that there have been bandits in these parts of recent, do you know anything of this?" he asked. I could sense the insincerity in his voice.

Anger rose in me immediately. "You know I do. You also know that they came here, because you have heard rumours of a man who could not be cut or pierced by blades of any kind. A man whose speed and strength seemed unnatural," I said as the captain remained silent. "I killed six of them, but not before they murdered my family. You are here to see if these improbable rumours are true. You are worried they may be. That is why you have brought forty men here and another twenty just over the rise there." I indicated the direction and noted his reaction. He moved his horse closer to me and I could see the other soldiers tense. The captain looked me in the eye as he spoke.

"I am to deduce if these rumours are true, by force if necessary," he stated.

Let them try I thought, and then they would know. I looked over to his men and all too easily saw a focus for the vengeance of my parents' murders. I was ready to make a quick example of their captain, but reflected on what my parents would have wanted – certainly not unprovoked bloodshed. I approached the captain and held out an outstretched palm. Giving the subtlest of nods in understanding, he drew out his knife, tested the sharpness of it on his thumb and, after a pause, ran it along the length of my palm. We both looked at my unmarked flesh and then at one another. He seemed completely taken aback, and it took him a moment to remember himself.

"I have orders that if the rumours were true, to inform you that the king commands you to come with us," he told me.

"What king is this?"

"King Alexander of Macedon," he replied as if I should have known. Perhaps my parents had, but I was just a little boy when the Macedonians came to our lands. Besides, what difference did it make to me which king ruled?

"Why?" I questioned.

The captain seemed annoyed and his soldiers outraged that I had questioned an order from the king himself.

"The king wishes you to help fight his enemies," explained the captain.

"I am sure he does. Tell the king I do not want to fight his battles. I only want to be left alone," I said, turning my back on them.

"The king commands it!" he bellowed. I could sense some of his soldiers had their hands that bit closer to their sheathed weapons at this point.

I turned on him. "The king was not here on that day when we needed him most. I owe him nothing." I could see he was torn between his unquestionable orders from his king and sending his men to fight an unknown like myself. In the end it was pathetic human arrogance that drove his decision.

He paced his horse back to his men and shouted orders for some of them to break flank to my left and others to my right. "Who are you to question your king?" the captain shouted back to me.

"I won't fight the king's wars for him. I won't murder those who intend me no harm."

"Take him!" ordered the captain.

Three of the soldiers jumped from their horses and made an attempt to grab me. With startling speed I struck the first to the jaw and hit the second with the back of my hand. Grabbing the third, I threw him hard to the ground, bringing up the dust. None of them got to their feet.

"Archers!" shouted the captain furiously. The soldiers directly in front of me drew their bows; almost twenty arrows were pointed at me.

"You fools," I whispered.

"Fire!"

Their arrows flew, and I could not help but turn my face away. The arrows ricocheted off my body and, as I looked up, I realised that another order had been given and the left flank was charging at me. I quickly turned to face them and, at the last possible moment, managed to dive out of the way of the charging horses. I was distracted from my surroundings for a moment and so did not realise until too late the right flank of horses as they ran me down beneath a mass of hooves. As I got up the mounted soldiers attacked me fiercely with their swords. They did not hurt me or cause me injury, but I was becoming very annoyed by what I considered to be pathetic distractions. Yet this was the intent. The captain wanted my attention drawn, so that his armoured horses could be brought from over the rise of the hill, without my realising it.

On another command the soldiers attacking me withdrew and a moment later I was hit with the full force of the charging armoured horses. The captain expected me to be dead, or at least severely injured.

I was neither.

The captain seemed at a loss as to what to do next but stubbornly issued a new command for another fierce sword attack from his men from both flanks. This time though I was aware of his strategy, and looked out for his real attack, amongst the commotion. I realised, to my horror, that three of his men had been dispatched to set fire to the farm; my parents' farm. This was enough. I had given them a chance to retreat and now, like the bandits, they seemed determined to destroy that which I loved and cherished most. I broke free like an enraged beast from the mass of men and dived onto the first soldier who held a torch, breaking his neck. I leapt high into the air, higher than the farm, I reached the second soldier, who received the same fate. The third soldier managed to throw his torch towards the barn. I jumped a moment later, intuitively guessing its trajectory, grasping it in my hand before landing on the roof of the farm. I dropped down onto the remaining soldier. He lay there unmoving as blood seeped from his brow.

Picking up the fallen soldier's sword I raised it into the air and bellowed to his stunned comrades, "Leave now and no one else need die this day. Stay and I shall be forced to kill every last one of you!" The wind was the only reply bringing up the dust around our feet as I looked over the frightened soldiers' faces. I pointed the sword at them as I shouted, "Well? Choose! Go and live, or stay and die."

"Withdraw!" shouted the captain his eyes not leaving mine as his men fell in. I wanted to believe that this would be the end of it, that humanity would fear me enough not to seek me out again; that I would be left alone.

Somehow, though, I did not believe I would be so fortunate.

Chapter 3. Garianne

As the days passed I had a terrible feeling of trepidation. I could imagine the king's fury from my refusal of his command and his response to what he would consider treason. Yet I felt justified in my position. I questioned his right to command me, even though he was a king, but the more I thought about it, the less that seemed to matter.

The animals had been grazing that day and I was in the process of herding them back to the farm. The sun was dropping slowly in the sky, soft serene oranges and violets spreading out across the wispy clouds, and a gentle breeze caressed my face. An impression of calm settled upon me until I sensed three people approaching from the hills. I presumed, like many others these days, they would simply go around rather than pass through the small valley, but I became aware that the three were heading straight towards me. I had no wish to interact with these, or any strangers. I scrutinised them with my acute senses, even though they were not yet in sight. I could tell that two of them were old, one male and one female, and the third only a boy. The old woman had an oddity about her that I could not explain. They were moving slowly and after some time they eventually crested the final hill and approached the farm. It was becoming dark and the stars were slowly emerging. The only other light was from the fire within my home.

The cart drew close to me, as the three of them huddled together. The old man looked welcomingly at me. The boy was wide-eyed, curiosity pouring from him. I envied his positive, hopeful outlook on the world, at the same time pitying him, for it was a lie that he would come to realise sooner or later. Yet his eyes, and the eyes of all humanity, I believed, would never truly be opened.

My attention fell to the woman before me and immediately I felt there was something different about her. Every time I tried to focus on her I became distracted by the cart, or the horses, the sky or the land, or back to her two companions; my focus seemed to slide off her. Unlike the others, I found her difficult to read. However, I relaxed a little at the warm smile she directed my way.

"Hello there," said the old man. "Is there room on your farm that we may stay and rest the night? As you can see we are getting on in our years and the young lad has not slept in anything but the cart for well over a season."

I did not feel my usual disgust at those before me. Was it the innocence of the boy? Perhaps I enjoyed the illusion of his fantasy – that existence was exciting and essentially good – if only for a fleeting moment. Or maybe it was because there was something odd about the old woman which intrigued me. With sadness growing heavy in my heart and soul, I realised it was probably because the three of them reminded me of the family I had once been a part of.

"We can pay you, if that is what you are thinking," prompted the old man.

"No, there is no need for that. You can stay," I replied.

They seemed relieved to hear this as I helped to guide their horse and cart to the stable. As I helped the old woman down I noticed that, despite her age, her movements were smooth and precise, as if everything she did were a beautiful dance, though so subtle as to be almost unnoticeable.

I readied them a place to sleep in the barn and asked them if they had need for anything else.

"No, no, you've done more than enough for us," replied the old man. "I think we are all tired so we will rest now, though the hour is early. We wish for an early start tomorrow."

"Very well." I managed to catch the eye of the old woman longer than was necessary as I said this and saw a depth of wisdom there that I could not possibly fathom.

I left the barn and finished my routine tasks for the night, before retiring to bed.

I always found it difficult to sleep and I had never dreamt as others do, except once. Being such a unique experience it stood out as a vivid memory. In my dream I was standing in a place of nothingness, no land or sky, no colour – if such a place can exist for it seemed featureless all around me. I felt as if I was nowhere yet I was obviously somewhere. Another stood behind me. I turned around and acknowledged her presence. She was tall and strikingly beautiful, with eyes gleaming with knowing. She was dressed unlike anyone I had seen before, in a manner which seemed both peaceful yet warrior-like. She was adorned in a material I did not recognise, it conformed snugly to her body and I felt that despite its apparent lightness it was exceptionally durable. Puzzled, I'd asked her who she was. She never opened her mouth but she did reply, one word, "Kinsmen". The dream ended there, yet it has always been with me and sometimes I feel it was the most real and significant thing I have ever experienced. Wrapped up in my recollections I knew sleep would never come and rose from my bed.

Stepping out into the starry night, I leant against the fence, and looked up at those wondrous lights blazing down upon me.

I sensed someone behind me.

"Admiring the view?"

21

It was the old woman. Her voice was unlike anything I had heard before and not what I had expected from one so old. It sounded young and perfected as if she were royalty of the highest order, like the voice of a goddess singing to me. From those first notes I wanted to hear more, the whole song.

Speak again so that I may soak in the delectable beauty of your words, I yearned.

"Yes," I replied eventually but abruptly, my own voice sounding woefully inadequate.

"Could you not sleep either?"

"No."

"Do you not feel tired?" she sang, as she turned to look at me with those incredible eyes full of intelligence and wisdom.

"No," I repeated simply. "I am never truly tired," I acknowledged.

"Then why do you sleep?" she asked.

The question seemed silly at first. But the more I thought about it the more intriguing and insightful it became.

"Because everyone has to sleep."

"People sleep when they're tired. But if you're never truly tired, then why do you go to sleep? Maybe you do it because you have always done it. Perhaps it's a habit," she said.

I thought on this. Although I never felt truly tired, I did sleep. Did this not suggest that I was like everyone else? Deep down though, I knew this was not true. I was not like everyone else.

I noticed she was holding a wooden cylinder and box. She followed my gaze down to the curious objects.

"What are they?" I asked.

"Ah, parchments and tools for writing – a passion of mine." I could see the delight in her face. As the melody of words sprang forth from her lips, I could not help but smile, something I did not do often.

"Would you like to see?" she enquired.

"Yes, shall we go inside? We cannot see much here in the dark. I will make us something to drink," I replied. Gods I could listen to her mellifluous voice all night.

Inside the house I offered her a seat, made a drink, and fed the dying fire which crackled in satisfaction. I sat next to her as she unrolled a piece of parchment on the table, and produced her simple writing tools. I was fascinated yet again by her exquisite movements, especially when she began forming symbols upon the parchment. It was as if her hand were performing a delightful dance, leaving an artistic trail of beauty in its wake. She turned to me smiling, offering the writing tool.

"Would you like to try?" she enquired

"I do not know how," I said.

"I could teach you," she replied almost mischievously. "Or maybe I should go now?" She began putting her things away.

For the first time since my parents' murders I wanted someone's company.

"No, please stay," I beseeched, the words feeling foreign on my lips.

She stopped what she was doing and looked me in the eye, for what seemed like an age.

"Very well, let us see what we can teach you. Give me your hand," she beckoned.

23

I was not enthusiastic about human contact but reluctantly agreed. Her skin felt strange, smooth but rugged. From the physical contact my focus, which had been sliding from her since we had first met, was now abruptly locked in place. We looked at each other as she began speaking slowly and purposefully, her voice taking on a hypnotic rhythm as she began teaching me the Aramaic alphabet. I repeated after her when told, and copied the symbols she specified. My mind absorbed everything she taught me with an immediate permanence. As the moments passed I noticed her pace was quickening, and to my surprise I was keeping up. As the lessons increased even further in pace and complexity, I felt my mind becoming hungry for more. The old woman's voice was getting faster and faster, impossibly fast. I became dimly aware that her mouth no longer moved, that her hand had stopped upon the parchment, yet the words flew across its surface like lightning. The lessons continued, and my mind exulted in the thrill of its own hunger. I do not know how long we sat there, in that bubble of accelerated learning, separated from the outside world, but eventually the pace slowed until the old woman's lips were moving again, and she reverted to her original speed.

Overcome with exhaustion, I fell back into my chair and oblivion took me.

I awoke with the sunlight pouring through the window hitting my face. Bewildered for a moment, I could knew instantly that it was much later in the day than my routine demanded. The memory of last night seemed like a dream, as some aspects of the night's events seemed impossible. I stumbled outside to the barn to discover to my dismay that it was empty. It seemed the woman and her two companions had left some time ago, as I could not sense their presence at all. I rushed back inside and suddenly noticed a small piece of parchment on the old wooden table. I approached it cautiously, like a hunter afraid to alert his prey, and slowly picked it up. I was instantly stunned to realise that upon looking at the parchment, I was able to read it. The clarity and pleasure of reading for what seemed like the first time was almost overwhelming. This is what the message said:

Jonas,

Consider, what I taught you last night, as a gift, in return for the generosity you showed to us. Do not attempt to seek me out. You will not find me, though we will meet again soon, I promise.

Garianne

That was the first time I beheld that legendary name, a name that would change my future forever. How had she known mine? I was sure I had never told her. After reading the note several more times just for the pure pleasure, I put it down, and despite what she had said, I ran from the farm in the hope of finding her. It took the better part of the day before I finally gave up.

As I stood there on the grounds of my parents' farm, I knew after my experience with Garianne, nothing could ever be the same again. It was time to leave and see what the world was about. I truly did want to be alone, but I knew that would never happen here. What I yearned for was to learn; to touch that purity of thought I had experienced with her – the incomparable joy of enlightenment when that which was hidden, was finally revealed to me.

I did not hesitate a moment longer. I moved about my home collecting only that which mattered to me. I filled the cart with tradable items and tethered the animals to it. Without looking back I left the only place I had called home and headed towards the nearest town, leaving my past behind me.

Chapter 4. The Battle

I made my way towards the nearest settlement, my purpose clear; I sought to escape from humanity and to discover new knowledge. Unfortunately, such a quest for the latter somewhat contradicted the former. Towns and cities were naturally to be the most likely opportunities for learning but they were also, by definition, places with the largest population density. I tried not to concern myself with the thoughts of enclosing crowds, and the inevitable interaction with others. It was to be unavoidable if I were to sell the animals and other produce I had brought with me.

I walked into the centre of this humble town , the surroundings sparking off memories of my parents. As I looked around, the words on signs (which were sparse at that time, as they were useless to an almost illiterate society) sprang forth with insightful flashes of meaning. I felt a well of pleasure from reading them and decided to make use of this good feeling to approach the sales master to discuss purchasing space within the market. He showed me a space; there seemed to be many.

"Why is the market so quiet today?" I asked him.

"Because of the war, of course," he replied, looking at me strangely.

"Which war?" I questioned.

His confused look seemed to become even more exaggerated. "The Macedonians are fighting on all fronts now. How can you not know that? No sooner do you possess something, there's the threat of losing it again," he said, shaking his head in dismay.

He turned away not waiting for a response. I could not help but allow myself a tiny smirk. Now it made sense why there had been no retribution for my actions against the king's soldiers; he had his hands full holding on to that which he had taken from the Persians.

Despite the relative quietness of the market, I was able to sell all my animals and produce. Perhaps it was my desperation to be away from the town that made me haggle considerably less, to the benefit of my buyers. As soon as I had my coins, I packed up my small amount of remaining supplies and headed east along the trail towards the next town.

I had been to the town of Erbil only once before with my father, when I was a small boy. The journey would probably take me several days and as I walked along the quiet, deserted path, the sun dropping slowly in the sky, the soft breeze caressing the dusty landscape, my thoughts turned again to the old woman who called herself Garianne; an unusual name I had never heard of before. Her beautiful voice echoed in my mind. I remembered she had suggested that I didn't need to sleep if I wasn't tired. That was what she had meant, wasn't it? I pondered her words and decided that I would only sleep when I really did feel tired enough, I carried on walking as the sun fell behind the horizon. The stars came out spectacularly as always, like wondrous candles in the heavens, and I found myself looking up at them in a new way wondering exactly what they were.

Since being taught how to read and write by Garianne, I now found my mind awake like never before, I was full of questions. I had become far more inquisitive of the world around me, and more self-aware of this inner dialogue. I was realising aspects about myself and my environment just by pondering on them. For instance, as I walked I thought that it was probably cold by now, but it did not bother me. Most people protect themselves from the cold because it is uncomfortable and can cause them harm and, in extreme cases, even death. I, on the other hand, registered the cold on my body, but it never made me feel the need wrap up, as I'd seen others do.

I then recalled working in what others deemed cold or hot conditions, wearing the clothes I would always wear. All this led me to the conclusion that I was more or less indifferent by any extreme temperature, in the same way I was unaffected by the swords of the king's soldiers.

As I walked through the night I concluded a great many other things from such similar logical deductions. With each new revelation, came a new flood of joy. It was incredible I could actually learn new things just by observing the world and pondering on past experiences. Why had I never questioned such things before? I suddenly stopped in my tracks, as I realised something. All around me were the unmistakable signs of sunrise. I had not slept during the night and I was not tired, nor was I hungry. Yet another difference about myself I had concluded.

The terrain had changed now. It had been somewhat flat when the sun had set the previous evening, now orange, sandy rocks rose on either side of me. I made sure my supplies were secure, and attempted a series of giant leaps up onto the high rocks above. Sitting down, high above the wide rocky vista stretching far off to the horizon, I carefully took out the precious gifts Garianne had bestowed upon me and began to write. I wrote of the thoughts I was having as well as my hopes and dreams for the future. I remember daydreaming of finding an abandoned city one day with buildings full of parchments containing vast amounts of knowledge. I could live for many years in such a place as that, unfettered by the rest of my kind.

Later the next day, as I made my way along the path, I became aware of a great many people to the north. My first instinct was to avoid them, but as the moments passed, curiosity got the better of me, and I decided to investigate, after all no one could sneak up on me. Yet, knowing where people are without seeing them doesn't necessarily make them easy to avoid. My progression was slow, but eventually I was able to make it to an outcrop of rock where I could privately observe what was occurring. What I saw before me were two vast opposing armies pitched in bloody battle, one I recognised from their uniforms as King Alexander's soldiers, the others I did not know. Up to the right were more soldiers and what I could only conclude to be higher-ranking commanding officers, sending out orders to different parts of their army.

The sight before me made me curse my abilities, for I could pick out every gruesome detail. Hundreds of men carving each other apart like animal meat. I could see it, smell it, hear it, and taste it. It felt as if I were in the thick of it. It was horrific that they could do this to one another, and for what? Land, riches, power? Again I felt revulsion and a need for complete disassociation from all of humanity. They were truly mad. Away from them I would go, away from them all. They could die and suffer for all I cared, drowning in their own insanity. What befell them was that which I had never personally experienced. Men's limbs sliced cleanly off, wounds torn apart, blood flowing or spraying about the battleground turning everything red. The noise was a terrible mix of war cries, and screams of pain and anguish. Would that human nature could change? Yet I looked upon these animals tearing into one another and knew in my heart that the human race had been abandoned by the Gods. Then something caught my eye amongst the bloody slaughter. Someone I recognised. It was the man who slit my mother's throat. I stared in astonishment.

It was him!

I saw again the moment he took my mother's life and looked to see if his two companions from that day were there also.

By the Gods they were!

One had recently been slain for he lay upon a mass of dead bodies. The other, the one I had thought of as the bandits' leader, was close to my mother's murderer and fighting fiercely. They must have given up the business of banditry and joined the king's army, perhaps seeking safety in such a well-trained mass of numbers. Before seeing them the last thing I wanted was to go down there and be surrounded by hundreds of men committing unadulterated slaughter. Now, at the sight of the last of my parents' murderers the fire roared in my breast and thunder filled my head. My teeth locked, my knuckles whitened as I ran down towards the battlefield.

I wanted to be in and out, with as little interaction as possible. I knew that a non-uniformed man, who could not be harmed by conventional weapons, could not remain inconspicuous for very long. Though I was surprised that within my first few steps my presence was already being alerted through a network of patrolmen far outside the perimeter. Thinking back, it would possibly have been a better idea to somehow acquire a uniform using stealth on an unsuspecting perimeter guard. However, with vengeance in mind this idea did not occur to me at the time, and despite their observation I was already rapidly approaching the battle, the roar of the fighting like a rising tidal wave. At ground level I reached the outer perimeter of the battle, consisting of sparsely ongoing skirmishes. The soldiers there hardly noticed me for they were too involved in killing one another and keeping their own lives. I had lost sight of my parents' murderers and the inner perimeter of the battle was densely populated. A moment before hitting it, I quickly made a guess where they would be and jumped high into the air. The combatants streamed under me as I suddenly had a bird's-eye view of the ongoing slaughter. I spotted them both before I landed in the middle of the battle, striding purposefully towards my enemy, tossing aside any who were in my way, ignoring those who attacked me. At the last instant one of them saw me, his face horror stricken. In his survivalist, adrenaline-heightened state, he managed a respectfully fast and incredibly forceful cutting attack against my head, the sword making contact with my temple with such incredible power that it broke the blade. A swift blow brought him to the dirty ground. Unexpectedly his comrades attacked, distracting me for a moment. Then I saw that two of the enemy soldiers were at the point of killing the other man – the who killed my mother. I couldn't allow it. I leapt on the attackers knocking all three clumsily to the ground. I was up a moment before them delivering a quick mortal blow with my hand to one of the soldiers. I then turned around to see the second enemy soldier skilfully put my mother's murderer to his sword. I quickly dispatched him and straddled over my fallen enemy inspecting his wound. Blood poured freely from his chest, his head lolled to one side. My hands urgently grasped around his throat.

No! He is mine to kill, I thought, tightening my grip around his throat, tears blurring my sight; falling, mixing with the blood on his body. I tried to kill him, but you cannot kill a dead man. My grief rose and exploded in a wail that echoed and pierced the entire battlefield. I realised my vengeance was completely taken from me, as my gaze fell upon the corpse of the last man involved in the death of my parents. I felt numb and cheated.

Disassociated from my surroundings, I was barely aware of the commotion I had created amongst the soldiers on both sides. They poked and prodded me with their swords, as if I were an animal, a beast in a cage. In their faces I saw how they despised and feared me.

The battle continued and some of them were trying unsuccessfully to injure me but I did not move a muscle. My mind was flooded with anguish and frustration, building to an unbearable degree. The animals continued to assault me until suddenly something changed within, a terrible darkness overcoming me. Another soldier attempted to pierce me upon his sword but, before he knew it, before any of them knew it, I grabbed his throat, snapped his neck and tossed him aside like a bag of bones to the ground. A few others tried their luck but, where I was concerned, there was no luck. Most of them now backed away.

"You cursed fools!" I shouted to them turning around. "All of you. Look at the slaughter around you. There is no reason for it. Man thinks itself better than all the animals upon the Earth. You think that we have created great things, great civilisations. We are not civilised. We are damned to kill one another in an endless cycle of death until that day when we are ultimately lost."

More and more soldiers turned to listen as my voice boomed in the air. Many witnessed what had transpired and the word spread quickly; they knew what I was capable of.

"From this day forth, I disassociate myself from all of humanity. From this day I stand alone."

Staring at them defiantly I began to walk away, the mass of soldiers parting before me, as if a mysterious force were pushing them aside.

Unbelievably, the battle had stopped, although no sooner had I left them, I noticed the Macedonians taking advantage of the short interval to launch a sneak attack around their enemy's flank. I looked back in despair, as I witnessed yet more waste of human life.

Everything I said had fallen upon deaf ears. I should have known better.

Chapter 5. Davern

I continued my journey in an easterly direction, this time following no particular path. The land became hillier as I headed towards the Zagros Mountains. As the days passed I became aware that I was being followed by a number of riders. I assumed them to be the king's men sent to keep a report on my whereabouts. The king apparently did not forgive infamous 'traitors' readily.

For a moment I considered using my acute senses to sneak up on them one at a time to stop them. However, I had had a bellyful of violence and wished for no more. Being on horseback they could easily send messages back to the king while I made my slow progress on foot. I could not out-pace them. Or could I? I felt it was time to test myself again. The last time I had slept had been four days ago and I hadn't eaten or drank much either – another self-experiment I was conducting. Nevertheless, I did not feel weary. Making sure my belongings were securely tightened, I began to run at the pace of a steadily galloping horse.

Over hills and across streams they pursued me, as the sun continued its slow arc across the sky. One by one I sensed them fall behind, while I continued my respectable pace unabated.

Finally, as I reached the mountains proper, only one horseman remained, his horse stronger or perhaps simply fresher from the offset. At the right moment I quickly hid myself behind a mass of huge rocks that made up the terrain. Long moments passed until I heard the slow clip-clopping of a horse heading my way. The rider was being cautious and I had the feeling he knew these mountains as a good place for an ambush, such as the one I had planned for him.

I heard the sound of a drawn sword, and then a voice. "I know you're here. I only want to talk."

"Then why draw your sword? You say you only want to speak, yet the only language you know is violence," I replied stepping from my hiding place. "Tell the king he need no longer worry about me, for I am leaving Assyria for good".

"I am not one of King Alexander's soldiers as you can tell. I speak for another," said the man. He was undeniably right, he did not wear the uniform of a Macedonian soldier, nor did he look like one of them.

"What is it you want?" I asked.

"We want to make you an offer, a very generous offer."

"And who are 'we'? The Persians?"

"No, believe it or not I'm not Persian, despite my current appearance. I represent someone from a place far away. Who needs your help, and in return we'll grant you anything you desire."

"Whatever I desire?" I asked, intrigued by his proposal. "And what can you offer me, hmm? Riches, power, women?"

"Is that what you want?"

"What would you require from me in return?"

"Fight for us."

"Do you want to know what I really desire?" I said, walking up to him and his horse. "To be left alone," I said through gritted teeth.

I turned my back and began walking away. "If you still persist in following me, I will have no choice but to hurt you."

He said nothing watching me go. I think he got the message for he turned his horse to go back the way he had come.

Finally, a man with some sense in his head, I thought, then I paused.

"Knowledge," I shouted.

"What?"

"Knowledge," I repeated turning back to him. "I am in search of it. Do you know where I can find writings?"

"Only records, such as those for trade, land, ownership, that kind of thing; nothing to compare with what is kept in one of your cities such as Arrapkha."

As I had thought, those mass congregations of humanity would be the only places I would find anything worthy of being read.

Rolling my eyes to the heavens I said, "So be it. If I must, I will go. I will go to Arrapkha." I began to walk in my original direction but suddenly stopped and turned to the horseman who was watching me curiously. "Ah, which way is it to Arrapkha?" I asked timidly.

He laughed out loud, which I tried to find irritating, though couldn't as I found the situation just as amusing as he did.

"Go directly south from here, cross the first river, at the second river follow it away from the mountains and you will come to it soon enough."

I found myself in the rare and unusual situation of being grateful to someone. There was something I was meant to say. It had seemed so long since I'd ever said it. After pausing for far too long I finally said, "Thank you."

He told me his name was Davern; another name I had never heard before. He'd offered and I'd begrudgingly accepted him as my guide to Arrapkha, which I was already beginning to regret, for he was irritatingly positive about everything.

"What a beautiful day, dost thou not think, Jonas?"

When he said such things I would just glance at him and roll my eyes. This was mainly because he kept repeating himself and often said words like 'dost', 'thee', and 'thou'; I think it amused him. Davern also laughed lot, a big bellowing guffaw, as if trying to get the attention of anyone around. Why I put up with him I have no idea. It was after one of our exchanges ending in his usual big bellowing laughs, that I asked him something that had been preying on my mind for some time now.

"You know, Davern, I am curious. How do you expect to walk into Arrapkha, when you are quite obviously their enemy?"

"Ah well, it is quite simple. I will be in disguise. You will see," he said mischievously.

This will be interesting, I thought. He was travelling light, therefore I found it very hard to believe he had anything with him with which to perform this miraculous disguise. Nevertheless, something strange occurred as we drew closer to Arrapkha. Little by little and almost without me realising it, Davern's appearance began to change. Things about him that I could have sworn were different the day before had changed to make him more acceptable as a Macedonian. As the days passed not only the uniform he wore, but his weapons had somehow been replaced, his steed subtly changed, and even his physical appearance seemed different from the man I had first met in the

Zagros Mountains days ago. If it were not for his irritating ways I would have believed this was an entirely different person.

When we finally reached the northern gates of the city, the guards barely glanced at him. He gave me a sideways peek and smirked, eyebrows raised like some child up to mischief.

I shook my head in disbelief. How had he done it?

Now within a city I found myself surrounded by unsavoury characters. I recoiled as I witnessed the inhabitants' behaviour, and tried my best to ignore what my acute senses were telling me. The square we stood in was awash with life; crowds of men and women moving around one another going about their affairs. You could tell it was a place of trade and business of every kind. The noise of all the shouting and yelling was very much like being in the middle of a battle, only without all the blood.

From the look on Davern's face though, it was obvious he was enjoying himself.

"What dost thou think we go have us some decent food, Jonas?"

"I'll be fine without, I think."

"Afraid thou might enjoy thyself? Would it really hurt for you to exhibit a sense of humour now and again?"

"Would it hurt you not to be so juvenile all the time?"

"Perhaps that may be so," he laughed, "though at least I have been known to be serious when the situation calls for it. I've never seen that stone expression of yours even crack a smirk."

It was true. I possessed barely a hint of what could be called a sense of humour. I've always thought we are what we are. Our perceptions of others are based relative to that of ourselves. To Davern I lacked humour, whereas to me he possessed too much. It made him appear foolish. As time passed I realised that this was far from the case, and I suspected he only acted the fool to disarm those he interacted with.

Davern had wandered off and was talking to the locals. I grabbed him and pulled him to me. "Listen, I don't want to be here any longer than necessary. I told a great many people I was leaving Assyria, so I don't want any of them seeing me sauntering around one of its major cities. Where can I find knowledge?"

"Look around you, there is knowledge everywhere. You can learn by speaking to people around you—"

"I don't like speaking to people," I interrupted. "Don't you remember me telling you? I want to be left alone. I don't want to speak to anyone and I don't want them to speak to me. I'd much rather be left alone to read and learn."

"Ah." Davern nodded his head in apparent understanding. "Well only priests, philosophers, and perhaps royalty are allowed such privileges."

"Let us forget royalty. The king, quite likely, wants me dead, though I think he'd find this particular desire rather difficult to accomplish. I am tired of pointless confrontations. That leaves the temples then. Do you know anything about them?" I asked.

Davern paused a moment as if listening to some inner voice.

"I know that they don't allow in anyone except their own and royalty. You aren't either."

"Somehow I have to read those writings."

"Well, I have noticed you do seem to have some extraordinary talents. Perhaps we could sneak in during the night when everyone's asleep, and take a look."

I folded my arms and gave him a quizzical look.

"How does a resident of the Zagros Mountains know so much about the temples of Arrapkha?" I asked.

"Know thy enemy?"

"Are we enemies then?" I stated, having not heard the expression before.

"The Macedonians are your enemies now and the enemy of my enemy is my friend. That makes us friends, don't you agree?"

I furrowed my brow. I wasn't sure about that.

Somehow I continued to tolerate his company and that night, with the use of my 'talents', we were able to enter into the temple undetected by the priest guards. I needed to concentrate hard to sense where in the structure the scrolls were kept, but before too long I had mapped out in my head the easiest route.

We made our way silently down the dim torch-lit corridors, our shadows dancing against the stone walls. Luckily, the chamber containing the scrolls was unguarded; the only thing standing in our way was a huge double door with an iron bar across it. I lifted it easily and stood it on its end securely in a corner. The doors made a drawn out creak as we opened them and I felt sure the guards would hear, for there were no other sounds in the dead of night. I looked back the way we had come and knew that no one had been alerted. We opened the doors no wider than was necessary as we both slipped into the chamber beyond. It was almost pitch-black inside save for a tiny amount of moonlight seeping through a tiny hole in the ceiling. Davern passed me a torch from outside the chamber and we used it to light another. We saw alcoves all around the chamber with shelves full of parchment. My heart beat a little faster in my eagerness to immerse myself in their contents. I reached out and carefully opened the first scroll, exhaling in delight. In the low light of my torch my eyes soaked up the words on the parchment, and within a moment I had memorised it. My hunger roused, I swiftly moved on to the next one. It did not matter to me the subject, the pure pleasure of reading and learning to any degree was enough for me.

Most of the scrolls were religious in nature, or records. Surprisingly though, there were a few fascinating parchments on mathematics and the movements of the stars. My mind was so enthralled, I never questioned the time, or perhaps more importantly my companion's lack of surprise that it took me less time to read a scroll containing hundreds of words, than it did for me to reach for it and unroll it.

Not long before sunrise, Davern nudged me from my immersion, "It is time to go. The priests will be rising soon."

We left the temple unnoticed and in the pre-dawn light we were on the quiet streets of Arrapkha. I felt stunned from all that I had learned that night.

"Are you alright?" Davern asked.

"I'm just a little overwhelmed. That was a lot to take in, in one night. The last thing I read was considerably shorter." I thought back to Garianne's note.

"Well, I think we deserve something to eat. I for one am starving, and there are places that open even at this hour to cater for tradesman or, in our case, knowledge seekers." Davern gave me one of his wide grins. I did not feel the need to tell him that though I hadn't eaten for a long while now, I was not hungry.

"Very well then," I agreed.

The establishment was heavy with the sweet aromas of food. Despite admitting to not feeling hungry, I could not help myself from sinking my teeth into some succulent cooked meat. Eating and drinking are two of the fundamental pleasures of life, after all. I was still in wonder from everything I had learned.

"Did you know," I began saying to Davern excitedly, "that the stars in the night sky are made up of patterns? They all have names, and that they move around the world once a night."

"Are you quite sure about that?"

"Oh, yes."

Davern looked slightly amused. "Then where do they go during the day?"

"Erm… The scrolls didn't say anything about that." I thought hard about it while Davern watched me curiously.

"Perhaps, perhaps they go under the ground," I pointed across from one end of the floor to the other, "and up the other side into the sky again."

"Perhaps they do," Davern replied smiling. "Well, if you'll excuse me I think it is time for me to indulge in yet another one of my little pleasures." Davern stood up and approached a group of men while I sat there baffled.

For some time I pondered all that I had learned from the scrolls. There had been maps which, to my delight, I found I could recall in perfect detail. I now had a very good idea of the lay of the land in this part of the world. I wanted to explore the lands of Mesopotamia, Egypt, and the Greek city states, especially Greece for I could now recollect hearing on many an occasion that it was renowned as a place of learning. I was also insatiably curious to see what lay beyond the lands and oceans of these spuriously made maps.

As usual my attention had turned inward, my surroundings seeming distant. So it took a little while for me to realise the trouble Davern had gotten himself into. I slowly became aware that there was a lot of shouting directed at my companion. The disturbance was escalating quickly and one of the fools had a sword which he was brandishing in Davern's direction. Time seemed to slow down as I considered whether to help him or not. Then in a flash my knife was sailing through the air sinking firmly up to its hilt in the attacker's wrist. The force of impact threw him to the floor. I was involved now, so I strode across the room and battered some sense into them.

"I think it is time we left," I suggested to Davern. Unfortunately, without my being aware of it, I had been attacked from behind with a sword.

Nothing travels faster than a rumour; as we exited we realised we were no longer inconspicuous. A crowd of people were gathering at the entrance, and I could see a couple of soldiers frantically talking, until one of them dashed out of sight.

"This doesn't look good," Davern said.

I remember thinking that with people being the extremist fools they are, this would go either one of two ways: They'd praise me as they would a king or a god, or treat me like a freak. Unfortunately, it was the latter. The first stone which came sailing from the crowd missed me, the second didn't. Anger rose in me instantly.

"Who threw that?" I demanded, but the crowd ignored me and continued throwing more stones and shouting obscenities. Some were even laughing. Why were they laughing? Their ignorance and disrespect drove me mad with rage. I would kill them. A firm hand planted itself against my chest, just before I began to move.

"No, Jonas," protested Davern, more serious than I had ever seen him. He impressively dodged something flying towards his head. "Spare them. My horse is just around the corner and I have seen how fast and far you can run. Let us be away from this place. Head north along the river and towards the mountains. I'll find you there. If you kill them you will be as bad, no, even worse than them. Be better."

I hesitated for a moment, though something in his eyes and his voice was so controlled I found myself calmed.

I nodded.

"Go. I won't be far behind," he said.

Faster than any horse, faster than anything, I sprinted through the streets and out of the city.

The sun was broaching the horizon when I finally decided to stop running. I was actually breathing a little harder so at least I was normal in that respect. Combining my new knowledge of what is known as astronomy and mathematics, as well as bringing forth the best maps from the temple at Arrapkha to mind, I was able to pinpoint my position precisely. I sat down wondering which way to head next, when all of a sudden I sensed a presence.

"No one managed to keep up with you then?" enquired Davern, as he appeared from the shadows.

"What? No one except you. Where, by the Gods, did you come from?"

"I am very good at sneaking up on people."

I looked at him unconvinced. "No one can sneak up on me."

"Well it looks like they can," he retorted, his arms open representing himself as proof.

I walked up to him, a mask of utter seriousness. "You don't understand. I can sense people approaching from a great distance. But you, one instant you are not here, the next you are. That is not possible."

"Many people would say there are many things about you that are not possible."

"Perhaps, but I cannot do what you just apparently did; appear from nowhere," I said.

Davern merely smiled, irritating me further. The question of how he had changed his physical appearance came back to me, and I was sure he had not slept the previous night in the temple, yet he stood from out of nowhere, fresh as the morning air. Again I had the feeling he was listening to something.

"Who are you really?" I demanded. "I *will* have a truthful answer."

Davern maintained his smile. "Be seeing you soon, Jonas." he said, and promptly vanished before my eyes.

Chapter 6. The Mountain Tribes

I sat there stunned for some time, staring at the spot where Davern had stood only a moment before. Something very strange was going on. I firmly believed I did not live in a world where people disappeared into thin air, or could teach an illiterate person to read and write in little more than a night. Then again I was, of course, including myself in this category of impossibilities. I suppose I had succeeded in losing my companion. Was that not what I had wanted? I fully suspected that Davern, if that was his real name, had been deceiving me about a great many things but I had no proof. Nevertheless, I still felt angry that he had obviously not been telling me something fundamental about himself. I felt as if the Gods themselves had taken an interest in me. Was Davern one of their messengers? I found this hard to believe for he had been such a buffoon of a character. Why would the Gods send one such as him?

After some thought I decided there was no point lingering; Davern was obviously gone for good. I would carry on heading north over the mountains out of Assyria, and head west towards Greece. The agonising conflict between seeking seclusion and places containing knowledge was as strong as ever, despite the joy and enlightenment I felt from the scrolls of the temple at Arrapkha. Hopefully I would decide which was more important as I travelled.

The area of the Zagros Mountains through which I travelled seemed to be rife with warring tribes, who were constantly fighting with one another – and anyone else who came into their territory for that matter.

The first ones I encountered were rather surprised to find themselves bruised and beaten unconscious by a lone man using no weapons. I managed not to kill any of them, as I was getting used to using just the right amount of force. Later, it happened again with a different tribe, ending again with them all unconscious on the ground. The next time it happened, a third option regarding my future suddenly came to me. I did not know if it would work, but if it did, it would mean that I would be able to attain my seclusion and access to the knowledge I so eagerly sought at the same time. I looked down at the twenty or so men on the ground, half of whom were unconscious, the others stunned and in shock at witnessing my apparent invulnerability.

"Who is in charge here?" I demanded.

"He is," replied a man holding his leg in pain, pointing to an unconscious man on the floor. "I am his first," he continued apprehensively.

I rolled my eyes. "Very well. I want you to escort me to your tribe, or I am going to kill every last one of you."

I really had no intention of carrying out this threat, but it definitely got their attention.

Having picked themselves off the ground, they led me back to their tribe; a primitive, fortified town made mostly of wood and backing onto the edge of the mountainside.

I was led past the gates and continued through into the town. I think some of the residents thought I was a prisoner, as they seemed ready to start throwing stones at me.

However they were quickly warded off by my escort. I was brought to the tribe chief in what would be described as his hut. It was dimly lit and smelt damp and musty and I could see that he had a number of women around him who stayed close by. They held furs around themselves, but it was obvious they were quite naked underneath.

The chief was a large, powerful man, and it was obvious why he was in charge here. The head of my escort party slowly limped up to his chief and recounted the one-sided battle. The chief gave him a disbelieving look before standing and approaching me.

"What is your name?"

"I am Jonas."

"What do you want?" he growled at me.

"There is a lot of fighting around these parts, is there not? Many tribes, enemies everywhere?"

"Yes, they are always attacking us, but we will get them one day and crush them." He smiled looking about at his people encouragingly. They laughed and shouted their approval.

"Of course. I am guessing that this has been going on for a while, and may continue for some time in the future. What if I were to help? Your men saw what I can do. Twenty men or a hundred; it does not matter to me; I'll tell them to leave you alone for good."

"Could you not just kill them?" he asked hopefully. A malicious smile slowly spread across his face.

I looked at him sternly, "I am not going to do that, I don't want to kill anyone if I can help it."

He thought about this rubbing his unshaven chin. "What do you want in return?"

"In return I want only two simple things. Firstly, I'd like you to venture to the nearby cities and bring me scrolls or parchments, anything with writings on them. I thirst for knowledge, so bring me whatever you can. Leave the ones in the temple at Arrapkha; I've read them."

"And the second thing?"

"Secondly, I want a place where I can be left alone. A place where the only contact I have with another person will be from those who bring me the writings."

The chief waited for a moment. "That is all?"

I believed he thought I was really after his position as leader of his tribe.

"That is all," I confirmed.

The chief grinned, for his fears had been unfounded.

It was after a little fine-tuning of the arrangements that the chief, whose name was Hamah, made the agreement, and shortly after a substantial part of his army and I went to confront their closest enemy. This was the part I was not going to enjoy – hurting a group of people I'd never met before, to gain that which I most desired. I admit the thought of what I was about to do left a bitter taste in my mouth. I could say that we crossed into disputed territory, but the whole region was so 'disputed', such a statement had no meaning.

Chief Hamah raised his hand and we stopped atop a rocky crest looking down into a shallow valley. I could clearly see that the enemy's town was almost twice as large as Chief Hamah's and that they far outnumbered his tribe. For him to attack their fortifications would be suicide.

I turned my horse around to face Hamah and his men. "I'll be back soon enough. Set up camp and wait for my return," I said, dismounting my steed. "If anyone goes down there and starts causing any trouble, they'll regret it. What is this tribe's chief called?"

"Saragon," replied Hamah spitefully.

"Right then," I said simply and walked away.

Nothing happened until I had come quite close to the town, when two horsemen attacked me. I dispatched them both without fatality and hoped I would be able to handle the rest as efficiently. However I foresaw that there would have to be quite a bit of pain and suffering for me to achieve my goal here.

The town had high wooden ramparts where I could see men with bows running around and predictably they fired a few perfectly aimed arrows at me rather than trying to talk first. Naturally they bounced harmlessly from my body and I stood there waiting for this occurrence to sink in. Obviously, someone in there was still in denial, as another round of arrows was let loose against me, resulting in the same effect. I decided to run full speed towards the gate. The door broke open with a massive crack, as I stumbled into the town. I took in the scene in a moment and saw a great many soldiers heading my way. I also saw frightened women and children too, and what I was about to do made me sick to my stomach.

Gritting my teeth I thought of my ultimate goal and began to work my way through the town's warriors, disabling them on the way. In such close quarters they could not really mount any major offensive, not that it would have done them any good. However, I was as surprised as they were that: an expertly thrown spear aimed at my head, masses of boulders dropped upon me, and a huge tree trunk sharpened into a stake charged at my midsection, had no effect whatsoever.

The assault took some time as I had to knock some of them down more than once. Eventually though, towards the end of the day, the town had been subdued, including their chief and, as far as I could tell, I had not killed any of them. I sat in what seemed to be the chief's throne room, waiting for him to wake up.

Eventually, Chief Saragon regained consciousness. He was extremely distraught to find I had single-handedly defeated his entire army's defences.

He stared at me wide-eyed. "Who are you?"

I ignored his question. "I could have killed all of your people if I so wished. As you saw, there was no way you could have stopped me." I let this sink in.

"What do you want?" he asked, his distress deepening.

"First of all you are to cease attacking Hamah's tribe."

"But they—"

A thunderous *boom* struck through the room as I pounded the stone floor with my fist. The room shook and the floor smashed into pieces, where I struck it, racks filled with spears clattered noisily down.

"But nothing! As I was saying, you will stop attacking Chief Hamah's tribe; anyone who does so will answer to me. Secondly, I want you to work with his tribe and all the others, to bring me writings from the cities, so that I may learn from them. I've given Hamah the same message. I will send someone to you soon. Think of them as a kind of ambassador, to help sort out the details for me."

"This is all that you want?"

I'd been through all this before and was slowly losing my patience. "I only want to be left alone, to read and to learn."

After elaborating some more I left the town and joined Hamah and his restless soldiers.

"It is done. All we have to do now is visit the other tribes, find me some remote place to live and we can all exist in peace."

How little did I suspect, how events of my life , were about to change.

After the initial settlement between the tribes, Chief Hamah had a huge feast arranged in celebration of what we had achieved. He made it especially difficult for me to leave as he seemed to regard me as his new best friend. I tried to decline his numerous offers of food, drink, and women, though eventually realised I was fighting a losing battle and began to eat as they did. Hamah roared with laughter as I declined the numerous women who came to me.

I finally managed to slip away into the night and the sounds of mirth dwindled as I reached the town's secluded outskirts. Again I found myself gazing up in wonder at those points of light in the night sky.

I sensed someone approach from behind. I turned and beheld the most attractive woman I had ever seen walk into the moonlight. She had long, dark hair and incredibly smooth skin. Looking at me with kind, exquisite eyes, my soul seemed suddenly filled with her presence. I knew I had not seen her before, for I would not have missed such beauty. I found myself taken aback and unable to speak or even move. The anguish and horror of the world washed away from me in her presence and I was like a child again, feeling a sense of awe and wonder. I could sense from her a focus of purpose I had never sensed in a being before, and the intelligence, the awareness in her eyes was fascinating. Her expression was one of total control and calm, reminding me of the mysterious old woman, Garianne.

"You do not find Hamah's hospitality agreeable?" she said in a voice that sang to me.

"I... I do not feel comfortable in crowds. I usually prefer my own company. "

"Oh, perhaps I should leave you to your solitude." She made to go.

"No, no..."

She turned back, eyebrows raised.

"... I said usually, not always."

She came back and stood next to me, though keeping a respectable distance. We both looked up at the night sky.

"Do you ever wonder what they are?" I asked.

She regarded the lights in the sky with a subtle smile. "The learned of the lands of Greece believe they are set against a giant celestial sphere." She outstretched her fingers. "Certain individuals are trying to ascertain its movement and trying to define and catalogue patterns."

I looked at her, mouth hung open. "Celestial sphere," I repeated, the term unfamiliar yet somehow comprehending the meaning. "Incredible. How do you know of this?"

"I get around," she said simply, as if this were answer enough. She looked again into the sky. "I must be going."

"So soon?"

"You can find me in the town. You remember the one where you beat all the men there black and blue?"

I was abruptly taken aback by this comment and looked down on the floor like a child, away from her impassive gaze.

"I am sorry. I wish there had been another way."

She looked at me considering my apology. "There is always another way, Jonas. We just tell ourselves there isn't because it is too hard."

"Wait, tell me your name," I implored as she turned to leave.

She stood upon the rock against the backdrop of stars. "My name is Min."

Chapter 7. Fallen Star

It was a cold night and many days later, when I stood outside the entrance to my new home, awaiting the arrival of my first writings. I could sense the lone horseman making his excruciatingly slow progression up the mountainside path towards me, the cold strong wind whipping around his fragile body. I had waited so long for this first taste of knowledge to arrive that, would you believe, I was actually salivating like a starving man being brought a succulent feast.

The submission of the other tribes in the area had gone the same way; Just a few had needed a little more convincing. A strained peace had settled over the land, and the chosen men from each tribe had pursued their missions to bring me as much knowledge as possible from the various cities in Assyria, Babylonia, and even further afield if they could manage it. I had drawn detailed maps from memory and sent them on their way.

Like many of the dwellings around these parts, mine was made from a combination of stone and wood. It had been left abandoned and had fallen into a state of disrepair. Its location far away from anyone, was perfect for me although I had, on occasion, invited Min to join me. She had declined my offer each time.

I set about making my new home into a place of rest, quiet, contemplation, and study, and was glad of the amount of work needed to complete the building, for I needed distracting from my impatience. After many days I had something resembling a satisfactory dwelling. It was small yet comfortable, and without even realising it, I had built something which closely resembled the home I lived in with my parents. I always felt a little sad when thinking of it, perhaps I missed the place where I had grown up far more than I dared admit. Occasionally, I wondered what had become of it.

The rider was very close, though he was plodding along even slower now.

My impatience got the better of me. "Bah! I could crawl faster," I said loud enough for him to hear. It was hard for me to comprehend exhaustion, having never experienced it myself. I stomped towards him.

"Where did you get them from?" I questioned the man, barely looking at him, my eyes and hands on the bags he carried.

"Erbil," he replied. "They were not easy to acquire."

"I'm sure they were not," I replied examining them.

At first glance the writings seemed to contain many subjects, though they mostly concerned recent history of the area.

"You can go now," I told the rider. He had been standing there idly and he paused before turning his horse to leave.

"Thank you," I said half convincingly, out of a feeling of necessity, rather than because I meant it. It did not occur to me until many days later that the man had paused probably because he was very cold and tired, and was perhaps hoping for some warmth and rest at my home before making the long journey back to the town.

Back inside my home I put down the scrolls and parchments in the place I had so eagerly readied for them. I stored them carefully away and then like an excited child, began selecting and reading through the writings from Erbil. I tried to read slowly, for I knew it may be days before more would arrive. Yet it was hard. I found that I could absorb their content in seconds. Immediately after would come sudden understanding and then reflection.

The days passed by and, one by one, writings from the other cities arrived. I scrutinised, catalogued, and pondered over the knowledge I attained.

Early one morning, so early it would still be considered night by some, I was standing outside when my attention was drawn by the most unusual sound. It was like the rumbling of thunder, though slightly higher in pitch and constant, rather than growing and fading. I saw that something streaked across the night sky. A ball of fire far in the distance, leaving a stream of smoke in its wake, was plummeting down towards the ground, towards the horizon line of mountains. Moments later there was a great blast light followed by a loud crash. It echoed horrendously around the mountain range. The light and noise slowly died, until the night was still once again.

I considered heading off in the direction of the fallen star, or whatever it had been, to investigate it personally. I had no idea if there would be anything there, or how far away it was. Just as I decided to venture out and have a look, I sensed two horsemen together, both with many writings with which to feed my ever-hungry mind.

As the men I had sent off returned, each with their harvest of knowledge, and as I immersed myself in these writings the question of the falling star became less significant. From my readings of the masses of scrolls and parchments I became extremely learned and even began speculating and developing my own theories, building on the knowledge I had gathered. No more was this true than in the subject of mathematics. Mathematics was not something man created; to me it was the most elaborate and fundamental language to learn, a landscape to explore, and it was as if I had only discovered about the terrain itself. The beauty of mathematics to me was that I could discover the trees, rocks, and mountains of this landscape – the other branches of mathematics, as it were. I grew even more excited from the fact that I may very well be the first and only person to have ever discovered these secrets of the natural world, for I had never come across any of my newly developed theories in the writings of others.

Looking about my study at the hundreds of scrolls and parchments, I became curious that these had been taken so easily. It began to make me suspicious, of what I did not know. It felt as if the whole venture had been far too easy.

I looked again at the treasure I had acquired. It did not belong to me, and I had no need to keep it, except for sentimental reasons and purely for the pleasure of reading something that was physically there. Everything I had read was perfectly memorised, ready to be retrieved as if I owned it, at any time. I could lay in the darkness and recall any of the writings and see them there in front of me, as clearly as if I had them physically in my hands. I would ask Hamah and the other tribes to return them to their rightful owners and, although I felt a pang of guilt for having them taken in the first place, what else could I have done?

The following morning I set off down towards Hamah's town, which took most of the day. This was of no consequence to me as it gave me plenty of time in which to pontificate my latest theories on mathematics, as well as other facets of the natural world. As I neared the town I could hear a great commotion. Hamah's tribe, it seemed, was in pitched battle with another tribe.

Damn them, I thought. I stood there looking down upon the town, upon their stupidity. I found I could understand everything I had ever read, instantly and completely, yet I could not fathom this sight laid out before me in the fading light. Again they were destroying everything and killing one another.

Then another thought occurred to me. *Min!* Suddenly I was on the move in an amazing burst of speed across the land, jumping great distances. As I entered the town, some of the combatants looked up and ran for cover like frightened rodents, though most had not seen me and continued their pointless violence.

"Min!" I bellowed.

Now they knew I was there, many more ran from me. I saw Hamah fighting Chief Saragon; they both looked towards me, terrified, though Hamah also had a sly look in his eye. I strode over to them across the long shadows, fire was everywhere, lighting my way.

"See, I told you, Saragon! Jonas watches over us. Are you and your men ready to witness his vengeance first hand?" shouted Hamah. Saragon now looked at me in horror.

"Where is Min?" I demanded.

"I don't know," replied Saragon.

I looked about the town. The madness continued around me and I was desperate to find her. I was about to shout for her again, when the thought erupted from my mind, *Min!* It sounded as clear as anything I had uttered out loud. Thoughts were usually quiet and private but this, I felt, had been broadcast throughout the town. It was immediately apparent that nobody had heard it, except one. I sensed her reaction and focused on it.

I found her in an underground level of an obscure building with a great many other women and children, who looked tired and frightened. She sat there in a corner of the room holding a couple of wailing children.

"Are they yours?" I asked uncertainly.

"No," she replied simply.

"Min, come with me. Let us leave this madness together."

"I can't. I have to look after these two; their mother is missing." She gave me a defiant look that told me that what she meant was that their mother was dead.

I drew closer to her. "Please, come with me. Let me take you away from all of this, I beg you."

She looked at me with genuine concern in her eyes, but nothing else. "I'll be looking after them until she comes back. So I can't join you, you see?"

I knew what she meant; she had taken it upon herself to be the children's guardian for good. What had she done? I gave her a despairing look.

"You heard what I said. I did not ask for this. This is the way it has to be. I am sorry, Jonas." Her face was stern and stubborn and I could see that there would be no way to convince her; she always made me feel like a naïve child. Why?

I looked at her and the children, she belonged to them now. I had lost her. What else could I say?

I stumbled back into the town, my senses numb, warm tears threatening to well up in my eyes. I saw Chief Hamah. Reaching out I grabbed him, then slammed him against a nearby wall. "What happened here?" I demanded.

"They attacked us without provocation," he said in his defence.

"That's not true," a voice said from behind. I turned around still pinning Hamah against the wall. Chief Saragon picked himself up from the ground.

He was shaky on his feet, rubbing his head he pointed defiantly at Hamah. "Hamah came to our town and started making demands for food and weapons. He said that if we did not agree, that you would come and lay waste to our homes. We believed him at first, but he underestimated us. We have spies and they eventually informed us that you do not have contact with his tribe anymore. We came here to claim back what is rightfully ours."

I turned to Hamah.

"He is lying, Jonas. Their spies have seen how you no longer concern yourself with our affairs and decided to attack us, as they have done in the past."

I could not fathom which of these stories were true, for they both sounded feasible. Why should the problematic affairs of others concern me anyway? I was not their keeper, their king, their god. My despair dragged me down like a plummeting weight in a vast cold ocean. I was part of their problem, intrinsically linked to the destiny of the tribes. I saw that there would never be peace amongst men. They would always fight one another, lie, and seek power. Trapped in the maelstrom of their chaotic madness, I would never be free of them. I had to walk away now or my life would forever be hopelessly intertwined with theirs.

"I am sorry Min," I whispered quietly.

I pushed Hamah away to Saragon and addressed them both. "Saragon, tell your men to leave. No one else will die this night. Tomorrow, when the sun rises, things will be different. I will have no more involvement in your pathetic squabbles, your destinies are yours, and yours alone. One more thing, anyone who approaches my home invites death." I had stumbled a little on the word 'anyone' – except Min – I could not help but think.

There was a stunned silence as I noticed the fighting had finally stopped and all eyes were on me. I looked at Saragon and through gritted teeth hissed, "Go now." He did so as I slowly followed them out. At the broken gate I looked back and saw Min still holding those children and it felt as though my heart were being torn apart – a piece left with her and a piece still with me – as I turned and walked away from them forever.

Chapter 8. Monsters

As the days passed I brooded over the incident in Hamah's town. I could never see myself as being part of humanity and I wondered if the place I now resided in would serve me well enough in the years to come, or would I have to search for some place even more solitary? There must be places where humanity was sparse, or maybe environments harsh enough where no one lived at all. Perhaps it would be prudent to move on.

I had often wondered what lay beyond the lands I had studied in those maps. If I travelled far enough would I find something beyond anything discovered previously by man before? An unexplored land devoid and untouched by their madness; what a wonderful place that would be. Surely such a place must exist. Humanity could not have filled every land in existence, could it? I will start preparations for my exodus tomorrow, I thought, as I stared into the fire in the room of my home. I did not need the fire for warmth or cooking; fire's movement and the sense of it always helped me think better, somehow calming me of my inner demons.

Something distracted my thoughts and I sensed someone approaching my home. They were still quite far away and moving slowly, though undeniably they were heading for my way.

"Those fools," I cursed out loud. "Do they never listen?"

This confirmed my decision to leave. They would always come, sooner or later, if they knew where to find me. For whatever reason this person approached, I knew it would be for selfish ones. I felt like I would have to commit an act of violence once again, to make an example to the others. Perhaps if I were quick enough I could pack my things and be away, avoiding any such undesirable confrontation. It did not matter if he pursued me, for I could outpace him and my stamina was unmatched. As I quickly gathered the last of my things, I sensed that the person approaching was not a man at all, but a lone woman. Was it her? Was it Min?

I focused my thoughts and felt her familiar presence. For a moment I could almost touch her, smell her and, something else, she was in pain. I rushed from my home and, as I turned the first corner on the path, I saw her. She held onto a large rock as if for support looking dirty and fatigued, though maintaining her serene beauty.

"Min!" I shouted. She looked up and stumbled towards me, suddenly falling to the ground. I was there in an instant holding her in my arms, supporting her head. She did not seem to be hurt, only dreadfully tired.

"What happened to you?" I asked. It felt unusual for me to care for someone so much.

She looked at me whispering, "You must help us. They came without warning."

"I told them, I would never involve myself in their affairs ever again, no matter the circumstances. It was inevitable that yet again you would war against one another."

She shook her head, a horrified look in her tear-streamed eyes. "No, not against one another... something else... something not human." She looked at me as though she was struggling with the memory of what happened.

"What is it?" I asked.

Her last word erupted from her mouth in a cry of whispered anguish, just before she fainted in my arms. "Monsters!"

Min did not regain consciousness until the next day. She lay in my bed not saying a word; at first she seemed only vaguely aware of the world around her, a terrible haunted look in her dark eyes. To my unnatural senses her mind appeared as if it were trapped in a nightmare. Had what she had seen permanently damaged her? As the hours passed into the night she became more focused on me and reality. Eventually I sat down next to her bedside, holding out a cup of water, carefully to her lips.

"Drink it all," I said firmly.

She did so. I put the cup aside and held her hands in mine. Her last words had made even me feel a little unnerved, and that night I admit I was a bit restless, my imagination running riot at every sound the wind could concoct. It was not only what she had said but more the way she had said it; that look in her eyes, so terrible. It remained there still. I did not think she would ever be the same again.

"Min, what has happened?" I asked as gently as I could.

Tears silently came to her eyes as she quietly spoke. "The children are dead, Jonas."

"I am sorry." Yet I was not and this made me feel horribly guilty. I tightened my grip infinitesimally on her hand, as I had no wish to damage her.

"You spoke of monsters, Min. What did you mean by that?"

She swallowed hard and her voice became even more strained.

"They came into the town silent and without warning, those terrible things; monsters. They looked… they looked like giant spiders with tentacles, their bodies smooth, black, and featureless. They were everywhere, so quick, their bodies moved unnaturally, as if they were made of water. I saw them kill the children, turning them to dust before my very eyes. Nothing could stop them, so I ran to you. On my way here I saw smoke in the distance coming from another town. Those things must have been there as well. We must flee or they will come here and kill us both. Not even you can stop them. We must go."

Min tried to rise from the bed, but I held her in place.

"Jonas, please I have seen what they can do. We must go."

"Be silent and let me think for a moment," I said firmly. I scratched my bristled chin as I pondered on what to do. I knew I would not run from this as I was far too curious and the danger didn't concern me.

"I have decided. We will head towards where I saw the fallen star the other night; that particular mystery has hung over my head for far too long now. I was about to leave my home for good now anyway. I think the falling star and these monsters of yours may be connected somehow."

"Then we must head in the opposite direction," pleaded Min.

"No. I am not afraid and I will not run from them. You must stay by me for now, for it is the safest place you can be."

Min considered this and begrudgingly accepted with a quiet nod of her head. I could tell she wanted to stay by me, though it did not seem to come from the desire I secretly hoped for. Puzzlingly, I sensed, it seemed to be out of a sense of duty.

We waited until the following morning so that Min could rest and regain more of her strength. Surprisingly, she seemed to have fully recovered from her ordeal, and was ready physically, though not quite so emotionally, to set off towards where I thought we would find the fallen star. What we would find there, I had no idea.

Min's stamina surprised me. She managed to keep up and never complained of being tired. It was strange travelling with a companion again, especially since Davern had ridden a horse, our maximum pace was very quick. I had to consider Min's need for food and water as well as her limited endurance. I, however, could not remember the last time I had consumed anything. After walking east only half a day through the mountains towards the direction I had seen the falling star, I felt something quite odd, a sudden need to hide.

I looked around urgently. "Quickly, over here, Min." I gestured to a deep alcove in the rock and pulled her in close to me. I felt my heartbeat quicken at being so close to her, feeling her breath on my neck and the radiating warmth of her body. I tore my attention away from her and focused my mind on our surroundings.

"What is it?" Min whispered.

"Something is watching us, something from above."

Min instinctively looked up. "What is it?"

"I don't know, but we cannot go any further without being seen."

It was then that I noticed something else. I could sense a large group of men on horseback almost parallel to our position, also heading in the direction of the fallen star. I waited until the inexorable feeling of danger had passed.

"Quick, follow me as fast as you can," I said. We ran to a position where I calculated our path would meet with the horsemen. Even having seen Min for the well-toned, athletic specimen she was, I was still amazed that she was able to keep up the pace I had set.

Min's tale of monsters seemed too fantastic for words, and yet I had to admit, I believed every word of it.

What were these monsters, really? I wondered. I knew something was watching our movements but it felt like nothing I had ever sensed before. It felt unnatural. The horsemen had stopped and were setting up camp, allowing Min and I to reach their position earlier than expected. I was disappointed to find how easy it was to walk straight into the middle of their quiet little camp.

"You need to post sentries around this camp, for something strange and unnatural is abroad in these parts," I shouted, my voice echoing around the hard surfaces of the surrounding rocks. All faces in the camp turned towards me, some drew their weapons in reaction, a few recognised me immediately and realised the uselessness of such an action.

A man stepped forward "We know. We have come to avenge our companions, who we found slaughtered not two days ago."

"Do you have any idea what you face?" I said.

"Talk of monsters, which I do not believe. But I do believe we will know them when we find them. And we will deal with them."

"With... what? Twenty men."

"With good planning and execution, twenty men can overcome a far greater number."

"I do not know what you face, but I fear they are neither men nor beast. Twenty or a hundred men may make no difference. Let me investigate this matter and I will see what these monsters are. Watch over her." I gestured at Min. "See that she comes to no harm, mind you, for if she does all your lives will be forfeit, of that I promise. I will tell you what I find when I return."

I turned to Min. "Stay with them. This may be more dangerous than I first anticipated. I cannot guarantee you won't come to harm where I am going. You will be safer with them."

"Will I?" she asked doubtfully.

"Yes. Don't worry, I will make sure they understand the dire consequences for touching you or causing you harm of any kind. I will return and…" I stopped mid-sentence as a dreadful feeling fell upon me like a dark shadow reaching from the horizon and into the camp.

"By the Gods they are coming!" I turned to Min, "Run and hide. Now!" The men were startled and on their feet in response to my words.

They appeared from nowhere, and for the first time my eyes fell upon these monsters. There were three of them and they were very much as Min had described. They were the blackest of black one could possibly imagine, with no discernible pattern on their surface. If it were not for the slight shine of their bodies, it would have been impossible to see any internal form at all. Upon their four legs sat a small spherical torso, and on this, what must have been the creatures massive head shaped like a rounded, tapered mallet. There were no facial features of any kind to be seen, yet upon appearance it was obvious they saw us and possibly heard us, too. They stood much taller than any man, which made them seem very menacing. Instead of arms they had three pairs of long tentacles which moved slow, almost hypnotically. Their movements were precise and fluid. They were, indeed, formidable foes. I took all this in, in an instant, for in the next they were within the camp.

I braced myself, ready for an attack from the monster making its way towards me and some other men. In a fluid motion I saw it point a tentacle towards us, the end of which seemed to blossom open. Suddenly, the world around us erupted into fire and light. I instinctively raised my hand and turned my face away, through half-closed eyes I saw a terrible sight; the men standing beside me were burnt to smouldering ash, their screams only lasting less than a second. The fire continued and, as my clothes were burnt to nothing, I became aware that the ground beneath my feet became molten and began to bubble. How could even I survive something like this?

Even though I had only an inkling of what hot and cold were, I did feel it, though neither had ever caused me any discomfort. Now, suddenly, I began to feel intense heat, a building pressure on my skin. I did not like this new feeling and began to panic. I had to act fast. I pretended to fall to the molten ground, the fire stopped and in an instant I had sprung on the foul creature. By the Gods it was as quick as I, its tentacles everywhere, beating upon my body, wrapping around my legs and arms. I held one in my grasp, as it tried to rip my jaw from my skull. We pirouetted and rolled across the camp in a mass of monster and human limbs, in a brutal and ugly hand to tentacle combat, slamming one another into the ground and into the rocks. I could sense the other two monstrosities watching us, but not interfering. I could not sense any of the men and knew that they had quickly been slain in the first moments of battle. Nor could I sense Min...

"Min, where are you?" I screamed. Nothing. "No!"

The evil thing before me was now attempting to crush my head and neck in its powerful grip. I wrapped my arm around one of its tentacles to make sure it would not get away and slowly drew my other fist back, waiting for the right moment. My first blow shook the creature, though it continued its attempt to kill me. Its body seemed unbreakable, but so was my resolve. Whether it took ten or a hundred blows this creature would fall before me. My anger at Min's death and my pounding on the beast increased, each blow more brutal than the last. I sensed some unseen barrier about to be breached that accounted for much of the creature's impenetrability. It failed and suddenly I saw the hide of the monster becoming palpable under my unstoppable blows. I finally broke the head of the creature and it went into spasm, flailing about furiously as if possessed. Suddenly, the huge cursed monstrosity, tentacles and all, went limp. I pulled it from me and threw its dead body to the ground. Its stink on my hands was like some foul, putrid fish.

The other two creatures stood there watching with no sign of emotion that I could sense. Were they wary of me now? I am sure they had never seen a man as strong and resilient as me. They should have feared me for one of them had killed that which I cared for and they would all pay.

"You killed Min, foul monster, and now I am going to kill you."

I launched myself towards the nearest creature but its reaction was instantaneous. It shot something at me, a small projectile that expanded out and transformed itself in mid-flight, casting itself like a net. Though I could see nothing it slammed into my body, and pinned me hard against the rock face. I could not break free! Nonetheless, I continued to vent my rage against this thing while simultaneously tearing apart the rock behind me in a bid to escape. The two creatures moved closer towards me, casting strange lights upon my naked person. This continued for some time, until one of them moved even closer and shone a bright red light directly into my eyes. The world went dark and, for the first time in many months, I fell asleep.

Chapter 9. Ethereality

I slept and I dreamt, for the first time in a long while. My apparent habit of sleeping had turned, in time, into a habit of not sleeping and therefore not dreaming. Had dreaming always been like this? I was aware on some level that I had difficulty recalling recent events. Something terrible happened, yet the harder I tried to remember the more elusive the memories were.

I was standing in my home, the moon casting a hauntingly blue light into the house. Also the fire was fading, emanating a faint orange glow. Other than that, the house was mostly shadow and darkness. I noticed Min standing a few paces away from me.

"Min," I whispered, sadness and yearning tainting my voice. "I am sorry I let you die. I failed you."

"I'm dead?" she replied puzzled. "I seriously doubt that." She dismissed the idea as if it were ludicrous. My sadness deepened, she was just another part of my dream, my poor Min.

"Listen Jonas, we need your help. Perhaps we shouldn't have left it this long. Perhaps we should have said something earlier, but she wanted everything prepared before we made contact."

"What do you mean?" I said.

"Not everything I'm going to tell you or ask of you will make sense; you'll just have to trust us," said Min.

"Us?"

"Us," repeated an unseen voice from the shadows.

"Oh no, not you!"

"Nice to see you've been developing that sense of humour of yours, Jonas," commented the unmistakable voice of Davern.

"This isn't a dream, Jonas. You need to understand that before we can continue," interceded Min. I could see her more clearly now not two paces away.

"How can you prove it?" I said

"I can't really; you just have to trust me." She reached out and held my hand in hers and touched my face gently with her other; it felt real enough. I considered her a moment. My father always told me to trust my instincts.

"Let us say that this is not a dream. Now what?" I asked.

"The creatures that attacked you are called Nacuerians, a name we have given them. You see we know so little about them; we don't even know what they call themselves. They are currently taking you back to their ship, where they are preparing to leave and go a long way from here."

"Where's that exactly?" I asked curiously.

"That's difficult to explain."

"Oh."

"This is going to be impossible. He has no frame of reference to understand you," commented Davern, shaking his head.

"Be quiet," Min ordered calmly but firmly, and surprisingly he did.

"We have to stop them leaving, this is the only way. Jonas, there is something inside you that can… break their ship, stop it working. They'll be curious about you, so they'll be… looking at you in different ways. That is when this thing inside you will attack their ship, and hopefully stop them leaving."

"What is it? What is inside me? How did it get there?" I asked.

Min gave me a gentle smile. "It is something incredibly small, which can be transferred by touch, such as when you touched my cheek when I lay on your bed. It is referred to as a cerebral implant and despite its size it has the potential to stop the Nacuerians. "

I was now trying to fathom something akin to magic. "How is that possible?"

"Do whatever you can to bring down that ship, my voice will still be in your head to help you, when you wake."

"This really isn't a dream is it?"

"No," they said simultaneously.

"Who are you both? What is going on here?"

"All in good time, oh impatient one," said Davern.

"First we must destroy that ship. Don't worry about getting hurt, you'll be fine," assured Min.

"You hope," said Davern

Min gave him a look that would have struck dumb any man; such confidence. "He will be fine."

"What about us? Garianne hasn't authorised any of this," protested Davern.

"She would if she were here. I've told you she won't get back here in time, we have to act now."

"Wait! You know Garianne? Who is she?" I exclaimed.

Min looked into the darkness. "We must go, be ready." Abruptly she was gone.

I stood in the darkened room feeling like the dream had ended and I had been abandoned. The details of my surroundings were swallowed up by shadow and I was left in a completely featureless, black void.

Where is Garianne? I thought, and then quite suddenly I was someplace else; a place I did not recognise. At first it struck me that I was in some kind of immense temple, for I had never seen a room so large that had not been a place of worship. It was almost the size of Chief Hamah's entire town, and high above me through a transparent domed roof I could see a multitude of stars and lights, which were as awe-inspiring as they were beautiful. I had never seen the heavens look like this. *Where am I?*

Even more shocking than the view of the dome were the strange creatures that occupied the room. They were all four-legged and covered in short, light brown hair. They stood almost nine feet tall; their front legs were almost twice as long as the back ones, setting its body up at a seventy-degree angle. Its shoulders, jointed human-like onto its neck which ended in a flat head. Its eyes were at least three times larger than a human's and closely resembled that of an ox, with heavy eyelids, except it had a keen look of intelligence in them. All of them seemed oblivious to my presence, and everywhere in the room there were strange and elaborate light shapes that the creatures continually interacted with.

There was also someone else here. They appeared to be human, and female. I thought this because her back was facing me and I felt I could not be sure of anything at that point. She was a tall, slender figure, dressed in some elaborate gown the likes of which I had never seen before. Power and authority emanated from her. She stood not ten paces from me and I had a nervous feeling that unlike everyone else in the room, she knew I was here; I felt very much the intruder. I was about to approach her when she turned around to look directly at me and smiled. She appeared to be around ten years older than Min, with a mild, flawless complexion and dark hair. She reminded me of Min; there was something so supremely confident about her. I managed to hold her unwavering gaze long enough for some kind of recognition. I knew those eyes.

She walked towards me; her movements subtle, fluid, and perfect. "Amazing, quite amazing," she remarked.

"Garianne! But you were an old woman when we first met. How can you be so young?"

"I have taken many guises in the past, that was one of them."

"Garianne, to whom do you speak? My sensors do not detect anything on the command deck." The voice, seemingly coming from nowhere, was deep, melodic, and in some way comforting. Strangely, it sounded to me how I would imagine a mountain or a large rock to speak.

"It is fine, Lom. Just an unexpected guest," replied Garianne continuing to smile at me. "Unexpected, though quite welcome."

I could see that the creatures had reacted now, and I believed somehow that they had been privy to this verbal exchange and my presence in the room. With Garianne's assurance they went back to their previous business.

"Garianne, what is going on here? Am I awake or am I still dreaming?" I asked her.

"Dreaming? You've been sleeping?"

"I don't think it was natural. One of the creatures I was fighting shone a bright light in my face; I felt my consciousness slipping away. The next moment I found myself talking to Min and Davern as if in a dream. They know you. How?"

"They work for me."

More questions sprung into my mind. I was becoming very annoyed.

"Something is going on here. Are you going to tell me what it is?" I challenged.

"First tell me what happened to you and what Min said to you in your dream."

Garianne pondered thoughtfully on all I recounted and I felt as though I were somehow fidgeting impatiently as I waited for a response.

"You must do whatever Min tells you to do, no matter what it is. I will see you soon, and then I promise all your questions will be answered."

"When will that be?" I asked rather desperately. I could feel myself starting to slip from this place as if I were suddenly on the edge of a cliff and something was undeniably about to pull me away.

"Any day. Now go."

I tried to hold on as Garianne turned away, her words seeming distant and muffled.

"Lom, we need to leave now, all departure procedures will be completed on route to the 'Sol' system," she commanded in that undeniable voice.

As I slipped slowly away I looked up. The stars themselves shifted and a monstrously huge, curved object heaved into view. *By the Gods, are those clouds that I can see? What am I looking at?*

The thoughts were lost, as again I was enveloped by oblivion.

Chapter 10. Starship

When I awoke, I was upright and submerged in some form of liquid, yet I could hear myself breathing rhythmically and everything was peaceful.

I heard a voice in my head. *Keep your eyes shut, remain calm, and do not move.*

Min! I thought, trying to do as she requested.

Not exactly, Jonas, I am a simulation of her in your head.

I do not understand.

Understanding is not essential at this point.

Where am I now?

Beginnings are the foundations of success, Jonas. Their systems have proved more complex than we anticipated and we have to be cautious. There's a much larger possibility for error now rather than later, so you must do exactly as I say.

Can you hear my thoughts?

Indeed I can. I am inside your mind, so you don't have to speak. In fact it is imperative you don't for if you do they will know that you're conscious. Think clearly and I will hear you.

I will, I replied, finding it surprisingly easy.

Good. We are lucky. The Nacuerians never scanned you. They aren't aware of your cerebral implant, or the virus which has already penetrated this ship's systems. But it may be detected at any moment.

I do not understand.

Please Jonas, don't worry about the details. Just do as I say.

I did the mental equivalent of nodding my head.

Where am I exactly?

You are aboard a Nacuerian ship, held inside a transparent cylinder of breathable liquid. Would you like to see?

Without confirmation an image sprung into my head. I could quite clearly see myself as she had described. It was an odd sight and felt unnatural as if I were dead, looking upon my own corpse. The liquid was eerily green, and I was breathing away, looking quite peaceful. I moved the thumb on my right hand ever so subtlety and saw my doppelganger respond in the same manner – incredible! I quickly noted my surroundings; nothing was familiar.

The liquid contains special properties, primarily though it keeps you asleep. The virus I have placed within the ship's systems has disabled that property and so you are awake. Do you understand?

I believe so. I'd given up the how, what, and why. I only knew that I truly trusted her and I wanted to get through this.

The Nacuerians believe you are still unconscious and therefore incapable of causing them any kind of harm, I want you to prove them wrong. I had the distinct feeling she was smiling mischievously as she said this.

What if they put me to sleep again? I asked apprehensively.

They can't if you don't want them to. The red light they shone in your eyes made a part of your mind think you needed to sleep, your consciousness simply obeyed. You can resist it; you only have to believe and fight it. This also goes for any other tricks or magic they might try to use against you. They can't stop you if you believe they can't. Fight them, Jonas, a lot depends on it.

Min, are you still alive?

I hope so.

How can you not know? I asked.

I'll tell you later. Get ready to follow my instructions, she replied.

I was even more confused than before. How could she not know if she was alive or dead?

I waited for a moment and then felt my surroundings move. A violent tremor was shaking me and I knew it was time to act.

Jonas break out of that thing, now, said Min's voice.

I opened my eyes and saw that I really was there, floating in that cylinder, green liquid colouring everything I could see. I pushed myself from the wall facing me and in a blur my foot whipped out hitting the cylinder as hard as I could. The force of it broke its surface, and the liquid with me in it poured from the container. I remember seeing a woman give birth once a long time ago; it was a little like that, though even more of a mess. I picked myself up from the wet floor as naked as a newborn. The world around me still trembled, and then suddenly I heard a new and very loud noise, the likes of which I had never heard before. For some reason I felt that they knew I had escaped from my prison and were coming.

The unfamiliar surroundings and the barrage of sounds were too much for me. *Min, help. I need you.*

I'm here. Look. I was suddenly aware of an elaborate map in my head of the Nacuerian ship and my position within it. I could make out all the intricate structures and components in an incredible three-dimensional image. More immediate than anything else was the fact I could see a substantial number of these Nacuerians moving about the ship, some of which were heading my way.

Fear welled up inside me. *I cannot handle them all, there are simply too many.*

Of course you can. You found it hard the first time because you weren't prepared; the unknown can be terrifying and make you question your abilities. You can do it.

I knew Min wanted to say more, but it was too late, they were here.

They came in like leaves in the wind, some kind of unorthodox battle formation. I think it was supposed to confuse me, while at the same time giving them an advantage to locate my position; very clever. There was no constructive way I could plan my own attack with the way they came in jumping around like that, so I did all I could do. I grabbed the nearest one to me and started from there.

Move quickly and stay on your feet, Min said.

I did so, but it was not easy. The fighting was extremely fast, vicious, and brutal. I suspect that if any normal man were in that room he would have been dead pulp immediately. My world was a mass of black shapes, trying to batter me senseless, pushing and pulling with incredible strength and speed unmatched by any human movement. My rage unencumbered, I matched their speed and brutality. I had never truly tested my limits. Fighting in this chaos was, for the most part, purely an instinctive and subconscious act. My own thoughts distracted me enough for a mass of the Nacuerians to pin me against a wall. With both my arms held and two others holding my head the red light shone into my eyes. I closed them quickly.

Closing your eyes won't make a difference. You have to resist it Jonas. With all your will, concentrate.

I opened my eyes and stared defiantly at them, at the red light. After a moment, my head lolled and my body relaxed, and so did the Nacuerians. In less than a second a Nacuerian by my right fist was flying across the room at incredible speed and another found his shell had been broken. They quickly reacted to my resistance by throwing themselves against me, pinning me once more to the wall. four of them pulled with all of their might against my right arm, over twenty strong tentacles intertwined with my arm – trying to literally pull it off, and by the Gods as much as I resisted, it felt like they would succeed.

I began to panic *Min. My arm!*

Jonas, concentrate! You are a super-sentient being; you can resist them easily. Three or three hundred it doesn't matter. They can't beat you, believe me.

There was such conviction, such certainty in her voice, I believed her, even though I did not know what super-sentient meant.

The pull on my arm no longer seemed so strong and something changed within me, as my resolve was renewed, invigorating my mind and body. Quicker than I had performed any action before, I tugged hard on the tentacles wrapped around my left arm, which in a spray of blood, broke off like a handful of flower stems. They buckled in apparent pain, yet as usual not making a sound, their blood, which was a dirty grey colour, pasting the walls and floor. The others attacked me once again, yet their movements no longer seemed so fast, while my mind and body were like quicksilver. Suddenly, perfectly straight lines of what looked like lightning emanated from the creatures towards me. I had just pierced the shell of another Nacuerian and in a fluid motion moved it in between myself and the path of the lightning. With barely any hindrance the lightning went straight through the Nacuerian. I looked down in shock and saw the lightning upon my chest causing me no damage or discomfort; it felt more like a concentrated jet of water, rather than something far more dangerous.

From this point on they produced more weapons, each one as ineffective as the last. Meanwhile, I was slowly but surely diminishing their numbers; all the while the room continued to shake and jolt.

Jonas, I'm almost ready, said Min's voice.

For what?

To crash this ship.

I do not understand.

You will in a moment. Clear this room of those last two abominations.

No sooner had she said this, than the two Nacuerians left of their own accord. Cowardice? I thought not. They had left something behind, something dangerous. The room around me exploded in blue and white light, jolting my body.

What was that? I asked Min, as I picked myself from the floor.

Something that was supposed to kill you, but didn't.

The room is undamaged, I observed.

The weapon was designed to destroy organic matter, not the ship. Now just sit tight. Your part is over; you've distracted them long enough for me to gain temporary control of their ship. I'm going to crash it.

I still had the feeling that Min was describing things as simply as possible, just so that I could understand a little of what was happening. Again Min made me feel like a child.

Crash it against what, Min? What about me, should I get out of here?

No, I think you may find falling to Earth a bit distressing. It's best you're not fully aware of what's about to happen.

Falling to Earth? What do you mean? I thought we were at sea.

Jonas, this may be hard for you to conceive but the ship is in flight not on a body of water.

She somehow showed me an exterior view of the ship in my mind. By the Gods, was this ship really aloft amongst the clouds, and now falling back towards the Earth at what looked like tremendous speed; I did not feel any such movement.

Min, this cannot be. How can something so large fly? There was a certain amount of desperation in my question, for it looked like this ship would not be in the air for much longer.

I'll explain later. I'm using all the ship's power to put an inertial containment field around you. It will protect you initially when the ship crashes. I don't think the Nacuerians will be so lucky though.

My body came off from the floor, as I experienced the strangest sensation.

Min, what is happening?

Stay calm. You're just weightless, because of the containment.

Weightless? I was slowly turning upside down, twisting and turning, my limbs flailing about. There was no way to stop myself.

Now hold on.

With an overwhelming noise, louder than anything I had ever heard before, I saw my surroundings instantly collapsed upon me, and everything went pitch-black. I tensed up and curled into a ball, screaming. However, whatever it was that Min had used to protect me did an exceptional job, for nothing made physical contact with me for that first initial moment. After that I was abruptly enveloped by the crashing ship.

After the sound had died down and the wreckage had ceased moving, I broke my way free from what was left of the Nacuerian ship. I was completely unscathed. I looked about the enormous crater I now stood in, as confused as ever. I could sense no other life anywhere near me; it appeared that the Nacuerians were all dead. An eerie stillness slowly settled across the crash site and I felt angry that I still did not know the nature of what had really occurred, I felt like a plaything to all those forces I had witnessed, though could not fathom.

Min? I thought.

Nothing. As quiet now as my surroundings.

"Min!" I shouted out loud, my voice echoing across the barren landscape.

Still nothing. She was either no longer there, could not, or would not respond. I looked about me at all the destruction. I had felt no sensation of falling and nothing from the impact either. Was it the containment field Min had spoken of? I spent some time looking through the debris that might offer any enlightenment, until I eventually realised that it was futile. All that was left of the Nacuerian vessel was in ruin.

Curiously, I did not feel a need to return to my home in the mountains. Instead I felt an irresistible pull back to the place I was born and grew up in – the place my parents had been murdered and buried. For days I walked as if I were half asleep. I did not know why I was going back; I only knew I wanted to go back there, where it had all begun. On the way I came across a camp of men and during the night, while they slept, managed to take some clothes with which to cover up my modesty.

On the third day of my journey, mid-afternoon, I finally reached the crest of the familiar sloping hills that lead into the small shallow valley of what had been my home. I looked down upon the house and saw something quite unexpected. Someone was on the roof. I also sensed something else down there, yet it eluded me.

The sun was hot the day I returned to the place of my birth and, even though its heat did not physically affect me, somehow it contributed to my already foul mood. As I approached the stranger, I decided it would be nice to get some straight answers for a change.

"You on the roof, what are you doing?" I shouted. Even though I had abandoned it sometime ago, I still felt it belonged to my family.

"Why, repairing it of course. Can't you see that, Jonas?" said a voice.

Garianne's head appeared from the other side of the roof. "Good afternoon. What do you think? It's taken a little while, but I think it looks as good as new."

"Garianne, by the Gods you are here!"

I then witnessed a most beautiful sight. She jumped from the roof spinning in the air, and landed with uncanny grace and agility, like sand dancing in the wind. I felt I had just seen something perfect in the world; the movement had been so exact, so precise.

I was at a loss for words. I could see now that she wore a simple two-piece garment, the likes of which I had never seen. The little there was of it conformed to her delicate well-toned curves, as if it were a second layer of skin. The heat of the sun seemed to cause her no visible indication of discomfort.

"Why have you done this?" I asked, trying to look at the house rather than stare at her – somehow what she wore seemed more revealing than if she were naked. It looked as she had described it, as good as new.

"It is an offer of goodwill," she replied, walking over to a small container. "Thirsty work," she commented as she finished drinking. "My companions were horrified when I told them I wanted to rebuild this place with my own hands. You see, where I come from, this kind of work can be done in a blink of an eye, with hardly any effort at all."

I found that hard to believe, though should I really, after all I had seen? These constant mysteries were intriguing yet becoming tiresome. I wanted answers.

"Then why do it this way?" I asked, shaking my head.

Her eyes became distant and even a little sad. "The more time you have, the less you have. Something is lost: appreciation, learning, understanding. Many take the most direct route, their view of the world, only a basic perception of what really is; they miss the finer details. However, concentrate too much on the finer details and you miss the larger view. The trick is to do both at the same time."

When I look back at the words she spoke that day, I realise, as with everything Garianne said, the significance of them, and the vast depths of wisdom. Unfortunately, at the time, I did not appreciate them much at all; I merely stood there and shook my head.

"You want answers? Very well, it is time for them. Believe me when I say this – when you see what I have to show you, when you have seen it all, your life can never be the same."

I merely nodded in response.

"Very well, let us go then," she said.

"Where?" I stood my ground.

"To the ship," she gestured to my left, past the farm.

"I do not see anything," I said baffled.

"But you sense it, don't you?" returned Garianne.

"How do you know that?"

"I can see the way you've been glancing in that direction. You scrutinize it; you know something is there, though you don't know what. Look harder, Jonas. There is something there, yes?" She encouraged me.

I could make out a shape in the air and it was monstrously huge, dwarfing the farm. As I tried to make out the details they appeared to me, until it finally stood there as clear as day.

"By the Gods, what is it?"

"The cloak is still on, Garianne," said a voice I thought I had heard before.

"And yet he can still see it, Lom. Incredible," replied Garianne.

"See it, how could I miss it?" I stared at the structure before me, as big as a mountain, shining in the sun, reaching towards the heavens.

Chapter 11. Orientation

Garianne led me onto a platform, which shockingly rose into the air and into what was their sky ship. Together we walked down bright white, wide corridors making several turns, until we came to another doorway, the two parts of which seemed to melt into the walls as we approached. They then sealed themselves up behind us as we entered a room even larger than the one I had seen in my dream with the strange brown fur-covered creatures. It was dimly lit and circular. I saw strange patterns of light on the floor and on the wall that surrounded us. The floor felt strange beneath my feet, like standing on grass, yet it looked shiny and smooth. I knelt down and pushed my hand against it. It gave way a fraction though still held firm.

"This way," gestured Garianne. She was now standing in the middle of the vast chamber, embodied by a large circle of light.

I joined her. "This place is so big, what is its purpose?"

"It has more than one, though today I think it's time we gave you a little orientation."

I suddenly sensed two other people in the room as they walked into the light.

"Min! Davern!" My emotions were mixed, seeing them both here together. Min was alive and Davern had that irritating smirk on his face.

"Time for the truth, big boy. Think you can handle it?"

"Leave him alone. Are you alright, Jonas?" Min came to me and inspected me with her stern eyes as one might examine a pet. Was that all I was to her?

"What happened to you? One moment you were with me the next you were not?" I said to her accusingly, my brow furrowed.

"It was necessary, I'll explain later."

"Later! It is always later with you people!" I bellowed. "I want answers now!"

Garianne's eyes flicked from me to a point in the centre of the chamber. Suddenly something exploded and I quickly covered my eyes, startled. When I withdrew my hands, I found myself dumbstruck. Around us, as if it were real, was my parents' home and the surrounding valley. The only indication that it was some kind of illusion was the fact that I could still make out the far side of the room through the image and I could feel or sense nothing of the air or heat I would associate with the outside.

"Here is a representation of the farm and its immediate surroundings," said Garianne. I looked about me, the detail perfect.

"This is a view as seen from higher up."

Suddenly the view grew smaller as more terrain came rushing in to fill the gaps. It felt like I had been thrown up into the sky at incredible speed. I stumbled and Min grabbed me to stop me from falling. Our apparent movement stopped and it seemed like we were all standing on nothingness high up in the air, magically suspended. I could not help holding tight onto Min's arm.

"Are you alright, Jonas?" asked Davern, chuckling.

Everyone ignored him.

"From up here you can make out most of the lands of Assyria and Babylonia, the two rivers Tigris and Euphrates, the major cities, the Taurus Mountains to the left of you and the Zagros Mountains where you spent some time, to the right," said Garianne. I stared, mesmerised at the land below me. I could make out the path I had taken the year before I had settled in the mountains.

I had to keep telling myself that although this looked real it was not. All my senses screamed to me that I would fall, except that extra sense that I possessed that others did not, revealing the truth, that this was indeed an illusion.

Again the current view receded below us, as it seemed we flew up higher above the land, at a slower rate this time.

"Make the view complete, Lom," ordered Garianne. The last parts of the room disappeared and the illusion was now in every direction, above me a beautiful clear blue sky and the land stretching off far in the distance. Something strange struck me though as we continued to rise up.

"Are you alright?" asked Min, distracting my attention. I had not realised how tightly I was grasping her arm. I tried to relax it a little.

"I am sorry. Did I hurt you?"

"No." She smiled at me and my heart sighed. I was surprised again by Min's strength and resilience, for I felt sure the grip I had on her was, unintentionally, enough to damage her. I still held her firm, though as gently as I could under the circumstances. She was my only anchor, keeping me from feeling like I would lose my balance and fall. She, on the other hand, was as steady as a rock. I turned my attention back to that which puzzled me a moment before. It was the horizon. It was ever so slightly curved – how odd. Below me I saw the seas, which I had never been to before. I marvelled at the immense bodies of water and at the great land masses surrounding my home country. I smiled as I realised I was finally seeing those lands I had dreamt and wondered about on the maps. Min nudged me and indicated that I look up. The blue sky was now slowly turning dark as if it were becoming night. Surely this was not due for some time. I looked back to the horizon and what now lay beneath me.

"By the Gods!" I exclaimed. "The Earth is curved." Indeed it did seem that the horizon was now bowed. Along the horizon the Earth glowed and above this the sky was now black and the stars had come out. The curve of the Earth continued to increase as we ascended even further and a kind of panic slowly rose in me. I imagined people slipping from the edges of the world, yet nothing fell and there were no edges as I saw with utter disbelief the two ends of the curve meet to form a self-contained circle – no, a sphere. I stared, breathing hard, my teeth gritted as moisture came to my eyes.

"There is your world, Jonas. The planet Earth. Not as flat as you expected but a sphere of land and water," stated Garianne bluntly.

"It's alright, Jonas, try to breathe regularly," Min reassured me. I looked at Davern expecting his usual smirk at my weakness. All I saw though was concern.

"It is what it is. Accept it," said Davern frankly.

"How is it that people are not... falling?" I pointed an accusing finger at the receding ball in the heavens.

"A force called gravity holds everything onto the planet's surface. All matter exhibits this attractive force, though it is only when there's a lot of it all gathered together, such as all the material that makes up the Earth, the sun, and the moon, when it can hold things, such as atmospheres, oceans, land, and people," said Garianne. The sun and the moon were also in view now.

"Why are the sun and moon not pulled into the Earth then?" I asked, trying to calm myself.

"The gravity of the Earth pulls the moon around it, similar to the way you might spin a weight around yourself using a rope. The Earth is only one of many planets that orbit the sun."

"There are other worlds in the heavens?" As I asked this question the speed of the receding Earth increased unimaginably. In a moment it had disappeared from sight and Garianne showed me other worlds in the Earth's solar system; worlds of fire and ice, of every kind, all in perfect detail. Masses of text appeared in the air describing the attributes of these planets, though most of the concepts I did not understand. One by one they came into view like the Earth, as if we could touch them, and then disappeared again. Eventually I looked at the now distant sun.

"There was no other life on any of those planets," I stated.

"There used to be, a long time ago, and it was very primitive. Nothing like human life though," replied Garianne. The view did not seem to change much. I could almost perceive the sun becoming even smaller and I wondered if we were still moving through the cold, black silence of the void. I sensed the others waiting for me to say something and I knew that there was something here for me to grasp, to puzzle out. I looked at the stars and then at the sun. From here they looked the same.

"The stars… the stars are all suns. Do they have planets, with life?"

Garianne smiled. "Yes." The overwhelming brightness of a sun flashed by and soon after we were above another planet with many lights upon its surface; signs of civilisation on another world.

"The chance of life occurring in a star system are very remote despite there being many, many stars in the galaxy."

"How many stars are there in the galaxy?"

We were whisked away from the planet at an incredible speed and, despite its vast size, it had gone. I could see other stars congregating in the area around that planet's sun. In other areas of the room yet more stars came into view.

Garianne glanced at a point just above her head and, as if by magic, a number appeared in the air.

10

"This is the number of digits on your hands. Multiply it by another ten and you get?" The number changed.

100

"You simply add a zero to represent this number. Do you understand?"

"Yes," I said nodding.

Garianne continued. "From this vantage point you can see roughly this many stars."

1,000

"Can you imagine that?"

"I... I think... I can," I stammered, unsure of myself.

"Can you?" she pressed. I was trying; it was such a large number though. She looked as more and more stars came into view. I was exasperated as I saw a central glow emerging from this endless collection of stars like so much sand upon the ground. The number increased terrifyingly above Garianne's head, staggering my imagination as I tried to grasp the reality, as the whole majesty of it was revealed to me.

"The galaxy we live in is a huge swirling mass made up of around this many stars," said Garianne, indicating the number above her head.

400,000,000,000

Now my legs were starting to tremble and I could feel Min holding me up a little.

"I cannot... that is too many," I whispered shaking my head.

"And that is not all," she went on. Even the galaxy now receded and horrifyingly I could see there were others, each one crying out its existence to me, each with its uncountable stars. I felt myself drowning in what I saw, yet I could not close my eyes.

"Garianne, he can't handle it. It's too much for him," protested Davern.

Garianne gave the smallest of gestures and he fell silent.

"Min, hold him up," said Garianne. Min did so, though I felt a slight reservation in her.

"The universe contains as many galaxies as there are stars in our own galaxy, and yet we are just one of innumerable other universes in all of creation." With these words my eyes witnessed something I could barely comprehend as I saw the universe as a whole – a bubble with the universe upon it, in it, within it? Floating in, I had no idea what, with innumerable others.

"Behold the multiverse an infinite number of universes, some very like our own, other vastly different," said Garianne.

I saw universes like sand in the desert, yet structured into great spherical arrays layered one upon the other, each one larger than the one underneath, At the centre was a dense light. As the view receded, more and more universe came into view, As many universes as there had been stars in our own galaxy and still it kept on going, It was too much, I felt my mind finally failing to grasp what my eyes were witnessing, as my body went limp and I lost consciousness.

It was dark as I sat by the kindled fire in my parents' house. I could not bring myself to look up at the lights in the night sky quite yet; I only wanted to look into the fire. It helped me think and relax. My soul felt fragile, as if the merest tap would shatter me into pieces and I would become a gibbering idiot or worse, I feared, a dumb beast merely chewing the cud barely aware of anything.

There was a loud knock on my door; I started shaking again.

"Come in," I answered. Garianne entered like an intruder with Min behind, looking concerned. I continued to shake, though I wondered what Garianne could really do if I suddenly decided to unleash my full wrath upon her. Though I found I could not even look at them, only into the fire.

"I insisted Min not come, though she was adamant she see you, Jonas," said Garianne. Min's beautiful face looked anywhere but at me, while Garianne stood calm and upright as always.

"I am sorry it had to be this way, Jonas. I did what was necessary, though," said Garianne.

"How can you say that? Look at what you have done to me; I am scared of... everything."

"It will pass soon enough and you will be the stronger for it. Remember that for the next time."

"The next time? Never!" I hissed at her, putting my chair between her and myself. Tears came to my eyes.

"Like metal upon a forge, the body and mind can be made stronger," said Garianne.

"I do not feel strong, I feel broken, in pieces, crushed and repeatedly trampled into the dirt."

She suddenly moved towards me. Before I could react she had grasped my hand; I had never seen anyone move so fast, not the Nacuerians nor even myself. I felt something, an inner focus and strength open up from the depths of my being.

"It can be made stronger, especially yours, Jonas," she drilled into me. "What can you remember from the simulation earlier today?"

"No! Do not make me think of that," I said.

"Garianne, don't hurt him," Min protested quietly.

Garianne ignored her. "Describe to me the ice-covered moon of the fifth planet of Earth's solar system."

I stumbled away shaking my head, yet she held tight onto me.

"You're hurting him," protested Min sternly, yet Garianne continued to ignore her. As strong as Min was, it was obvious that Garianne was in charge here.

"Now!" demanded Garianne calmly but with an assertiveness I had never heard before.

"The moon has an average distance of 670,900 kilometres from the gas giant and it has an orbital period equal to that of 3.551 Earth days. It has a diameter of 3,130 kilometres and…" I said. As I went into even further depth about the moon, my shaking subsided. My posture and confidence were restored too and I began to feel like my old self again. Garianne let go of me.

"How does he know all that?" asked Min after a stunned silence.

"It was all there during the simulation. Jonas took in every detail, didn't you, Jonas?" said Garianne. I merely nodded, my head was awash with information I had until now not been conscious of. I also sensed that there was yet more underneath the surface.

"I do not understand half of it, though," I said.

"Only because you haven't yet been educated," replied Garianne. "Now we have given you a basic grounding in orientation, we will tackle mathematics, physics, chemistry, and a multitude of other areas of study."

"I think it is time you told me who you are and what it is you want of me," I said firmly to her.

"I think so too," she agreed smiling once more.

Garianne said the best way to explain would be to go back to the simulation room. I flinched ever so slightly when I went out into the night from my parents' house. *No,* I thought, *I will not cower from the stars like a man gone mad.* Despite my fear I stood up straight and stared back defiantly at those vast spheres of fire in the void.

Aboard what I realised now was a starship, we again entered the simulation room and I felt more than a little trepidation at being there again. The galaxy was already waiting for me, looking like some monstrous sand jewel suspended in the dark.

Davern stood there, his arms folded, watching me. The smirk gone from his face. "Are you alright?" he asked.

I nodded to him.

Garianne approached me. "My name is Cieshella Garianne Phulum. I was born on the planet Kylia a little over four thousand years ago." As she spoke we moved into the galaxy at an impossible speed until I could see we were above a planet in orbit around a star similar to Earth's sun. The planet also looked fairly similar to Earth, though I could tell it was not for it was mostly covered in a vibrant green and did not possess very much ocean.

"Over four-thousand years ago. How is that possible?" I asked.

"We'll get to the details later. Simply put, we have found a way to copy a person's mind and body, and recreate that person into a new form, fresh from the ravages of time. If you repeat this process, a person can live for a very long time."

"Forever?" I asked disbelievingly.

Garianne smiled. "Ah, well that is an interesting question. It is theoretically possible to repeat the process indefinitely, as long as there is no chaotic disruption that interrupts the process. A person could live as long as the multiverse."

"Will the multiverse last forever?" I asked her.

"Jonas, you do ask the most interesting questions. You've only just been introduced to the idea of a reality so much larger than the one you originally perceived, and already you are asking some very profound and fundamental questions. Any other human mind on this planet would have taken so much longer, if ever, to recover from the experience you had. The answer, most believe, is yes, yet it has not been proven beyond all possible doubt," said Garianne.

"You have been watching me all this time. First you, then Davern, and then Min," I stated simply.

"I came to see if you were truly what we had hoped for. I knew as soon as I met you that it was true. I had to leave Earth shortly after that, though, so I left Min and Davern to watch over you."

"And pretend to be human?"

"I instructed them that we would tell you everything when I returned. If you want someone to blame for the deception, then blame me, though believe me this way is best. You will see the truth of it one day."

"What is it you want from me then?" I asked. I had many questions, though I believed this particular one would unlock a great many truths.

"To answer that, I think we need a quick history lesson."

The planet below and all the stars faded away.

Min took my hand. "You might want to hold onto me." I looked at her. "Remember it's only a simulation. It's not real."

"I am not afraid." I replied determinedly. I refused to be afraid of whatever was to come. I took Min's hand from mine and walked defiantly to the centre of the room, stealing an equally defiant look at the impassive Garianne.

The room was plunged into darkness, before abruptly exploding in light. I could not help but momentarily flinch, yet I gathered all my will and held fast, standing tall against this unimaginable sight. There was no sound, though it felt as if there were, for I could not imagine all the light spreading throughout the room without a deafening rumble or roar.

"What you are witnessing is a simulation of the creation of our universe, almost fourteen billion years ago," said Garianne.

This time I consciously sensed the information from these events in the room. Even though I did not comprehend the numbers, I still had a fair perception of the underlying concepts behind them.

"After a considerable amount of time the universe cooled and gravity attracted matter together to form the first stars and eventually star systems. We believe that life may have first formed around twelve billion years ago. It 'evolved'."

Though I previously had no understanding of the idea of evolution, as she said the word I found I had somehow gathered a vague understanding of the concept.

"We went from primitive to higher, more intelligent forms, and eventually began venturing out into space," Garianne continued. "For reasons we do not understand we have never had any contact from earlier spacefaring species; their existence is pure speculation on our part. The oldest species we know of seems to have begun its venture into space only as recent as seven thousand years ago. This is very recent when you consider the galaxy has been capable of supporting life for billions of years, and yet only now, in cosmological terms, has the first species explored into space. Others have followed. Now there are over a hundred different spacefaring species throughout the galaxy. The oldest in the galaxy, is called the Galacien. The Galacien and the younger sentient species work together for the betterment of all sentient life in the galaxy. They are called, the Galacien Conglomerate of Worlds (GCW)."

"I still do not see where I come into all of this," I pointed out.

Garianne continued unabated. "As the Galacien and other species spread out across the galaxy over thousands of years, the galactic population increased vastly. We realised something that had previously gone unnoticed, due to populations previously being relatively small. We noticed the emergence of super-sentient beings."

"Min, you said I was a super-sentient when on the Nacuerian ship."

Garianne replied before Min did. "Yes, Jonas, Min may have been a little premature, but all signs seem to indicate that you are."

"There are others then? Others like me?"

"Only one amongst billions will be born super-sentient, so it was not until the galaxy's population was significantly large enough that we noticed this phenomenon. There was once, what we of the Galacien consider, the Golden Age, a time when there were hundreds of super-sentient beings made up of various species. They possessed incredible powers and working with the Galacien they did things then that we have never been able to match. You see there are no more super-sentient beings in the galaxy."

"What do you mean?" I asked.

"Over two thousand years ago the birth rate of super-sentient beings began to fall until eventually it had reached zero. The others lost their abilities when they reached an age where they needed to transfer to new bodies. A super-sentient's life is exceptionally long, but they do not live forever and once copied into a new form those abilities are lost. The last super-sentient existed nearly two thousand years ago, and no one has encountered another since, until now."

"Me," I said simply. "I am the first in all that time."

"It appears so," replied Min. "Though the situation is a little more immediate than that."

"It has something to do with these Nacuerians, doesn't it?" I replied.

"Indeed it does," said Garianne. "We need your help, Jonas. The galaxy has been invaded by the Nacuerians and we are losing the war against them. It was fifty-seven years ago when we first detected their presence in the galaxy. They are a brutal war-like species unlike any we have ever encountered before, seemingly interested only in destroying life and establishing themselves in its place. We are unsure of where they originate from. I am the Galacien's supreme strategist in this war and I believe that, if applied in the right manner, you can help turn the tide in our favour."

I looked at them disbelievingly. "I know I am quite different from anyone else, but what can I do really?"

"If you don't help us they will destroy all life within the galaxy. They will kill Davern, Min, and me. And then they will come for you. There will be no more sentient life left in the galaxy, except them," said Garianne.

"I can't do this. I have never experienced anything like this."

Garianne's smile was like a blanket smothering the fire of my anger. "Jonas, the Galacien has been a spacefaring species for thousands of years, most of the others, almost as long. This is the first time this has ever happened. No one has experienced the unimaginable enormity of such a thing as a galaxy-wide invasion before. We are all in over our heads here."

Again the view of the galaxy appeared. This time I could see it was broken up into patches of red and blue; there was a lot more blue than red.

"The blue represents the Galacien and any other sentient life indigenous to our galaxy. The red represents the Nacuerian-occupied territories," said Garianne. The red then began to spread, replacing the blue areas of the galaxy. A number of Earth years, as I now understood them, were played out in a matter of seconds.

"Our simulations show that, at this rate, the Nacuerians will destroy all life in our galaxy within six years. That's trillions of sentient beings, on thousands of planets."

Min approached me, placing her hand gently in mine. "She's right, Jonas. No one is safe and so consequentially everyone is involved. If we leave you here on your own, they will find you one day."

"Let them, I will make sure they regret it," I said stubbornly. I was reluctant to be at the mercy of their whims.

"No Jonas. Without our help they will come. And even though at first you may be able to slow them down a little, eventually they will overpower you. They will come and tear you apart, body and mind, for any useful information and you will be unable to prevent them. Only together can we stop them." said Min. Something about her words chilled me to the core.

Now Davern approached me and spoke. "Can't you see, Min, he cares only for himself? Let the rest of the galaxy suffer and burn, it doesn't matter to him."

"And what do you propose as the alternative?" I replied.

"Come with us," said Garianne "we will teach you, train you. We don't know how you can help yet, but we can prepare you for an opening, an opportunity. We can offer you all the knowledge you've ever sought, Jonas. That must be worth some sacrifice." I stood there for a long time regarding the sea of stars before me, while they waited patiently.

Eventually I spoke. "You know, there was a time when all I ever wanted was to be left alone. Until I met you Garianne. Until that night you taught me to read and write. I do not know if that was a blessing or a curse you bestowed upon me, for now I find I hunger for knowledge, and it is a hunger I cannot escape. It seems I cannot have both knowledge and solitude," I said, with great sadness in my voice.

I looked hard at Garianne, her unwavering gaze, those eyes pushing mine away, yet I held firm for a fleeting moment; it was enough for now. 'Supreme strategist for the Galacien Conglomerate of Worlds', she had said. I could see why. She had certainly done very well with making sure this had all gone exactly as she planned from the very start. I must watch her closely from now on, I thought.

She seemed to hold my gaze easily, while I struggled. One day I would not I swore to myself. I felt Garianne could tell what I was thinking, yet her reasoning was undeniable. There was nothing on Earth compared to what was out there. I only hoped I was strong enough.

"Very well, I will go with you," I said.

We both knew I always would.

PART 2. Chapter 12. Amelerians

It was time for us to leave Earth. I had changed recently, finding the inner strength that Garianne had spoken of. My mind had opened, ready and eager to learn that which I did not understand, and there was much I did not understand here.

Garianne, Davern, and Min entered what they called the command deck of this ship. I had been here before. This was the place my consciousness had come to when the Nacuerians put me to sleep and, on reflection, I could now make sense of what I had seen. The ship had been high above another planet and then had come to Earth. Given what I had recently learned, the distance must have been great and the speed to get to Earth that fast would have to be almost beyond belief.

"Ready for departure, Garianne," said the unseen voice of Lom.

"Very well, Lom. Are you ready to leave, Jonas?"

I looked around the command deck and there were many pairs of eyes upon me, only three of them were human.

"To leave Earth and humanity? Oh yes, why not?" I replied. Those were my words, yet, despite my bravado, I felt uncertain. Why? Was it the unknown? I had no idea of what was out there, but it had to be better than what was here on Earth.

Min came to me as I felt sure that the huge structure of the ship had begun to move upwards. She bore that same serene smile she had on the night we first met.

"I admire your courage. I'm sure this can't be easy for you," she said.

For some reason I felt angry, for again I felt she treated me like a child. Perhaps that was how they all saw me. I looked about at all of these beings, who traversed the stars as easily as humans might ride a horse. I sensed in them all a confidence that lacked arrogance and an intellect that lacked superiority. I sensed in them, none of the qualities I detested most in human beings.

Here, I felt embarrassed to be human. Despite my abilities could I ever hope to be their equal, spiritually and intellectually?

I felt very conscious that I was not like them at all. My stance, slumped; my awareness, numbed. I was quick to anger, spoke before I thought, and often thought of only myself. I thought of what I had done recently to acquire knowledge and felt shame. No, I would not continue to be that which I found so distasteful in others.

I calmed myself before speaking. "I am fine, Min," I said, managing an uncharacteristic smile. "Let us see what the universe has to offer."

I walked confidently forward until I stood next to Garianne. The ship rose in the air. I could see this quite clearly, for most of the walls and the ceiling seemed to have become transparent. I knew this to be another illusion as such, for we were deep within the ship. What I saw was somehow displayed upon the inner structure of the command deck.

The journey out of the Earth's atmosphere and into space was extremely quiet and steady; it did not feel like we were moving at all. If it had not been for my experiences in the simulation room, I believe I would have found this quite overwhelming.

I noticed that the creatures worked in silence, manipulating the complex light shapes I had seen before, and they did not seem to communicate with one another in the running of the ship, yet they went about their business as if by some unseen coordination. I felt it was time I started making a habit of asking questions. After all, how else was I to learn and rise above the base-creature I felt I was?

"Min, tell me about these creatures running the ship. Where are they from and how are they communicating with one another?" I asked.

"They are called Amelerians, originally from the planet Dethus."

I thought of the planet and could somehow place its position in the galaxy and the neighbouring planets their species had colonized. All this and so much more knowledge I had acquired from my experience in the simulation room. I did not mention this to Min for it felt good to know something they, perhaps, did not. Suddenly similar images of their planet and species invaded my mind.

"What was that?"

"Your cerebral implant – it opens up many possibilities for anyone who possesses one. Don't worry, it is very small. In this instance I instructed my implant to transfer some information about the Amelerians."

"Through thought alone?" I asked astonished.

"Yes, that's why the Amelerians might not seem to communicate with one another. But they do, through their implants. Would you like me to grant your implant access?"

I then heard a strange series of grunts and sighs.

"That is how they talk to one another?"

"That's everything that's happening on the ship right now, but we are able to single out communication between two of the crew."

Again I listened, this time it seemed like two intelligent creatures communicating, although I could not understand.

"This is what they are saying," said Min. I heard the grunting and sighing suddenly change to the language of my own tongue, completely comprehensible.

"The implant knows your language and the language of the Amelerians and translates it instantly," explained Min. "We'll show you how to use your implant. With it, you can communicate with any species, access an almost limitless amount of information, and control machines. I can't overstate the significance of how useful it is."

"Incredible," was all I could say. I felt like a mouse attempting to climb a mountain with these people. It seemed an impossible feat to reach their level of understanding but I was determined that one day, I would.

One of the Amelerians approached Garianne. "Greetings, Garianne, we are ready to leave orbit. What is our destination?" it said.

"In a moment, Lytpniuph. First, let me introduce you to Jonas. Jonas this is Lytpniuph the captain of this vessel."

"Greetings to you Jonas. I am honoured to meet a super-sentient and glad to hear that you wish to help us in our fight against the Nacuerians. You give us all hope."

"Speak and your implant will translate," said Min.

"Well, I will do what I can," I replied, sounding unsure of myself. I was not finding the idea of placing their hope in me a comfortable one.

Lytpniuph tilted its head upward; a gesture I sensed was one of gratitude and respect, It seemed the implant was also translating and giving me the impressions of the Amelerians non-verbal communication.

"Ship's destination is Galacien Prime," announced Garianne to the crew.

"That is eleven thousand light years away. How do we get there, might I ask?"

Min gasped and the Amelerians reacted in a similar manner.

"How did you know that? How do you have any idea of the concept of light years?" Min asked.

I attempted to subdue a smile at her astonished face. Garianne, to my disappointment, remained impassive. She had known. She always knew.

"From the simulation, of course. Somehow the entire galaxy and to a lesser extent the universe is all stored in my head. I only have to focus and I can pick out which part of this vast library of knowledge I wish to come to the fore. Though it is not as if I am reading or seeing it for the first time; I know it. It is like I have only forgotten it for a while until that moment when I recall it."

For the briefest of moments I sensed some significant yet almost unnoticeable reaction from Garianne, a look about her that should have stayed hidden. In an instant it had gone, but something I had said had had an effect on her.

"Jonas, I've just given you full access to your implant, it will teach you anything you want to know," said Garianne.

"Anything?"

"Yes. Lytpniuph, make the jump into hyperspace."

"Yes, mistress," replied Lytpniuph, returning his attention back to his crew and the ship.

"Min, how do I use it?" I asked.

"The same as on the Nacuerian ship. Just think."

Hello I thought. *Can you tell me about hyperspace?*

Hello, Jonas, of course I can.

"Min, is that you?"

"No. It's just the implant's interface. That was what you were talking to on the Nacuerian vessel."

"You mean it was not you I was speaking to?" I was disappointed. I thought she had been with me.

"The implant has been given my personality traits – a simulation. In fact, if it were complex enough for you to believe it to be me, then in a way it is. Think of it as my offspring," she said with some amusement, "with more information at her call than you can imagine."

Suddenly, I saw a huge tunnel of dazzling white light appear and engulf us. It was everywhere and it felt as if we were falling down into the farthest reaches of reality, like that terribly beautiful experience in the simulation room when I had seen our universe as a whole. My extraordinary senses tried to give me some kind of impression of what was going on. It felt as if we were above, beyond, and outside reality. Min could see my discomfort and beckoned me over to sit down in a chair. It was extraordinarily comfortable, firm yet yielding ever so slightly to my body. How ironic. I was intrigued by their chairs, and here we were travelling down the corridors between realities.

"Ask the implant," Min urged.

I obliged. "Implant, what is hyperspace?"

Not out loud, Jonas. Addressing me verbally will only confuse those around you and is considered bad manners by all cultures. We use verbal communication selectively. Just think as you did when communicating on the Nacuerian ship.

I did.

Hyperspace is another region of space which exists above, so to speak, normal space-time. Travelling through hyperspace allows us to travel the equivalent to faster than light speeds in normal space. I have a feeling though that you're going to need a little more than that aren't you, Jonas? Here, let me show you. I can sense how quickly you learn and adapt accordingly.

For me to really grasp the answer the implant had to teach me a lot about physics and mathematics. The more I asked, the more there was to learn. I felt truly humbled sitting there, the implant opening up the secrets of the universe, mine for the taking.

After some time I approached Garianne and the unsuspecting Min and Davern.

"Do you have a basic idea of how it works now?" asked Min in an unsure manner.

"Yes, I understand it completely."

"Completely?" Davern retorted unconvinced. "I hardly think that you have a firm grasp of the intricacies—"

"I can write out and explain the equations proving the existence of hyperspace, or build you a drive without the implant's help if you like," I interrupted him.

"How is that possible?" said Min

Garianne smiled.

"I am a very quick learner, Min, or have you not noticed?"

Chapter 13. Lom

The vessel's crew worked in shifts and the ship was constantly managed. However, I soon found out that 'Lom' was the ship and needed minimal supervision. I was aboard an extremely complex, thinking, living ship whose natural habitat was the void. Lom did not sleep and never tired, a bit like myself in that respect. It felt good that there was someone with whom I shared that kind of existence, even if it was a starship.

Min escorted me to my living area, seemingly aloof and cold.

"What is your part in all of this then?" I asked.

"It's not a conspiracy, Jonas."

"Is it not? The night we first met, you said nothing of this. Why?"

"Duty. I did as I was instructed."

"By Garianne?" I asked exasperated.

"Yes."

 "Why?"

"I don't know. Though with her there is always a good reason. She ordered me to do it, not to question her, only to trust her."

I continued walking neither of us saying another word, until we reached my quarters.

The door slid open. I walked inside and considered her a moment. She hid her emotions well; the same could not be said of me.

"Your implant will tell you anything you need to know. As you said, you are a quick learner. I'm sure you will figure it out."

I mentally instructed my implant to close the door and regarded my quarters. It was far more spacious than I imagined, though I should not have been surprised really when I considered Lom's immense size. I conferred with my implant, constantly asking questions about the use of just about everything I could see. Even the most basic of devices or domestic appliances to these beings seemed strange to me, grounded, as they were, on thousands of years of research, change, and adaptability to reach such a level, that humankind would deem miraculous. As I moved about the room scrutinizing the functions of my surroundings, my implant bombarded me with information, familiarising me quickly and efficiently, with my environment, until I did not feel so ignorant. I soon learned from my conversations with the implant that the Galacien and every other sentient species in the galaxy had begun as primitive beasts on their own planet of origin, millions of years ago. Since that time, they had evolved to primitive tool makers, then going on, using their minds more than any other quality they possessed to advance their capabilities. They had all passed through a similar, though not identical, phase to that which humans on Earth were now experiencing – a phase of simple societies and simple tools. Simple compared to what would come next, which were the technological revolutions that would gain pace as time went on. At first they were gradual and took many years to spread and revolutionise the lives of a particular species. They also usually came in bursts and in particular areas, whether it was such things as steam power, nuclear energy, or space travel.

I found the thought that man and all the other thinking beings in the galaxy were once dumb beasts, a disturbing one. I had always thought man to be, as he had always been, and always would be forever. Now, though, I saw that all sentient beings were on a different level of evolution, akin to rungs on a ladder, with human beings close to the bottom and the Galacien near the top. Garianne said the Galacien were the oldest species in the galaxy, though I found it strange that there was nothing out there older than the Galacien species.

I consulted the implant *Are the Nacuerians an older spacefaring species than the Galacien?*

We aren't entirely sure, though we believe that the Nacuerian species is younger than the Galacien. Every species has an evolutionary rate, which relates to how quickly they can adapt and develop their technology. The Nacuerian evolve at a slightly quicker rate than the Galacien and so, even though they may be younger, they may soon surpass the Galacien's technological level.

I still wondered about the galaxy, devoid of sentience for all those billions of years. I had already been told by Garianne there were no others and yet...

I thought about the wording before I asked the question. *Is there information anywhere that suggests there are, or were, species older than the Galacien?*

The implant seemed to pause, for its answer was not as instantaneous as usual. *The Galacien are the oldest known species in the galaxy.*

What does that mean?

It means that there are rumours, myths, and legends heard throughout the galaxy. The Galacien investigate anything that may be more than just whispers. Unfortunately, no evidence has been found of a species older than the Galacien living or dead.

Perhaps there are higher beings that you do not know about, though, perhaps they know of you, in the same way that humanity is unaware of the Galacien.

Perhaps, though without evidence such things are nothing but speculation.

When I think of all that I have seen, the immensity of the universe, the multiverse, I cannot believe that the Galacien, as advanced as they are, are the most evolved species in all of creation.

Are you referring to gods?

I believe there are gods even if you have not encountered them. I take it the Galacien do not?

You are human. It is part of your conscious make-up at this stage of your evolution to believe in gods. The Galacien have identified this behaviour in almost all species, but they grow out of it after a while. The Galacien stopped believing in a deity a long time ago.

What about faith?

Faith is good. I understand that faith in your gods can be beneficial to you in times of crisis. It comforts and helps you, though it can also be detrimental on an epic scale. Entire species have destroyed themselves or one another, due to this kind of faith. Faith in yourself and one another is far more beneficial than in something that has not been proven to exist.

I made no reply and found myself changing the subject to something a little more straightforward, such as the evolution of artificial mechanisms. However, I couldn't stop my mind buzzing with questions of gods and other such unknowns.

Hours later, as I sifted through the mass of information that was accessible through the implant, something caught my eye. The implant had proved useful and enlightening during recent debates, yet despite being given Min's personality as an interface, I found it still lacked a certain quality. Lom was an interesting being, I could converse with him (despite his lack of gender I had noticed others still referred to Lom as a he), and I had learned he was capable of performing a great many tasks simultaneously.

"Lom, there was a species that existed on a planet which orbits a star you call Heilanes, not far from our current position."

"Yes." affirmed Lom

"They are extinct; they destroyed themselves with some kind of biological weapon they created."

"True. Just over three thousand years ago now. it was a terrible waste of life. You can access all of the information through the implant."

"I know that. You knew everything about them. You had been watching them for centuries. You could have stopped them, yet you didn't. Why?"

"The Galacien believe that a species must prove it is mature enough to survive, much like an individual or tribe does. This tribe wasn't mature enough to handle the technology it had developed, and so destroyed their entire species."

"And you did nothing! There were over eight billion of them!"

"They were inherently destructive, Jonas. It was in their nature. They fought one another from the first moment we detected them, until the very end. Any kind of intervention on our part would have worsened the situation. Have you ever seen what kind of an effect full-scale extra-terrestrial contact has on an immature species?" said Lom in his usual calm nature.

"No."

"Disastrous, I'm afraid. We tried it long ago, when there were still enough amongst the Galacien to believe it might work. Again, even though the records are very old I can find them for you. You can see for yourself, exactly what happened. Though I must warn you, it is painful to witness. Our simulations always said that they would destroy themselves, that it was just a matter of time."

"There must have been something you could have done?"

"What would you suggest? Change their nature? Take away that which makes them who they are? We do not accept them as a part of the galactic community, and we do not accept them unless they show us they have matured as a species."

"How do they do that?"

"I can't tell you that, Jonas, for you are human," said Lom.

"So?"

"The human race is also considered immature, ergo our simulations predict you are more than likely to destroy yourselves sometime in the future, in a similar manner to the species of the of the Heilanes star."

"Stop including me in that term. I am not one of them," I snapped.

"I am sorry."

I felt unsure as to what Lom was apologising for. Was it because he felt he had insulted me, or was it for the fate of humanity?

"I am beginning to lose my patience."

"You can find the answer by looking through the Galacien records. I am not allowed to tell you for the aforementioned reasons, however, you are also super-sentient and we have need for you in this very unique situation. Garianne has given you unbounded access to all Galacien information should you require it. There is a rare opportunity for discovery and enlightenment, should you look in the right places. Compare species histories throughout the galaxy; the answers are there."

Taking Lom's advice, I spent time looking at many different species the Galacien had observed. Some were like the species of the Heilanes star, who had destroyed themselves, and were now long dead. Others, such as the Amelerians, had also reached that inevitable point in their technological evolution, where they had the potential to destroy themselves. Yet, clearly, their difference in behaviour from the Heilanus was astounding. The more species I compared to one another, the more I could see the difference between an immature species and a mature one, from the benign to the horrifically malevolent. Again, I felt ashamed and embarrassed to have been born human, for we were obviously the latter. With a thought I called upon the information pertaining to the human race. My implant confirmed what Lom had already informed me – as far as the Galacien were concerned, they were destined for self-destruction. I thought back to what Lom had said earlier.

"Lom, you have helped some species in the past whom have shown maturity?"

"Correct."

"Show me."

Through my implant, Lom presented the records for me to access in my own manner.

"Most of these seem to tell the same story – the species faces extinction, they try and prevent it, yet ultimately fail. You then interfere, you save them. Why?"

"I can't give you the answer, Jonas," said Lom.

"Yet I will have it."

I focused on the question which lay before me. The answer must lie in the details, for these species seemed fairly immature at first glance.

Then without warning, I saw it and was sure it was the truth.

"The species that you leave to destroy themselves do not help themselves in any way, to warrant external help. They fight amongst themselves until the very end, proving they are a danger to themselves and to others, hence immature. If they have not matured by this time in their development they never will, their end is inevitable. Those few species that come close to destroying themselves but unite together, despite past differences; those who can truly rise above it all and show true maturity as a species, despite the fact that they may fail, will receive the Galacien's help, for they have shown maturity. Also, such a species should find it easier to assimilate the galactic community into its collective mindset."

"There is your answer, in your own words," Lom said.

I could sense that there was, of course, far more to it than the summarised version I had given. Even now it was still coming to me like an elaborate vista – the more I looked the more detail I could pick out.

"It seems ruthless, monstrous at first," I said.

"The alternative is to let a great many immature species with extremely dangerous weapons roam around the galaxy killing, possibly, a lot of perfectly innocent sentient beings. That cannot be permitted."

I could see his point.

"However, there are some alternatives being considered even now. One way is to stifle the intellect of an immature species early on in its development, so that they cannot reach any kind of technological development. This is favoured by some, as it does not result in such huge loss of life. Others in the Galacien though, say this interference denies them their natural progression. There is no telling for sure what will happen to a species, for not all forces in reality are controlled and everything is in a constant state of change. Our simulations have proven to be correct so far, though they are not infallible. Of course there is also the delicate point of super-sentients."

"What do you mean?"

"It is still unknown how or why super-sentients are born. Interference with any species may cause a problem with this process, so it isn't worth the risk, despite the fact there are no more super-sentients anymore. Except yourself, of course."

I shook my head slowly as I thought back on my various negative experiences with humankind. "I cannot imagine humanity ever forgetting their differences and coming together enough to qualify as a mature species."

"Neither can we, I'm afraid."

It should have disturbed me to realise that the human race was destined for self-extinction, yet I found it did not. True, I did not want them to die, though it would be they who would doom themselves, not I. Perhaps if we somehow survived the Nacuerians, when humans reached the technological stage where they were capable of self-destruction, they would surprise us all, and show enough maturity to forget their differences and come together in harmony. Somehow, I did not think so, and obviously neither did the Galacien.

Chapter 14. Assault

The journey to Galacien Prime would take several days. At first I thought I would not be allowed to roam the ship unaccompanied, however, I soon found that this was not so. Lom was only too happy to let me explore his interior, as it were. Of course, my every movement was observed, and I would not have been surprised if Garianne herself was keeping a very close eye on me.

Despite our recent uneasiness, I decided to go and see Min. My implant told me she was in her quarters up and about. As I walked down the corridor I thought I would impress her by showing her how adept I had become at utilising my implant. Through it I requested to speak to her.

Jonas? I heard her voice respond in my head. *Obviously you've learnt how to talk with others using the implant.*

It is my first time, yet... I realised my thoughts were laced with emotion and immediately knew my mistake.

Be careful what you think Jonas. Her words made things even worse and I could feel the warmth rush to my cheeks. She never seemed to get embarrassed. In fact, from what I had recently learned, Galacien citizens did not suffer from such childlike attitudes towards sex and sexuality. It was stupid really. I was only twenty years of age and here was a woman in her hundreds, despite appearances to the contrary.

Are you well? Min asked.

Yes, I replied a little too quickly, wanting to change the subject. *Can I see you?*

It looks like you are about to.

Obviously, she could see I was on my way.

The door to Min's quarters opened as I approached and closed behind me as I entered. No longer did the workings of this puzzle me, for this had been one of the many things I had come to comprehend during the night. There was still an almost insurmountable amount of knowledge for me to learn, yet at least I was now familiar with the workings of my surroundings; no longer did I feel like a frightened beast wandering blindly about.

Min strolled through from an adjoining room, her clothes settling around her and her hair tying itself neatly into a complex pattern down her back.

Ask me about nano-machines later, my implant communicated, sensing my puzzlement.

No, now. I can do more than one thing at a time, I commanded.

I'm sure, replied the implant.

Strangely, I found my constant companion quite a comfort.

The implant continued to give me insight into how unseen microscopic machines in their millions were, at this very moment, working in perfect unison, using a combination of different kinds of subtle energy fields to manipulate Min's hair and clothing.

"I'm guessing you didn't sleep last night?" Min said smiling. "What did you get up to?"

"Why ask me, when you can simply find out from your implant?"

"I could, only it's far more pleasant talking about it with you."

"I learned a great many things, however, there is something that puzzles me. Garianne, Davern, and yourself, you are not human. Garianne herself told me she was originally from Kylia. I looked into that, her species isn't even remotely human. What about you; who are you really?"

Min turned away. "Why didn't you just find out?"

"It was tempting. But, like you say, some things are better done face to face."

She looked thoughtful. "I am 1,313 years old, Jonas, and this is my nineteenth-generation life. On my home planet there are three different sexes: one similar to the role of a human male, one similar to the role of a human female, and another who, though not involved directly with conception, is the child's chief carer. This was my original sex and that was why I found it hard to part with those children on Earth. It is inherent for me to care for the young, especially if left alone. Some habits never truly leave you," she said looking out into the depths of hyperspace. "Since my first life I have chosen to live again both as male and female of my original species, however, this is the first time I have chosen to live as an altogether different species. This is how I have looked now for the last several years and will be for some time to come."

"What do you look like really, then?"

"This is what I really look like. It's not a disguise; the change is biological. I'm still the person I've always been, though one is not completely unaffected psychologically by becoming another species. Being human has changed me like any other life experience. I can only imagine the effect, living so many lives, has had on Garianne."

"I meant, what did you look like originally?" I said, dreading how she would respond to the question. I knew she would show me and feared how I would react. I admit all kinds of strange and repulsive shapes infiltrated my imagination.

"Like this," she replied.

What stood before me was a representation of a humanoid bird-like creature, almost as tall as the average human, with smooth, short, dark blue feathers. Longer feathers sprung forth from the back of its head, looking almost like a headdress. There would have been nothing horrifying or ugly about the creature standing before me, except for its eyes. Its eyes were as black as night and there was nothing of Min, nothing human that I could identify in them. I could see in its eyes the keen look of intellect, but it lacked humanity of any kind. Its gaze upon me was totally alien and I looked away. The image disappeared and Min looked herself again, now very human, her face stern.

"It's what I was physically, and it will always be a part of my psychological make-up. I became a new species to expand my mind, to learn. No one in the Galacien Conglomerate of Worlds had been human before. Garianne made a passing comment once that there should be at least one of us who has become every one of the pre-spacefaring species, to know what it truly feels like to be one of you. I was the first to become human, then Davern, and a handful of others we left behind.

"The old man and the boy I encountered on Earth, the first time I met Garianne?" I said.

Min nodded. "Finally Garianne herself. She, of course, is far older than Davern or I, living more lives than both of us combined. Check with your implant sometime. I can't think of anyone who has lived as so many different species. You need to accept this if you are to move on. You're still limiting yourself to the human perspective."

I nodded my head but all I could see were those featureless eyes staring at me, haunting my mind. I felt I would never be able to look upon her the way I had done before. However, I still found I could not help but care for her, despite seeing what she was. An uncomfortable silence descended between us.

Jonas, Min, come to the command deck immediately, Garianne's voice said in my head.

"Did you hear that?" I asked Min, grateful for a break in the silence. She nodded. Violet shapes appeared in her quarters and I could see them down the corridors of the ship as we left.

"It means there's an emergency," said Min. "Lom, what's happening. Do we need to teleport?"

No. Though get to the command deck as fast as you can, I'll explain on the way.

We made our way swiftly through corridors and anti-gravity shafts, while Lom explained what was happening. *The Nacuerians have launched a full-scale assault on the Amelerian home system.*

Min looked at me. "No, they can't be hitting such a major system. We never expected them to do anything like this so soon."

"Maybe that is why they have done it," I said.

We entered onto the command deck which was a mass of hectic commotion. I could sense the fear from the Amelerians. From my short time with them I had already judged them to be a species far nobler than humanity. The Amelerian home system was seventy-two light years from our current position. I could not understand why the Nacuerians had attacked the home system first. I thought it would make more sense to cautiously take their outer systems and slowly work their way in. Lom confirmed that we had not changed course, and were still heading for the Galacien system.

I sensed from Garianne that she was having some kind of inner dialogue, and I realised what it looked like to an outsider when they are not privy to a private communication. I remembered on Earth how Davern would cock his head in an odd manner and now understood why.

I suddenly heard *... need him as soon as possible. How can we use him in the battle and what is the nature of his abilities?* coming from an unknown voice.

He is not ready. If we involve him now he will not survive and we will have no hope of winning this war, replied Garianne.

But they are attacking the Amelerian home system.

Garianne motioned for us to follow her into an adjoining circular chamber. When inside a number of very different alien-looking creatures joined us. Their sudden abrupt appearance caught me off guard – it was almost too much for my senses to take in. Forms unimaginable stood before me on two legs and four, some with none at all. Some had limbs sprouting from every part of their unusual bodies, yet there was anatomical sense to it when broken down to its basic concepts. There were parts for locomotion, tool manipulation, internal organ housing, and sensory organs, yet there were others that were more mysterious. Also, I had to differentiate between biological and technological additions they had implemented themselves, and external additions such as tools, clothing, and cultural adornments.

Garianne had done something to me when she opened the doors of my mind and I found I could not help but take in every minute detail I was exposed to. Even now I could feel my mind making thousands of deductions about these creatures, simply from their appearance. I asked my implant to bombard me with as much information as possible, to feed my quenching thirst for knowledge and the floodgates opened.

I observed that they all looked as if they were physically present, except for the fact that they were all surrounded by a faint white glow. I quickly confirmed that this was an added effect to help tell who was here and who was merely a projection.

An Amelerian now addressed Garianne. "Please, honoured Garianne, you must come to our aide."

"I would if I could, dear Pheltheam, yet we have the super-sentient. He has to be brought to the Galacien system, so that we may prepare him."

"Can he not offer his help now?" asked Pheltheam.

"He is not yet ready. If he joins the war now, the Nacuerians will become aware of his existence, and more than likely seek out a way to kill him before he can be ready to help us. He is an unknown factor in this war and that makes him dangerous to them."

"I agree with Garianne," said a soft voice. It came from a creature that was tall and slender in the limbs. It was completely white from head to toe, and just beneath the surface of what must have been its skin, which had the appearance of polished stone, I saw faint patterns of lights moving swiftly about. What struck me most about this creature was how symmetrical it was. My keen senses could tell that it was perfect, as if a mirror had been held up to its body so both sides were exactly the same. It seemed too perfect to be a natural form. It was a Phalinon, a species that had evolved from machines into something far more. My implant informed me that they had no home planet as such but preferred to congregate on ships that moved about, for the most part, in hyperspace.

"I am honoured to meet you, Jonas," said the Phalinon.

Sevine Anoor my implant informed me of its name.

"I, too, am honoured to meet a Phalinon, Sevine Anoor," I replied.

It and the others seemed surprised by my response.

"He does learn quickly for a pre-spacefarer, as you said, Garianne," commented one of the creatures.

"Though, unfortunately, not quickly enough," Garianne said and I felt irritated that, yet again, I had been unable to impress her. "Are we in agreement then; for Jonas to help us now would be disastrous and more than likely cost us our existence?"

There were a few that seemed reluctant to agree with this statement, however the majority did and that seemed to decide it. I was further irritated not to be consulted and that my fate was being decided by others.

"How many sentients are there in the Amelerian system?" I asked Min.

"Ask your implant," she said, not looking at me, far more interested in the ongoing conversation between Garianne and the others.

"I am asking you!" The slight raising of my voice attracting the attention of some of the creatures around me.

She looked at me sternly. "About eighteen billion." I could sense her frustration. "Not that many when you consider there are over six hundred and fifty billion in the Galacien home system."

And yet a staggering number. Eighteen billion. My feelings toward humanity bordered on hatred, I did not care much for them, but the thought that eighteen billion of these noble creatures were about to be exterminated by the Nacuerians was just too much. I felt the reality of it and found myself biting back tears. What could I do? Again I felt that control of my own fate was at the mercy of others. It was time that changed.

"We are going," I said walking to the centre of the room.

Everything went quiet.

"Excuse me?" said Garianne.

I turned to her. Gods, I still could not hold her gaze, nevertheless I continued, "You heard what I said. Either we go now, or you can forget about me helping you."

There was no external reaction from her. No one would have sensed the raging fury she held in check. Only I could and I admit I was fearful of it. Nevertheless I held on tight with all my might to the eighteen billion reasons I was doing this. I held steadfast.

"You don't know the consequences of what you are proposing. The risk is too great," she said slowly with unbelievable calmness and control. "If you are killed it's all over. Do you understand? Everything."

I tried to hold her unwavering gaze again. Eighteen billion I repeated over and over in my head.

Garianne exhaled, slowly glancing down in thought, every eye upon her.

"Lom," she announced, "change course for the Amelerian system."

Yes, Garianne.

I heard the subtlest of sighs from Min behind me, and realised that I, too, had been holding my breath.

"Have you begun his training yet?" asked a tall, elaborately dressed grey-skinned creature trying to break the tension in the air. It was completely hairless and what was apparently its mouth hung open exposing a mass of gum fibres. Its other most pronounced feature was its backbone, which continued over the head, ending at the bridge of its nose.

His name is Bur Messel, informed the implant.

"Nothing substantial. He hasn't received any warfare training as yet. It would be too dangerous to do it on the ship."

"You must begin soon, Garianne."

"It cannot be done on a ship," Garianne repeated. "I do not know his full potential, it is feasible he could accidentally destroy the ship. It must be done on a planet or a large habitat, under controlled conditions."

"You still think artificial reality training isn't good enough?"

"Absolutely not. It may seem real enough to us, however, Jonas seems to have extraordinary senses. He will know the difference. It has to be real, otherwise he will not learn."

Again they conceded to her will. Garianne had a knack of getting her own way.

I could not help but shake my head showing my disapproval.

"Believe me, Jonas is our only chance of continued survival," said Garianne.

"There are still the many survival missions," said Bur Messel.

"What are those?" I asked.

"We have a number of specially commissioned ships, with a large enough crew and necessary resources to set up a new home on a planet in another galaxy," said Bur Messel. "Some have already left. If the worst should come to pass, they will ensure the continuation of a species' existence."

"Perhaps, but the Nacuerians are numerous, breaking away from the herd, as it were, could make them easy prey." commented Garianne

"Our ships are faster."

"For now."

"They will outpace the Nacuerians and lose themselves amongst the stars."

"The missions you speak of will take many years. I think you underestimate our foes. When we first fought them our technology was far superior but recently we have noticed it has become more difficult to infiltrate their systems. Any day now they will be our equal, and then they will surpass us. Time is not our ally, it is theirs," Garianne said.

"As long as they have some chance, there is hope," said Bur Messel, but I could see he was visibly shaken by Garianne's words; they all were.

Discussion followed about the upcoming battle. Things were apparently not going well. As Garianne had indicated, the Galacien technology was a little more advanced than the Nacuerians', yet the Nacuerians seemed to have the advantage of numbers. Where did they come from? My implant informed me the answer was unknown, however it was speculated they were not of our galaxy.

Completely realistic images of the battle floated about us. The council of war manipulated the images to illustrate possible strategies. I could see how they all looked to Garianne for guidance. She had obviously well earned her title of supreme strategist, for she saw that which they too often missed and her insight could not be matched; I had to admit, I was impressed.

Min dragged me away from their discussions. "Informative?" she enquired with a raised eyebrow.

"Very. What is the matter?" I asked, finding her easy to read.

"I've been asked to fight in the forthcoming battle."

"But you're a…" I suddenly realised how archaic my attitude was.

"I'll have you know that there's a lot more to me than some simple human female."

"I know that, Min. What I meant to say was that I don't feel comfortable with you fighting, while I stay here."

"I think it's only fair to tell you that I'm one of the most highly qualified warriors on this ship. In fact fourth from a crew of over two thousand."

I was stunned. Min did not strike me as a fierce warrior. My implant started presenting me with her combat history and it seemed, even to my untrained eye, quite impressive.

"Are you doing that?" I said.

"I just thought you'd like to see; my record speaks for itself."

I sighed and shook my head. "Min, are you sure? This battle looks like nothing the Galacien have fought before"

"No, but I'm needed. It's my duty. I must do it for everyone and everything I hold dear," she said.

Min invited me along with her to prepare her combat SIBAT. It hung there, at least twice my height, looking exceptionally threatening, in one of many rows. I saw other members of Lom's crew inspecting their own SIBATs in a similar fashion to Min.

"Sentient Integrated Bio-Technological All-Purpose Tool" she announced. "More commonly known as a SIBAT."

"It's alive?" I asked.

"To a degree, though not in the same way as you or I. It is a creature created for a multitude of tasks including combat in any environmental conditions. The user can download a copy of their mind into the SIBAT, in order that it may perform actions that would be impossible to do without harming or killing a carbon-based life form within."

I watched as Min continued to expertly check over and configure her SIBAT's systems.

"What do you mean?"

"It can metamorphose into any shape, even split itself up into parts. Destroy up to ninety per cent of it and the other 10 per cent will carry on functioning, to a limited degree of course. Only the user's mind is downloaded into the SIBAT, no physical form exists within."

"And what happens to you if the SIBAT is completely destroyed?"

"Don't worry, Jonas, the worst that can happen is that I'll get killed out there," said Min.

I looked at her in astonishment.

"I won't die. My mind will be safely stored back here waiting while I'm away. If I'm killed, the last thing I'll remember is being ready to go. If I survive out there then I'll retrieve my memories from the SIBAT."

"I hope you do."

"I'm very good. Why do you think I'm so highly qualified? I've survived to retrieve the memories, which give me the experience. The greatest warriors are those who have survived the most battles."

I thought for a moment. "During the battle there will be two of you," I said.

Min turned to me and smiled. "In a way, yes. The original me here in my body, unconscious and a copied, conscious version of me out there."

"And if the ship is destroyed?"

"I'm backed up on Galacien Prime like everyone else."

"And if Galacien Prime is destroyed?"

She stopped her work, considering the unthinkable for a long moment. I could sense a deep sadness pouring from her being.

Finally she spoke. "Then nothing will matter anymore."

Despite learning everything I possibly could about the SIBATs, I still could not bring myself to feel comfortable about Min going out there.

Standing there in a moment of silence, I noticed something peculiar about Min's emotional state. "Do you always feel frustrated and angry, or is it only since you met me?" I was surprised to find myself asking this, for I feared the truth.

She immediately stopped what she was doing, though did not look at me. "It's to be expected when you consider the death that's been going on around us for years now."

"Yes, but why is it specifically directed at me? What have I done? You hide it incredibly well, but you cannot hide it from me."

I could sense her struggle. She did not want to speak her mind. "I will do my duty, yet I cannot help how I feel."

"How do you feel?"

After a heavy sigh she said, "I have always believed in her, in Garianne. There is no one like her, at least no one I've met, and I've met a great many people in my time. To put it simply though, this time I think she's wrong,"

"About what?"

"About you. Dead wrong. You're super-sentient and you can help, I'm sure. I've studied what your kind could do in the past and it was extraordinary, yet I can't see how you can stop them all, or even come close. There's just too many of them. We'd need a lot more like you to make a difference. She scares me, you know? She has so much faith in you... it scares me."

"I asked."

She nodded. "For what it's worth I'm sorry. But like you said, you asked."

Chapter 15. Insight

I parted company with Min, for she needed to go through the process of downloading her mind into Lom's memory stores. I asked Lom what would happen to her memories if the ship were destroyed. Lom replied that all their memories after their last copy would be lost. Not me, though. If I were killed here and now, there would be no chance of revival. Unlike everyone else in the Galacien Conglomerate of Worlds I would not get another chance, just like my parents. My mood was melancholy as I slowly walked down the corridors of Lom.

"By the Gods, Jonas, are you alright?" asked Davern approaching from behind.

"Do you have to speak like that, it's not who or what you are?" I said.

"Not true, I am human like you."

"At the moment, maybe. You weren't before and you probably won't be after this."

"Probably not, though it helps my understanding of what it is to be human, not that there's anything special about that."

"Now there is something we agree on."

"You really hate them, don't you?"

"I do not hate them it's just…" I found it difficult to explain.

"What is the matter?"

"Do you think Garianne's right about me?"

His face became serious, which for Davern meant grim. "I don't know. I really don't. All I can do is have faith and hope. I do know one thing, though."

"What?"

"If she says you're our best chance, you are."

He started moving down the intersecting corridor.

"Where are you going?" I said.

"I've been called aboard one of the other ships which have joined us. Don't worry, I'll see you again soon, you can't get rid of me that easy," he said with a large grin.

Garianne and the war council were to direct the battle from a safe distance, probably, I thought, to make sure that I would not get involved. However, from the moment I had first met Garianne, I was involved; it was too late now. At her request I joined her and the other war council members, in the simulation room, when we were less than half an hour from reaching the periphery of the Amelerian home system.

Unbelievably, the Nacuerian forces continued to arrive in vast numbers spaced out evenly on the edge of the system beyond the orbits of the outer planets. They waited while battles on several major fronts were fought around the key artificial habitats, moons, and planets. Each side had the capability to destroy any one of them, even the Amelerian star itself. The Galacien could not allow this to happen. The destruction of even an outer planet would cause terrible consequences for the Amelerians. The destruction of their star would mean an end to all life within the system. Therefore, the main focus of attack and defence was taking place around the star. The destruction of a star! My implant explained in horrific detail the devastation such a weapon, these 'world-destroyers', could produce. For such a weapon to even exist was an abomination.

The situation was very worrying. The Galacien technology was generally more advanced but the Nacuerian forces outnumbered them by more than ten to one.

Skirmishes were being fought and won by the Galacien resulting in the Nacuerians sending in another small fraction of their vast force to continue the fight.

"What are they waiting for?" said Bur Messel. "Why don't they come in force and finish us quickly? Despite their vast numbers they nevertheless throw their lives away in skirmishes that gain them nothing,"

Some of the others looked to Garianne and she looked in turn to me. I was shocked. How did she know that I had a working theory?

"They are testing you," I said. They all looked at me unconvinced, except for Garianne and the Phalinon, Sevine Anoor.

"Go on, Jonas," said Garianne, encouraging me not to feel intimidated.

I walked into the centre of the room. "Look, it is information they want primarily, not the Amelerian system or even its destruction. Not initially anyway. They do mean to take it eventually, but not before they have got what they are really here for."

"And what is that?" asked Bur Messel.

"They want to know how you fight, what your resources are, and what you do when something as valuable as the Amelerian system is at risk." I looked at Garianne and slowly nodded. "To see if you are holding anything back." We were both thinking the same thing – something like me.

"How we fight? They're taking incredible, and might I add unnecessary, losses. How can you be sure?" said Bur Messel.

"I do not know, though the more I think about it the more it makes sense. I do not think they care about their losses, only gaining information about you, something you are sadly lacking on them. Once they have all the information they need, then they will come in force and decimate the system."

"I believe he is right," said Sevine Anoor.

"I for one am not sure. Jonas still possesses the mentality of a human, despite being super-sentient," said Bur Messel.

It took me some amount of self-control to ignore this rebuke. I would not lower myself. I would not prove them right and have them think of me as primitive.

As they were discussing amongst themselves whether I had the faculties to grasp the intricacies of the situation, Garianne's voice cut through.

"Jonas is right," she said.

Their expressions became as one. Now they believed it. Now it was fact, for *she* had said so.

"They readily sacrifice or are sacrificed for a greater purpose: information. To learn how to better defeat us. I don't think a Nacuerian's psychology allows it to think of its own life in the same way we do."

Again Garianne looked at me and I felt her give me a mental nudge to pick up on her train of thought.

"Yes, in my first encounter with the Nacuerians, there were three of them, yet only one attacked me. Even when it was obvious that I would kill the foul creature, the other two merely looked on, watching me. I sensed no contempt or blame from the one I was fighting, towards the other two for not helping it, and in turn I felt no pity or desire to help, from them; only a single purpose from all three," I said.

I got an idea of some kind of code of confrontation from this, which I now tried to put into words: *Reveal nothing more than is necessary to your enemy, lest he realise the measure of your true potential.*

The sentence had formed perfectly in my mind and I could see the wisdom of it, despite being a summary of an idea that meant so much more. I was momentarily stunned and felt sure that Garianne was scrutinising me, even though she did not look in my direction.

Something significant had just happened. I felt as if a veil had been lifted and I was aware that the others were still watching me, sensing that I still had more to say. My mind raced and I felt like the room was truly mine.

"The first Nacuerian I fought used purely physical force, when it engaged me in personal combat. For a technologically advanced species, this was a primitive way to defeat an enemy. It was purely a controlled experiment, for the greater whole to learn from, as is this particular battle. By the Gods!—" I faltered a little for I knew how the Galacien thought of such beliefs "That's it!" Some of the war council looked irritated by my outburst. Garianne seemed mildly amused and intrigued by my enthusiasm.

I tried to control my manner and win back some kind of decorum. "May I?" I gestured to the use of the simulation.

"Please do," said Garianne.

Using my implant to link to the perfectly realistic three-dimensional imaging system, I illustrated my analysis of the battle so far over the Amelerian system.

"Do you not see?" The subtlest smile of delight quivered upon my lips, insight flared beautifully within my mind. "It is all an experiment, a game to test our strategy."

I glanced at Garianne and saw subtle realisation on her face immediately. Her reaction only lasted an instant and then was hidden.

I heard her in my mind, *Go on, Jonas, take it through to its conclusion.*

I did.

"They could have attacked us anywhere and in any way. Why the Amelerian system and in such an illogical fashion? It is for them to learn, to make sure they can overcome us for something more significant – their next major target. They will know how we will react before we do, before the battle even begins."

The Amelerian system hung in the air to my left, with my right hand I manipulated through other systems on my right. I already knew the answer, as of course did Garianne. I stopped when I came to it.

"Galacien Prime?" Bur Messel sounded exasperated "Not before so many other systems; not so soon?"

"Min said the same about the Amelerian system and look what is happening there," I pointed out.

"Why there? The Galacien system is nothing like the Amelerian system," said Sevine Anoor. "It is unique."

"Yes it is, though, look at its surrounding systems in comparison to Amelerians," I said.

Through numerous examples I compared their surrounding systems while they looked on in astonishment.

"They are almost identical, enough for them to foresee what should happen when they hit the Galacien home system. When jumping to a home system it is just as important to be aware of what is behind you as it is, what is in front. That is where defeat is most likely to come from when using such a bold strategy. The Galacien system is unusually strong from the inside, yet weak from the outlying systems – just like the Amelerian system. "

"By the stars, he's right!" said Bur Messel.

The others could not help but agree.

"The question still remains my friends. How do we stop the Amelerian system from falling?" said Sevine Anoor.

Garianne and I looked at one another. We still had no idea, considering the Nacuerians' overwhelming numbers, how to prevent the death of billions of innocent sentients, and the fall of the Amelerian system.

We were now moments from officially entering the Amelerian system. Garianne found a trajectory that would hopefully let us pass undetected by the net of Nacuerian warships. Even though like most ships in the battle, ours possessed stealth technology, it was impossible to hide a ship completely if the enemy had sophisticated enough detector sensors aimed in our direction. It amused me to think that, despite all this advanced technology and counter technology, our final strategy came down to the equivalent of sneaking past our enemies while they looked the other way.

Min, or should I say Min's mind and all the other SIBATs were waiting in their launch tubes. Using my implant I could see them all in lines ready to launch into their prearranged squadrons. How odd to think that something that looked like a malleable egg with stubby arms and legs trying to push their way through the surface was, to all intents and purposes, Min. I requested to have a partial sensor feed with her SIBAT, but she promptly denied me, telling me that I would only distract her.

Garianne wanted to drop off the SIBATs on the other side of the Amelerian star, before moving to a safe location at the outer areas of the system, somewhere where the chances of being detected were very small.

I stood at the back of the command deck which had become darker and quieter than usual, studying and playing out possible scenarios on a smaller representation of the simulation.

Garianne approached me to watch. Did she look upon my tactics as simple or were they worthy of something close to respect? It angered me that her opinion mattered so much to me.

"Take a break, Jonas. Give your mind a rest," said Garianne.

"I cannot see how we are going to stop them; what is going to happen?" I said.

"It depends on whether they wish to wipe out the system itself or just those that live in it," Garianne said, with a calmness that I simultaneously admired and despised. "Either way, if we fail to stop them, our chief priority is to get you out. Lom has been focusing on enhancing the efficiency of the engines. If the worst should come to pass we need to get you out and heading to Galacien Prime as quickly as possible."

"You still think that I can do something to stop that? I don't see how," I said pointing at the representation of the increasing number of Nacuerian ships surrounding the system. "Where are they coming from? We desperately need information."

"Rest for a while. I suggest a walk outside."

Chapter 16. Ambush

The illusion was perfect, though of course it could never fool me – an alien landscape, an alien sun shining into my squinting eyes, strange rolling shallow hills of pastel yellows and purples. I broke away from a mass of bulbous plants, each one almost as large as myself, into a clearing. Strange purple grass grew in patches, their perfumed aromas soothing my troubled mind.

The sun was warm and for a while I forgot about Garianne and the Nacuerian-Galacien War. All I could hear was the peaceful whisper of the wind rustling the grass and, in the distance, tall thin trees. The calming, slow rhythm of the wind emptied my usual troubled consciousness.

Inevitably, my thoughts returned to the present crisis, though my mind now felt less agitated and far more composed. Perhaps it was because I seemed to be all alone, something I still yearned for in my heart. I had to make a conscious effort to ignore the others on the ship, for I could sense them moving about not that far away, like mice behind the walls.

I hoped that inspiration would come to me here, but it was not to be. As the moments slipped by, the chance for a possible solution seemed to seep away like sand through a sieve. I still could not understand how the Galacien had been out-manoeuvred so easily. The galaxy had belonged to the Galacien for thousands of years; they had a presence everywhere, even if that presence was a lone probe on a never-ending orbit around an unimportant star. The galaxy was under their scrutiny and I found it impossible to believe the Nacuerians could have infiltrated so easily and quickly, without the Galacien noticing.

Lom, why is there such a lack of information on the Nacuerians? Have the Galacien never captured one of their vessels or extracted information from one of them personally?

Only fragments, that which we have observed directly. Vessels that are captured, become totally useless as a source of information, as are the Nacuerians themselves. As soon as any attempt is made to gather information from a Nacuerian or any of their data-technology, it simply shuts itself down and becomes completely useless.

Yet you have been able to infiltrate their systems before?

True, but anything we take from them becomes corrupt.

There must be a way.

We are having a little more success lately. Remember on Earth your implant was using the Galacien's very latest development in system infiltration. It had far longer than anything previously to probe their systems, and exercised a degree of control over the Nacuerian ship and, most difficult of all, cleansed a little information from its flailing system. Remember though, the Nacuerians, no doubt, may have also evolved their technology on a level comparable or beyond our capabilities.

I stood there in silence, the gentle breeze washing over me, whilst I turned the problem over in my head like a stone, trying to smooth out the dilemma. My mind became more troubled. At first I thought it was my frustration inevitably returning, though as the moments passed I became aware it was far more immediate.

Garianne the ship is in danger! I mentally called to her.

Are you sure?

Yes. Lom replace the current environment with the exterior view, three-hundred-and-sixty-degree view.

The alien landscape was instantly swept away and in its place I saw we were surrounded by stars, our five ships very close to a moon orbiting a gas giant. With a flash of light and a sharp expulsion of air, Garianne teleported into the simulation room, soon followed by some of the members of the war council.

"Lom, bring all the ships to a stop and make a passive sensor sweep," said Garianne.

"It is too late, they already know we are here," I said.

Hundreds of focused beams of energy erupted from the moon's dark shadowy surface fiercely bombarding our ships. Our surroundings shook violently, despite Lom doing his utmost to compensate from the pounding we were taking. My implant fed me the ship's report – our shields were up and holding, just.

Bright light flashed intensely. I looked behind in horror as I saw the ship following us being sliced to pieces by the Nacuerian energy beams; pieces which, in turn, exploded or fell away from the main bulk of the destroyed warship, all played out before my eyes in a surreal and terrible silence. I saw many flailing Amelerian bodies pour from the open wounds of the dead ship, until suddenly it all receded at great speed as Lom accelerated us away from the onslaught.

Our surroundings began to spin as I realised Lom was rolling and the SIBATs, which were spaced out along the axis of the ship, were launched in turn when faced away from the enemy fire. I tried my hardest to maintain my sense of balance while the ship went through its complex evasive manoeuvre coupled with its 360-degree spin in order to launch its entire complement of SIBATs into space. I managed to catch a glimpse of the other ships performing the same manoeuvre, splitting off in different directions.

Nacuerian ships were now flooding out from the moon like a swarm of angry insects, filling space with their weapons fire. I needed to know how many there were. Lom informed me that its sensors could pick up well over ten thousand ships. Almost all were fighter class with a few heavy cruisers hanging back.

Garianne kept me privy to the orders she gave to the SIBATs and our own cruisers. She sounded completely calm and in control of the situation. Could she not see that we were all dead, they were simply too many?

Blinding flashes appeared around us as the Galacien let off some of their more devastating world-destroyers, though there were few opportunities to do so, as the Nacuerians and the SIBATs were so densely intermingled now, moving in every direction conceivable.

I instructed my implant to show me where Min was amidst the apparent chaos. In my mind I could see a SIBAT. She was moving at incredible speed, hugging expertly round the surface of one of our huge cruisers. Nacuerian fighters attempted to swarm in on her position and overwhelm her, brutally trying to destroy the SIBAT.

My fists tightened. How long would she last out there? She fought well, skilfully cutting a path of destruction in her wake using her SIBAT's superior weapons system, beams of lethal energy swiftly pinpointed their targets in an impressive frenzy of fire; her skill as a warrior was clear to see. However it concerned me that she, and the others out there, had never fought such a battle before.

The Nacuerians never let up on the pressure with their greater numbers, and my implant informed me that they were slowly but surely putting a strain on both the starships and the SIBATs. Despite every tactic and weapon used by the Galacien, no matter how advanced or elaborate, it would not be enough. The Galacien did possess an edge, I could see that, but unfortunately it was not enough to break down the Nacuerian numbers.

No wonder Garianne looked to me as a possible, perhaps the only, solution.

As I looked at the ongoing battle, it was plain to see that only some external force, something unaccounted for by the Nacuerians, could win this war. The battle continued unrelenting and I needed an answer to my question. The question I had only now come to realise, that which would decide the fate of the galaxy. I could see no other option, no other way to continue.

I turned to Garianne "I need the use of one of your SIBATs."

"Why?" she said not looking at me. I could sense her issuing constant commands, concentrating on multiple tasks at once. Conversing with me was just another and did not appear problematic for her.

"I believe I can get some information from the Nacuerians, but I cannot do it stuck in here. I need to get out there; I need to get close to them."

"If your mind is transferred to a SIBAT, your abilities will not follow. Remember what I said about super-sentients? Your abilities cannot be copied into another body, or any technology for that matter."

"That is not what I meant. I have familiarised myself with SIBAT systems and know that it can meld itself to me physically."

"An out-dated method to wear this class of SIBAT, with a number of disadvantages," said Bur Messel.

"I believe I can compensate for them," I said.

"Out there amongst that madness. Our greatest warriors are falling against them and you've never interfaced with a SIBAT before. You'll be killed in moments."

Garianne scrutinized me with her piercing eyes, as if she were studying my very soul, her fingers rubbing her delicate chin. "If you are killed out there... then you are gone forever. And be under no illusions, Jonas, you can be killed and then we would lose something unique. You are the only super-sentient in the galaxy. The risk is too great."

"I am going to have to get involved sometime, and when I do I am sure there will be great risk. Whether I take it sooner or later makes no difference, except that if we leave it, there may be no later. "

My words gave Garianne pause.

"Garianne, you can't be considering this?" said Bur Messel.

"We both know there is no way to save the Amelerian system; the Galacien home system is next." I said.

She stood there, her intense gaze never wavering. I waited for what seemed like an eternity for her to say something. Who knew what thoughts were being played out in her mind? All the others I could read to some degree, not her though.

"Garianne," said Lom, "the Nacuerian armada is finally moving into the system."

Slowly she nodded in agreement.

Chapter 17. Belly of the Beast

The SIBAT teleported into the simulation room before Garianne and I arrived. She had taken one of the least skilful warriors from the battlefield and timed it so as not to endanger the others still out there. On the ship, someone's mind and memories of their experiences out there were, at this moment, being transferred back into their body. I wondered if they were frustrated or relieved, or perhaps they merely accepted whatever was expected of them. I had to remember not to think of these beings in human terms.

I could sense the war council members grumbling quietly amongst themselves, all except Sevine Anoor and Garianne, both of whom remained silent while I quickly configured the SIBAT for the unique purpose in hand. As Bur Messel had pointed out, the Galacien rarely used the SIBATs in this way anymore, so I had to re-educate the SIBAT's quasi-sentient systems. Already it was beginning to remould its shape and open itself up, so that I may step into it. It almost perfectly resembled my body's profile now, and its white exterior seemed to soften as it began to peel back to reveal a deep red interior like a dark, beckoning womb.

"Work with the SIBAT's systems. If you let it, it will automatically protect you, hopefully making up for your lack of experience and get you to where you need to be," Garianne said.

"I need to get inside one of their cruisers," I said.

"You're hoping to interface with them directly then?" said Bur Messel.

"Yes, one way or another."

"They'll kill you before you have a chance."

"Perhaps not. He may be able to get close enough to them," said Garianne.

"What can he do, really, Garianne?"

"What he does best, learn. Are you ready?" she asked me.

I nodded.

I stepped into the SIBAT and it quickly moulded itself over the rest of my body, feeling like a thick, second skin. My orifices were catered for by the SIBAT's systems allowing me to still breathe and hear, though everything was covered and protected. All my functions worked through the SIBAT now. My eyes were covered shut by the SIBAT's firm though flexible fit. However this did not matter, for I was afforded more senses than I had previously had access to; the entire electromagnetic spectrum for one. It was no wonder that some Galacien citizens had chosen to use similar technology to more permanently house their minds.

My implants presence became more prominent as the SIBAT's sentience used it to link itself to me. The feeling of dual-presence in my mind became greater, as the SIBAT finished its integration, and its final systems came online. We were now joined, my awareness filled with the possibilities of this new symbiosis.

As I waited for Garianne to get everything prepared for my insertion into the battle, I informed Min of my plan. It was met with a predictable reaction.

"Jonas, you'll be killed," she said.

"What do you care?" trying to match the coldness she had so often showed me.

"I worked very hard to get you here, a lot of people have, and now you're going to throw all that away."

"I have been through all this with Garianne. The Amelerian system is mere hours away from being totally overwhelmed or destroyed by the Nacuerian armada."

"Then we need to escape now, while we still have a chance. The longer we leave it the less likely we are to get out alive."

"I know that. If I don't do this now though, we may just be delaying the inevitable. I am sorry Min, it has already been decided. My insertion is moments away. I just have to wait for my backup to assemble and reach their coordinates."

"I know," she replied. "I'm one of them. I just received my orders."

"What? No, Min, you cannot do that."

"I'm afraid I can."

There was a stubborn silence between us. Those who were with me were to sacrifice themselves and their short-term memories, if necessary, so that I could get through to the Nacuerian cruiser. My main concern was that Lom would be destroyed attempting to escape from the Amelerian system, in which case all those that I knew would suffer memory death.

Out there on Galacien Prime were their earlier memories, from which they could live again. Yet these memories, including those of Garianne, Davern, and Min, would have no memory of me. I could not have her forget me, any of them. There was no question of how I felt for Min. Garianne however, was another matter. Never had I encountered such an extraordinary being, but my emotions were conflicting whenever I thought of her: respect, annoyance, admiration, fascination. I was shaken from my reverence by her appearance before me.

"Something you'd like to share?" she asked.

"No, I am fine," I replied bashfully.

"It's time, Jonas."

In her eyes I saw something that gave me a sense of foreboding and then, suddenly, the cloud lifted and there she was smiling, her eyes deep with insight. "Into the belly of the beast," she said.

I and the suit nodded as one.

Ahead of me I saw the ghostly images of the battle outside as Lom superimposed my insertion view into the room. Thousands of Nacuerian fighters zipped about like angry insects attempting to hunt down the Galacien SIBATs. Energy beams flickered about in apparent chaos, while behind vast capital ships held their own against one another. A trio of SIBATs came together, moving through the mass of the battle's combatants. There they waited for a dangerous moment to pass before I teleported.

As I left, something passed between Garianne and myself and I knew for certain that she was keeping something from me.

Then I found myself moving at great speed, in the cold vastness of space, with only the skin of the SIBAT protecting me. All around me, above and below, stretching off into the endless distance amongst the stars, were ships of all sizes seeking to destroy one another.

There were four of us, including Min. We quickly made our way through the mayhem towards one of their capital ships, focused energy beams pummelling our SIBATs more and more frequently as we approached.

Nacuerian fighters joined the fray, some of which were dispatched by my comrades. Every moment that passed attracted more of them to us. The SIBATs were reaching the limits of the amount of energy they could either absorb or reflect from enemy fire. We had to constantly shift our formation, to take on fire for one another, to ensure the survival of the group.

All of the SIBATs were fairly weak now, though we were almost there. The Nacuerians surely knew there was something significant about our goal, for the cruiser's focus, looming monstrously before us, was predominantly on us now. I cursed myself, wishing I had taken my time to be more cunning for now I doubted whether we would make it. There were only seconds before our SIBATs would be destroyed, and I briefly considered my own death after all this time having only recently become comfortable with my apparent invulnerability.

We sped headlong for the cruiser and were almost upon the ship's shields, when the three other SIBATs formed up in a line in front of me. The first two at the head of the group shone a brilliant blue and I knew they had converted all of their SIBATs' matter into energy making them very effective projectiles against the Nacuerian ship's shields. A shockwave of light erupted ahead of Min and myself, as the two SIBATs were destroyed by the impact, though they had weakened the Nacuerian cruiser's shield long enough to give us a chance to get through.

Min's SIBAT had taken on a conical shape as she broke through what was left of the cruiser's shielding and I quickly followed her through.

"Come back to us," said Min a moment before her SIBAT tore through the hull of the great ship, destroying it in the process.

I continued to break through the way she had made for me, tearing through the inner layers of the vessel. Finally I brought my SIBAT to rest in a large cylindrical chamber; the only sound was that of my own breathing. Through the SIBAT I could sense that the ship was now sealed off from the vacuum of space and that there were many life forms heading my way. Not surprisingly, they knew I was here.

I readied myself. One way or another I was going to get what I wanted. I ordered the SIBAT from my body, its quasi-sentient mind recommending that I make use of its weapons against the imminent attack. After a second ignored order it reluctantly left, standing next to me like a silent sentinel.

I could feel them coming long before my ordinary senses would have noticed the Nacuerians. Then, the chamber was filled with black writhing shapes, over the floor, the walls, and even the ceiling, all approaching in a mad dash to render me limb from limb. They were truly abominable creatures and it took me an extraordinary amount of will to control the fear threatening to choke and overwhelm me.

They surrounded me. No animal sound escaped them, no shouts or screams that suggested their violent intent, only their almost hypnotic gesticulation of tentacles. As the swarm descended, I firmly commanded the SIBAT to shut itself down; its involvement would only momentarily delay that which I sought. Like the sword the moment before it strikes, they almost seemed to pause, and then the world was a terrible violent flash of dark alien shapes.

I fought back against the beast that seemed one rather than many, an overgrown mass of pulsating limbs. I could feel its alien thinking forcing impressions upon my mind, cold and merciless.

I could not understand how a sentient creature could feel the way the Nacuerians did – fundamentally wrong somehow. I was sure nothing else in the galaxy had the same mental make-up. What was it that had made them this way?

Was it really natural that creatures such as this existed in the universe? These thoughts raced across my consciousness as I fought back hard against them and I sensed that they, too, could feel me in their minds. The brutality continued and I had still as yet received no injuries, while I had managed to dispatch a few of them – a few out of so many.

When I did kill one of their number, though, I sensed nothing from the rest. No anger, no overwhelming need to avenge the death of a comrade; they simply did not care. Their feelings were closer to cold curiosity.

The more we fought the more attuned I became to them. I sensed them to be different, wrong. Something unnatural, yet I couldn't understand what. A small clearing broke out before me, and for a moment I thought they were afraid. I saw one standing alone there. It predictably drew my attention, as it was intended to, and the red light I had seen before shone into my face. For a moment I was unsure what to do, such was my determination to do battle with them. Then I remembered, and against every natural instinct to fight, I let go and let the red light take me.

Chapter 18. Enlightenment

I had no idea how long I had stood there. All I knew was that it was night on the farm and I was watching my mother and father whispering in the distant moonlight. Something was very odd, though. I was experiencing a sensation I was completely unfamiliar with, as though a thin layer of my skin had been peeled from my body. I looked at myself and could see quite plainly that my arms and hands were a lot smaller than they should be. I also appeared shorter. I touched my face which felt smooth, not even the merest hint of bristle on my chin.

This seemed familiar and yet not quite right. I did not feel myself and yet I could not remember how I was supposed to feel. In fact it appeared I had no memory of recent events.

The wind suddenly swept against my body, drawing from me a sharp intake of breath. The strange sensation I felt suddenly increased to a shocking degree and I now perceived the very air around me as an enemy. causing great discomfort. It then occurred to me maybe I was feeling cold. I had never experienced the sensation before, even though the concept was a common everyday experience I sensed in others.

A second attack beat itself against me, as I braced my small frame, grunting through gritted teeth until the gust subsided. Through this horrible sensation the landscape seemed to spin around me, changing, shifting until I could no longer make sense of my surroundings. Something solid caught my eye and as I turned I found myself face to face with the captain I had met in another life. I remembered that incident, but it was fragmented. I was merely a boy and he had come to ask me some questions. Something bad had happened but I could not remember what. My arm was outstretched and, before I could move, he had knelt down and taken it in a vice-like grip. I could not break free, no matter how hard I struggled. His hold on me did not seem natural, as if the very air around my arm had somehow solidified into a dense material, making escape impossible.

With deliberate and unnerving slowness he drew out his knife and tested its sharpness on his thumb. Satisfied, he duly ran it slowly across my palm. A sharp fire of pain exploded along the point where the knife cut into my hand and, as I looked down in shaken disbelief, I could see my own red blood pouring freely from the wound. A sly smile spread across the captain's face, apparently pleased. He wiped his blade clean with a rag and tossed it at me. Now free, I quickly wrapped it around my hand bringing about another wave of pain that made my whole arm ache. I stared at all the blood in shocked silence.

After considering me for a moment longer, the captain turned away towards his men as if to take his leave, when he suddenly turned back, roaring and raising his sword high in the air. I stumbled back and fell in surprise and terror on the ground, my body a mess of blood and sand. His men laughed and he snorted his contempt and wry amusement. I hid from their eyes, and when they had finally gone I found I could no longer hold back the tears and wept.

I dragged my feet along the dusty ground heading for home. I must have looked a pitiful sight – dirty, bloody, tear-streaked face, broken, and tired. As I drew closer to the house I saw my parents and a group of bandits standing together, not moving, as if waiting for something. Confused, I approached and walked amongst them. Then the silence was broken as they suddenly broke into movement. I watched as my father was pushed from one bandit to another. One finally took a swing at him, hitting him squarely on the jaw. He dropped down in a heap on the dusty ground and I could see that he was exhausted and badly beaten.

I heard my mother screaming, shouting for me to run, when one of the men grabbed me roughly by the scruff of the neck. I yelled at the searing pain as he twisted me this way and that on shaky legs. I found to my despair that I did not have nearly enough strength to stop him, to stop them any of them, from doing exactly what they wanted to me and my family. The bandit dragged me across the floor, his strong arm immovable, throttling tight around my neck. My mother continued to shout my name as my eyes bulged from their sockets, streaming tears down my face blurring the nightmarish scene before me. Just when I thought the man would choke me to death, he released me, pulled me to my feet, and threw me hard against the stone wall of our house, the force of it knocking me senseless.

When I came around it was to a world of pain, the likes of which I had never experienced before as if I was being slowly cracked open like a dead carcass. I became aware that part of this pain took the form of a great weight bearing down upon me, making me gasp for breath. One of the bandits was sitting on me.

My vision focused a little more and I saw my father lying dead upon the ground. Ignored, forgotten like he was nothing. A frenzy took me as I writhed like a man possessed. The creature upon me was like a rock, immobile. I would not stop though, I would never stop until exhaustion or death took me. The man who sat on me struck me hard on the head with the pommel of his weapon and darkness took me.

They left me during the night tied to a tree, the ropes cutting into my naked flesh, bruising and burning my skin. I stared almost catatonic in shock at what was left of my poor father, a dark lump left on the ground, unidentifiable in the gloom. I could see it, even though the light had faded and hidden the macabre scene.

I could see it, forever burned into my mind.

My eyes slowly drifted to the house where the dim candlelight bled from the window shutters. Inside came the sounds of shouting, laughing, and the occasional fight breaking out. Of my mother I could hear nothing. Either they had already killed her, or she had become like me. Every so often some of them came out of the house to beat or degrade me in some manner. They sneered as they told me what they had done to my mother, their words causing me more pain than their physical assaults, my entire being screaming in vengeance. It was all useless though. I was a dry leaf in the hands of a giant. They told me what they planned to do to me the next day. Terrified, trapped, I could not comprehend why any creature would expend so much time and energy on another's suffering. Eventually they left me, returning to the house. I watched them go completely accepting what would happen to me the following day. The rain came down and an almighty thunderclap heralded the beginnings of a storm.

I shivered abruptly, alone in the dark.

It was the middle of the night when I heard her voice through the rain, a soft whisper in my mind so beautiful it brought tears to my eyes.

Jonas, the voice said.

I raised my head and looked about. No one was there.

"Who... Who is there?" I mumbled.

Garianne, said the voice.

"Where are you?"

In your head, don't you remember me?

"No… Should I?"

Indeed you should. They have made you forget, Jonas. They are trying to break you.

"They have," I admitted. My head lolled, the constant downpour soaking and freezing me to the bone. I felt like my mind was finally about to shut down, fleeing headlong into madness.

Not them, the Nacuerians.

"Who?"

We planned for this, you and I, remember?

With her final word it all came back to me – all of it. I shook my head momentarily disorientated.

"I remember. Damn them, they have done this to me, Now I know the truth."

It's still down to you, Jonas. There's nothing any of us can do to help you now, wherever we are.

She was right of course, as always. The Garianne program in my head was very limited compared to the Min quasi-sentient program. Created only to deliver a message, respond to my basic and predictable questions, and, of course, to give me access to that which the Nacuerians had taken from me – my memories. A simple program by Galacien standards, the better to elude detection, yet still immensely complex. It had completed its task, and was even now efficiently deconstructing itself, until there was nothing left to detect.

I was alone again, painfully aware of the cold sapping the life from my boyhood frame. I knew now that there would never be someone to come for me, no gods to appeal to, to save me. Not now, not ever. These thoughts began to spread like a fire in my mind. Somehow this was connected with significant thoughts I had had before. A puzzle that required a solution, yet so much more than that – an answer I had been searching for. The idea, vague at first, filled my mind with an almost prophetic purpose and my path became clear. I raised my head against the rain as it battered upon me and opened my new eyes on an existence, changed forever.

Chapter 19. The Nacuerian System

Like a small mammal clutched in the talons of a bird, I was still at the mercy of the Nacuerians. That would change. I now knew that the world around me was merely an illusion, created to distract me, to break me, crushing any resolve in believing I could overcome them.

But I knew the truth now and I would make them pay.

I remembered what Garianne had said about forging my heart and mind in fire. The Nacuerians had sought to burn and cripple me by the scars it left, yet it made me stronger. My previous mistake was obvious now – trying to use physical force in a place where it did not matter; a place of the mind. I had always relied on my physical strength to establish my mental strength and, when they took that away from me, my mind had crumbled. Mental strength was the true power in this world – in any world – not the physical. Sentient beings are creatures of the mind, that is the place where we truly live and die, not out there.

"Give me a lever long enough and I will move the world." I had heard something like that from Garianne and pondered its mental equivalent. As I pontificated, I felt my resolve harden beyond anything I had previously experienced, the world of illusions lifting from my consciousness, like peeking from behind a veil. I could sense the Nacuerians in the room, with me held in the grapple of some machine.

Talons indeed, I thought.

I was there only a moment, letting go of the fabric and coming back to their false reality. They had not noticed, though a moment longer and I believed they would have. I needed to make them think I was still here while my consciousness was elsewhere.

I remembered the time I had spoken to Garianne light years from my physical body on Earth. I tried to remember what it had felt like, in an effort to reproduce it. I smiled; it came so easily. I could sense their machines monitoring me. Part of their purpose was to look for any signs that I was regaining consciousness, and then make sure that I was again sedated. With a little practice, I managed to leave enough of myself tied to that tree for their monitors not to register my conscious state.

I perceived the world of the ship's computer system and knew how to configure that part of my consciousness so that an interface was possible. My mind could now move into their system, yet it was securely guarded by a number of extremely advanced defences. I inspected them passively from a distance, so as not to give myself away.

Like any advanced system, the Nacuerian ship resembled a living organism, with information running throughout, and a form of energy maintaining its working existence. The more I observed its workings, the greater an understanding I had, until I felt confident that I could move freely through the ship's systems and not be noticed for the foreign entity I was. Although it all seemed too easy, for I had taken the measure of their systems in so little time. I remembered Garianne's suggestion that it was my ability to learn which made me special, not my physical strength or my durability. That which I had just experienced proved again that it was mental and not physical strength which was superior. This great truth continued to blossom and expand into many ideas as I began to move at great speed through the ship's systems. My thoughts had become like lightening and the merest fraction of a second was strewn out and slowed down.

In my enhanced awareness, the Nacuerians aboard the ship barely moved. I was on the ship's time now, where many tasks could be performed in less than the blink of an eye. I made myself appear like one of the systems' programs in every way becoming one of the multitudes. Like a giant hive of insects they went about their various tasks, quickly, efficiently, and unquestionably. Every so often another program would look me over and then quickly move on, for my understanding was too great now for any of them to know what I truly was.

In my arrogance, I nearly missed their all-seeing, network, a super-system which supported the whole and had foiled all the Galacien's previous attempts at retrieving information. I was not surprised, for it was a formidable super-system. The Nacuerians understood the value of secrecy and I had discovered that they did not care for one another, like other sentient creatures did. The network would disable and sever the ship's systems if it detected me as a threat. I realised that my overconfidence had nearly cost me dearly. It would not happen again.

I made sure I was patient, biding my time, scrutinising the intricate workings of the Nacuerian super-system. Seconds passed by in the outer world, though in the world of the ship's systems they seemed like hours.

Eventually I felt I had taken its full measure, and became confident again, yet cautiously, I moved on. Reaching the ship's data-core I went through what the core perceived as the correct procedure for data retrieval. The hardest thing I'd ever had to do since entering the system was to stay calm and therefore in control, while the information I sought flowed freely into my mind. Any strong emotions on my part could have shown up as some kind of anomaly and warranted curiosity and some kind of alert.

I purposefully ignored looking at the data, as the seconds dragged on, shunting it to the back of my awareness. When the transfer was finally complete, I duly began to move back to the other part of myself. On my way I encountered two of the super-system's guardian programs. I remained impassive and compliant as they probed me. It was a routine check for I had already altered the ship to make me seem as if I were a legitimate program. They were being thorough though, scanning deeper. Another fraction of a nanosecond and they would see the information I had retrieved.

I had no choice. I took a sublime hold of them, and when they knew something was definitely wrong with me, I was ready. They instantly tried to send out an alert, however it was too late and I subdued both of the guardian programs. I quickly went about altering their perceptions of the encounter and sent them on their way again, both convinced that nothing out of the ordinary had occurred.

That other part of my awareness returned to the world of illusions and I felt myself tied to the tree again. I knew I must remain in the emotional state expected of me at all costs and that I must not exhibit any feelings such as hope or elation. A part of me felt incredibly empowered by the revelation I had discovered about the universe as well as my newfound ability to interface with the ship's system. I prepared myself, and calmly accessed the valuable data I had retrieved but, despite my best efforts, I could not remain completely unemotional at what I had unearthed from the Nacuerian data-core. Irrespective of its effect on me personally, I managed to keep my emotions in check but knew their monitors would sense a change in my physiology no matter how insignificant.

I heard the door of the house being kicked open as the bandits carrying my mother began to walk towards me. I needed to escape with the data-core's valuable information. It provided insight into the Nacuerian species but, more significantly, I had discovered that there was a traitor within the Galacien, someone the Nacuerians had been working with all this time, ever since they had begun to invade the galaxy. Now I needed to act out a part of my own, a deception that would convince the Nacuerians and the traitor, that their secrets and schemes were safe.

I waited for the men to come, dragging the illusion of my mother behind them. I knew she was not real, yet to see her even as a representation treated this way stirred a deep ire that the logical part of my mind was forced to quench. However, these feelings would help convince the bandits and hence the machines monitoring me that I was still their pawn to play with.

The bandits punched and kicked her as brutally as they did my father, I let the pain of the sight of it affect me, to complete the illusion. I could have easily broken free of this place but that course of action would give everything away. Deception was the way now, my way – deception was the key. I endured a little more suffering at the sight of the brutality forced upon my mother, until I felt that the system was satisfied and it was time to get out.

I plunged a part of my consciousness into the ship's systems, and a quick look through the interior sensors showed the Nacuerians motionless, as if frozen in time.

I manipulated the ship into believing that I was one of the Nacuerian super-system's guardians, giving me practically unhindered run of the ship. I looked in on my physical self to confirm that I was undamaged and whole and saw myself held faced down, unconscious in some kind of suspension field. If I returned to my body now I could see

169

no way of breaking free by any physical means, I had to rely on another way. There were a number of options. I could usurp the ship's system, taking complete control and navigating back to Lom but this, again, would lead to the traitor discovering that I had gained access to the Nacuerian system and possibly found out their identity. I needed something less obvious and more sublime.

I had come to the conclusion that I would need help. I hated to admit it, but there was no way I was going to be able to do this alone. I found out that hours had passed since I had been captured and the Amelerian system was now completely overrun. The Galacien conglomerate warships had apparently fought until their last ship helping as many civilians as possible to escape. It had not helped much as the Nacuerians' vast numbers meant they could easily be hunted down. The Nacuerians had come and slaughtered all life in the Amelerian system. But what about Lom and the others?

Chapter 20. The Kinsmen

The Nacuerian ship I was on was part of a small fleet which had left the Amelerian system, and left quickly. Apparently they had encountered a being that defied explanation – me. Now they needed to take me away and study me.

Using the ship's sensors I passively searched to see if there was any indication of surviving Galacien warships in the vicinity. I tried not to worry about Min. I knew her mind had returned to her body the moment her SIBAT had been destroyed, though she would have no memory of the mission to get me on board this ship. No doubt she had been brought up to speed though. Yet I had no idea whether she had survived the Nacuerian invasion of the Amelerian system. I suppressed an urge to smile when I detected an Amelerian cruiser following from a great distance, I was sure it was them and that Min was with them.

Again I was faced with the dilemma of how to proceed without my new knowledge being discovered. It was vital they must remain unaware of my ability to infiltrate their systems, for their ignorance gave me the advantage. However, I had already mastered an ability to separate my consciousness from my body, this, I thought, was my best chance at contacting my allies.

I reached out with my senses across, what seemed like, a vast ocean. Incredibly small yet bright, shining out like stars in the night, were the minds of those on board. Lom itself, containing these many pinpricks of light, shone paler, yet the light ran throughout the entirety of its immense being; it was beautiful. I brushed against many minds briefly, curious as to how they differentiated. I could tell the Amelerians were all very similar, yet they were all still individuals. I found myself taking the equivalent of deep breaths when I spotted Min. My attention bore upon her and surprisingly I could sense her worry. She, like the others, had no idea I was on the command deck watching her. I was invisible, moving about the ship reading their emotions, their thoughts; so alien, yet at the same time something common in all of them. Again I was struck at how different, how wrong in nature, the Nacuerians were.

They were indeed tracking the group of Nacuerian ships, though they did not know if I was alive and, if so, which ship I was on. Then something invisible to my senses entered the command deck. Different to any of the others, how I did not sense it as I approached Lom I do not know, exhuming power and confidence. The same kind of strength of will I had felt build in me on the Nacuerian ship existed as a part of this creature, though, by the Gods, the strength it hinted at was unnerving. I could sense nothing more for it seemed to have natural defences that I had no hope of getting past. A will of something indomitable.

It was Garianne and there was something else that differentiated her from the others. She was looking at me.

Garianne did not say a word, although I knew she was aware of my presence.

Garianne it is me, Jonas, I said nervously. Can you hear me? She made no reply, although I could sense that she had somehow heard me.

Garianne I know you can hear me. Why will you not respond?

I'm just making sure, thought Garianne.

Of what?

That you haven't been tampered with, that the Nacuerians aren't… manipulating you.

I assure you they are not.

I can tell that now, though it is possible that you yourself may not have been aware.

Was that true? Could the Nacuerians do such a thing? I quickly checked through my newfound knowledge. There were a number of ways they could have accomplished this, though Garianne herself had said they had not, and I was sure I would have known.

Tell me what's happening, Jonas, asked Garianne.

I knew that I must be cautious and provide plausible truths so I told her of my battle with the Nacuerians, my submission to them in the hope to learn more about them, and of the world of illusions. I did not tell her of my revelation and the fact that I had gained access to the Nacuerian data-core.

I had hoped that you might have found some way to acquire the information we so desperately need, thought Garianne.

I paused for a moment, fearing that she already suspected something. I remembered that I had to be careful of my thoughts during this kind of contact, and so focused on a more altered version of events on the Nacuerian ship.

I was able to sense something from them while in close proximity and have continued trying even while being held a captive. However it is limited and vague. I am sorry, I replied.

There was a silence, and I had a horrible feeling that I had not convinced her.

Very well then, Jonas. Let us see what we can do about getting you out of there, shall we?

I heard her address the crew. "May I have everyone's attention… Thank you. Jonas has made contact with me and, despite the circumstances, he is alright. Lom, he's on the furthest of the four ships, we are pursuing. Prepare to bring the new engine enhancements online."

What was that Garianne? I asked.

I mentioned it before. Lom and the ship's engineer have been working on the engines recently, upgrading them. We should be able to muster up a little more speed.

What for? I'm sure Lom is already faster than any Nacuerian ship.

We're going to try and out-manoeuvre them; you'll see soon enough.

I kept my sense of the ship and what was going on in the space between us. Garianne obviously had something planned. The Nacuerians had four warships, Lom was alone – it was not a definite as to who would emerge victorious in a battle between them. I noticed that Lom was exerting around ninety per cent of its potential speed, though still gaining on us. Suddenly I sensed that Lom had launched some kind of energy projectiles towards us. The Nacuerians moved to avoid being hit but the projectiles were tracking us. Almost a minute passed before they impacted on the Nacuerian shields, draining them of energy.

The other three Nacuerian ships decelerated and spread out to engage Lom, while our ship continued at its maximum speed. The three Nacuerian ships could not keep up with Lom so they had to make the most of it when they entered their own weapons range. Three against one did not seem like fair odds at all, even though Lom had been bombarding the ships while they quickly tried to reach their optimum firing range. As soon as they did, they let loose with everything they had. Lom did not try to pass them, rather decelerating to engage them. What was Garianne up to? Then it dawned on me, the Nacuerians had played into her hands by presuming that Lom would pursue at its top speed. Once Lom started firing on them, the three ships were forced to engage it. Garianne had Lom fall back and was only playing for time.

As the battle raged on, the distance between us and them became greater and greater, until Garianne decided enough was enough. Lom engaged its engines and soon reached a hundred per cent of its attainable velocity and then increased it further. Now the Nacuerians became concerned. Their three warships were left far behind while Lom was quickly closing the vast distance between us.

I must go, I communicated to Garianne, sensing a lot of commotion now on the Nacuerian ship. *They know you can catch them now and I am not sure what they will do.*

They will try and render you useless or eliminate you, if it is within their power, and corrupt their own network, to prevent us from learning anything from them, she replied.

I will try my best to make sure neither of these things happen.

I brought my mind faster than light back to the Nacuerian vessel and plunged myself into the system.

I spent some time looking over their current status. There were a number of procedures to go through when capture was imminent – transferring all data to the Nacuerian network super-system, which existed somewhere in hyperspace, was one of them. Once done, the data-core would then infect the ship and the Nacuerians on board with a virus, destroying them. That process was being prepared, and even now I could begin to see the signs of it throughout the system.

There was another factor to consider in their procedure now, though. The fate of the so called super-sentient. Perhaps they had learned the word from the Galacien traitor? Or maybe they cleansed it from my mind in the same way that they had extracted the memories of my parents, and Earth, in which case they knew everything I knew, up until the moment of my deception.

I was not about to allow this knowledge to be communicated to the rest of their kind so I moved to where the data was being prepared to be sent onto the Nacuerian super-system. I quickly found the data package which contained my memories and altered it in such a way that, when next accessed, it would corrupt itself beyond all possible recognition.

That taken care of, I now took steps to make sure that my physical self would come to no harm. The Nacuerians had been studying my physical form for some time now and were desperately thinking of ways to destroy me. I had to admit some of them were rather ingenious, although interestingly enough, even though they felt confident about destroying my physical form, they had serious concerns that my mind would somehow survive. There were a lot of theories and speculations which basically came down to the fact that they did not know what I was, and therefore could not be entirely sure as to whether they could kill me. Some of their ideas seemed extremely lethal and I was definitely not going to wait around to see if they could accomplish their goals. I saw I had plenty of time before they were ready to make an attempt on my life, so I left, and spent a little time looking around the system making sure there was nothing I had missed.

There was.

Something subtle and elusive within the system itself that I hadn't noticed before, not just another program going about its various tasks. This was something else entirely. I could not pinpoint its specific location, I only got the feeling that it was in there with me, watching. It definitely did not feel Nacuerian in nature. I checked to see if it could be something left here by the Galacien traitor, for it felt as if it was observing the system, collating data for some purpose as yet unknown. But I did not think that was it either. It felt completely alien.

I did not dare attempt to search for an answer directly, for I had no idea of its capabilities. Recent events had taught me the error of arrogance. I must be patient, even though time was running out.

Carrying on through the system I let my natural senses absorb this entity as much as possible. It seemed aware of my true nature, yet so far, had chosen only to observe my actions. I kept myself aware of its presence while I finished my business in the ship's systems. The last of the ship's data had been retrieved by the data-core, including that infected package containing my information. I also saw the form of my execution had been decided upon – a particularly nasty virus, which they felt confident could destroy my mind. They were not taking any chances. I studied the virus for some time and covertly consulted the ship's medical sub-systems, before making it think that it had been given instructions to alter the virus and make it benign.

The altered virus entered my body orally and would not cause me any harm. Lom had almost reached us and drained the ship's shields. The Nacuerians did not care though, for they fully believed they had collected and delivered all possible useful data intact to their precious network, while eliminating me at the same time. The rest of the Nacuerian species did not care for this one ship and its crew.

I had only seconds now with which to return to my physical form and considered whether to confront the foreign entity. It had observed everything I had done, though was unaware that I knew of its existence. I was not sure how it would react if I attempted contact. Secrecy did seem of paramount importance to its purpose here and, if

I confronted it, who knows what would happen. I sensed it was very powerful and feared that it could potentially wipe any memories and any data I had acquired since entering the system, and then send me on my way. If I did not confront, it, however, I would never know what it truly was. I had been searching for something that was not a part of the Galacien Conglomerate of Worlds, when looking for species older than the Galacien. Now it seemed I had found a potential candidate.

I made a decision to take the risk. I had to find out what it was, for I believed I would never get anywhere otherwise. The system was shutting itself down around me and I thought it prudent to initiate an automated return time program which would take me back to my body should something undesirable happen.

The entity seemed to exist in many places at once, though more in one non-descript place in the system, than anywhere else. I moved to where I sensed it strongest and attempted communication.

My name is Jonas. Who are you?

There was no reply.

Now I was this close to it, I could sense its power and it unnerved me. I had a terrible vision of being manipulated, that my free will was only an illusion. Something deep within the core of my being told me this was not so, though the idea could not be shaken so easily. Just because this entity had such power did not mean it would choose to utilise it. But why did it stay in the shadows?

I was unsure; something was not right.

I know you desire to keep your existence unknown. I will tell no other of our encounter if that is your wish, though perhaps an exchange of knowledge may benefit us both.

A low rumble that sounded like rocks falling preceded a voice in my head:

Is that what you desire, Jonas, knowledge?

Yes, knowledge and solitude.

Yes we know of you, Jonas, better than you know yourself.

Had they already taken that which I offered without my consent?

It seems then that you have me at a disadvantage, for I know nothing of you.

Few do.

Who?

The Phalinon know, yet they do not.

What do you mean?

They possess the information; awareness of its significance is another matter.

Why don't you just tell me?

This is part of the necessary process, Jonas. One day you will understand.

My time had almost run out and I sensed the entity drawing all its parts together becoming one, ready to depart the system, To where, I could only guess. The Nacuerians had realised that their virus had had no effect on me, and were initiating a self-destruct of their ship in a desperate attempt to kill me.

Who are you? I asked.

A remnant.

My automated return program was pulling me back to my physical form but I managed to ask one final question. *A remnant of what?*

I heard the echo of their reply, as I felt myself return to my body while simultaneously being teleported back onto Lom.

The Kinsmen.

Chapter 21. Traitor

Min and Garianne entered the medical bay, where I had spent the last hour since my return to Lom.

"You came back," Min said approvingly, unsuccessfully trying to hide her pleasure at seeing me.

Nodding, I smiled. Of course she cared for me but I could not tell if there was anything more.

"Are you alright?" she asked.

"Yes, fine," I replied, like a son to his doting mother.

"Is he?" she directed at Sevine Anoor who had been looking me over since my return.

"He is fine so far as I can tell," said Sevine. "They did introduce something into his body, though it doesn't seem to have had any effect on him."

"Apparently you're as impervious on the inside as you are on the outside," said Min. "It is good to see you are well, Jonas. What were you able to learn from the Nacuerians?" asked Garianne.

"I was able to establish some kind of telepathic rapport with them, when I first fought but, unfortunately, it was rather limited. I'm afraid to say that my attempt to give myself to them in the hope of gaining more information has failed," I said feigning disappointment. I told them of every thought and impression I was able to get from them, to show that I had tried, wanting to sound as convincing as possible.

"A little information can reveal a great deal if scrutinised correctly," remarked Sevine Anoor.

The mood in the medical bay was grim to say the least, not surprising considering what had just happened and the path which lay ahead. I could sense that Lytpniuph and his crew were in shock from the fact that their home system had been laid to waste by the Nacuerians. As for Lom, he had been created in the Amelerian system, I could sense that he too had a similar reaction; the feeling permeated the ship.

"Where is Davern?" I asked.

"Killed in the initial attack," said Garianne.

I remembered the destroyed cruiser. "His memories?"

"They're safely stored on Galacien Prime," said Min.

"What will he remember though?"

"Nothing of the last few months. He won't remember you."

Davern had been a constant annoyance, a little too human, yet I had to admit, I missed him already.

"What happens if the memory stores on Galacien Prime are destroyed?" I asked.

"You know the answer to that. Permanent death for anyone whose memories reside there, including Davern's."

Min tried to smile. Her positive attitude was her way of keeping herself going through these difficult events. Sevine Anoor was more difficult to read being a Phalinon. I was eager to find out what knowledge the species had stored concerning the Kinsmen entity I had encountered, the Kinsmen from the only dream I had ever had.

Not quite yet though.

The traitor was here on the ship. The thought of this made me want to do what had always come naturally, though I was such a fundamentally different creature now.

Garianne looked on with her usual calm, controlled expression. I needed to play this perfectly, for the traitor was here in this very room – again deception was called for. The Galacien traitor was extraordinarily clever so everything I said and did must be calculated, to ensure nothing was given away. Only I and the traitor were aware of the Nacuerians' true plans and timescale. I had to act soon; I had to get Sevine Anoor alone. I feigned a stumble as I moved from the treatment bed.

Garianne had her hands under me before anyone else in the medical bay had made a move and lifted me back onto the bed in one fluid motion. "I think you should rest a little more," she said.

"I do not require rest, as you are no doubt aware," I replied.

"Nevertheless, the Nacuerians put you through an unusual experience. Sevine will you see to him?" she insisted in the voice that was difficult to deny.

"Of course."

Perfect.

"Don't feel bad about it. You did everything you could. Garianne will find a way, won't you?" said Min.

Garianne merely nodded her head, in reassurance before they left. Sevine and I were alone, as I had hoped. The silence felt like a great pit waiting to be filled.

I jumped into Lom's systems, so different from the Nacuerian's, and in moments I was familiar with his workings. I made a slight, though problematic, disruption to the internal sensors on this part of the ship, giving me the privacy I need.

"Sevine, there is something private and of utmost importance that I wish to discuss with you?"

The Phalinon automatically glanced towards the door.

"Don't worry, the room is secure."

It cocked its head studying me.

"What about Lom," Sevine said.

"Lom will not be aware of what transpires here."

"Are you sure?"

"Yes, I have infiltrated its systems and made sure."

Sevine paused, obviously taken aback by the extent of my abilities. "We helped create that which makes Lom possible, no one can match our technology."

Of course this was true. All realms of technology were their area of expertise. Yet I felt confident that to all intents and purposes we were alone. I finally felt secure, for now anyway.

"Trust me, there are no witnesses to what transpires here."

"Very well," replied the Phalinon, finally satisfied.

"Sevine there is a traitor amongst the Galacien, someone who has been collaborating with the Nacuerians all this time," I said.

"Explain your reasons for believing this."

"When I was on the Nacuerian ship I was able to infiltrate their system and download everything from their data-core."

For a moment the Phalinon remained motionless. "Why did you not tell the others?"

"I do not know who could be working with the traitor. I know who the Nacuerians are in communication with, yet that does not necessarily mean she is working alone."

"Who is 'she'?"

I found it hard to look at Sevine, for the answer still deeply disturbed me.

"Garianne. How can that be possible?"

Sevine looked introspective. "Anything is possible, you of all people should understand that. You are a creature from a primitive planet who possesses extraordinary abilities, far in advance of what would seem logical. Don't you agree? Garianne is one of the oldest beings of the Galacien Conglomerate of Worlds. Perhaps she wants to ensure the continuation of that long life, a kind of immortality in the face of the galaxy-wide genocide we now face, by conspiring with the enemy."

"I always sensed there was something she was keeping from me. We must be wary. She is extremely clever and I've never encountered such a being before," I said.

"She has acquired and mastered many abilities during her long life. Not all of them are immediately understandable," said Sevine.

"I encountered something else in the Nacuerian system, an entity which referred to itself as Kinsmen," I said.

"Kinsmen?"

"It told me the Phalinon have knowledge of them," I waited a moment, noticing that the Phalinon was consulting his own knowledge base.

"I personally know nothing of your Kinsmen," he said eventually.

I could not hide my disappointment.

"However, that does not mean that we are not in possession of the knowledge you seek. We have vast data stores, which we could gain access to. There may be something there concerning these Kinsmen. May I ask why you believe them to be of such importance?" asked Sevine.

"I believe that to win this war we need to appeal to some greater power. The Kinsmen are the only clue I have that it may exist; I must follow it, wherever it may lead. I need access to your people's records."

Sevine nodded his head. "There are numerous locations for our archives, all exist in hyperspace and all locations are secret. If Garianne is indeed betraying the Galacien, I do not want her to have knowledge of these places. Fortunately, the nearest archive to our present position has its own propulsion system, therefore we can move its location. It is not something we do often, but these are special circumstances."

"What do you suggest?" I said.

"We are back on course for Galacien Prime, expected time of arrival, twenty-two hours. Garianne will not accept another detour, unless it is for a very good reason," said Sevine.

"I believe I can convince her," I said.

"No, she will know if you are lying to her. It is a talent of hers. I will speak to her as she cannot sense deception in my kind. I will exaggerate the fact that you are weak from your ordeal, and push the importance you have stressed in consulting our archives. I will find a way to persuade her."

Sevine Anoor made good on his word returning less than an hour later confirming that Garianne had begrudgingly agreed to let us go to the archive to try and find a way to defeat the Nacuerians. After all, I was a super-sentient who could assimilate and use vast quantities of information. What did she have to gain from this, though? Sevine had given nothing away and believed that she suspected nothing.

Sevine told me that I would not have to deceive Garianne indefinitely, only long enough to get aboard the archive, which was only a few hours away. The Phalinon would protect me there. However, Garianne possessed many mysterious abilities and was a master strategist, always seemingly several steps ahead of everyone else. Was she at this moment predicting the possible outcomes of my visit to the archive and preparing? What did she have planned for me? I still could not see the sense in what she was doing; what could be gained if the galaxy was consumed by death and destruction?

For a while I struggled with my anger. I felt like confronting her here and testing her high and mighty abilities against my own. How would she fair, I wondered? I was super-sentient; unique in known space, yet Garianne had the kind of experience I could only guess at, and knew exactly what I was capable of.

My experience on the Nacuerian ship had taught me that mental will was superior to physical power, if utilised correctly. My will was stronger now, but how strong was the will of a being, forged through thousands of years of experience, out here amongst the Galacien? No, I dare not make a move yet. Caution and careful observation were called for.

My intellect was growing at an exponential rate and I felt confident that I would soon be able to surpass Garianne.. Not so long ago I had learned to read in a night. Now I could learn thousands of languages in that same amount of time and knew more than some citizens of the Galacien. My ability to learn matched the tools I had been given access to. I had gathered vast quantities of data from the simulation room, and the implant had made my evolutionary leap possible, so that now I was on the same level of the ladder to those beings around me. I never had truly let it be known how much I had learned and grown from the use of the implant.

My enlightening experience aboard the Nacuerian ship and the series of revelations bestowed upon me in the world of illusions, had opened my eyes in more ways than one. Now it seemed that I was to have access to, what was possibly, the most advanced and largest archive in the galaxy. I needed time to assimilate and ponder all that I had learned, for I felt that there were many implications to all that I had discovered, in such a short time. I could only hope that there was a way to stop Garianne and the Nacuerians.

Curiously, it was Garianne who instigated all these events in the first place; it was because of her that I had evolved so far. Something did not feel right. I knew the danger, yet felt I had missed something.

I went to the command deck, deciding to get to Garianne before she requested my presence. Here, more than in the medical bay, I felt the pain and loss of the Amelerian species. I made sure that all my anger was focused purely on the Nacuerians, for I knew that to direct even the barest hint Garianne's way, would make her suspicious. I knew the level her mind operated on, and could not overestimate her enough. I would have to play my part well.

Garianne and Min approached me.

"Are you feeling better?" Garianne asked in her usual professional manner.

Min's emotions, in contrast, seemed to be in a state of conflict.

"I am now. I just needed a little more time to recover than I initially realised," I replied.

"What is it you believe you will find in the Phalinon archives that can help us?" asked Min curiously.

"I am not entirely sure," I lied, feeling bad that I had to but, I had not ruled out that even she could be working with Garianne. I ignored this for now, for it led down a path fraught with suspicion, sadness, and fury. I could not trust anyone yet.

"I have studied the Galacien archives with the use of the implant, now I must study the Phalinon archives directly as I feel I have only scratched the surface," I said.

"For what purpose?" asked Min.

I noticed again how Garianne let others ask all the obvious questions, perhaps so that she could better understand and manipulate a situation to her advantage.

"I have been searching for a greater power, beings that precede the Galacien. The Galacien knowledge base does not seem to possess anything… substantial."

"That is because nothing substantial exists," commented Garianne.

"Nevertheless, I am going to see if the Phalinon archives have what I seek."

"Why not ask them to consult the archives for you, while we continue to Galacien Prime?" asked Min.

"I do not believe that will suffice. I am sure you are aware that information in itself does not always lead to the truth. However it can lay hidden beneath the facts, undiscovered, even though it may have always been there in plain sight. You know I have a talent for assimilating and interpreting vast amounts of information, and quickly. I may be able to uncover something that the Galacien and the Phalinon have overlooked."

"Careful, Jonas," said Garianne, "there is a danger that you may see patterns that aren't necessarily there."

"What do you mean by that?" I said, aware that I had nearly let a little of my anger show.

"Only that if the answers are not as forthcoming as you wish them to be, you may find yourself seeing truths, which don't exist."

I hid my anger perfectly behind a calm exterior. "I will try to make sure that does not happen."

Garianne accepted my explanation, though convincing her and Min that I wished to go to the archive alone proved to be an impossible task. Finally, I had to resign myself to the fact that at least Garianne would have to come along. The Phalinon would be able to keep control of at least one traitor, if the need arose, no matter how resourceful she was.

New information concerning the archive flooded into my implant, supplied by Sevine Anoor. Apparently it was very secure, housing a vast array of highly advanced external and internal defences.

"Well then, Jonas," said Garianne, "if we are going to do this, let us be as quick as possible. We still do not know when the Nacuerians are going to strike and we need you there for any crucial opportunity that may arise in the coming battle."

What crucial point? I thought. Now that I knew Garianne for what she was, I was struck that her plan to save the Galacien by utilising me in some way was yet another deception. She had them believe that she had found a super-sentient being to use against the Nacuerians in such a manner as to bring about victory.

I believed Garianne had set this up to fail from the beginning. There was no hope of victory from my intervention; it would have to come from something that existed outside the Galacien-Nacuerian experience. The Galacien's hopes rested with me, mine rested with the Kinsmen.

Chapter 22. The Archive

The Phalinon archive hung in hyperspace, displayed perfectly on the command deck by Lom's three-dimensional holographics. It was a metallic sphere, almost fifty kilometres in diameter, with numerous equidistant short protrusions. Lom waited a hundred metres above its shining surface, while a docking port metamorphosed its shape to Lom's configuration.

Perfectly adaptable, I thought, looking forward to gaining more insight into the Phalinon's advanced and elaborate technology. They had contributed some frighteningly destructive weapons to the Galacien war effort, the most effective of which were the defence platforms distributed around the boundary of the Galacien home system, but my intuition told me it would not be enough in what now seemed to be the final upcoming battle.

The port finished its reconfiguration and Lom duly docked himself with the archive.

Sevine Anoor addressed the crew. "As you know my kin and I value our privacy. Only Jonas, Garianne, and I will be going aboard the archive itself."

Lytpniuph approached Sevine. "You honour us with this visit. It has been many years since anyone has even seen an archive."

"And I know of no Amelerian ship which has ever docked with one," added Lom.

"We feel for your recent loss and hope this experience will make it fractionally less painful for you all," said Sevine as he beckoned for Garianne and me to follow.

The three of us walked from Lom into one of the archive's airlock chambers before entering the archive. Unlike Lom, a living ship, this place felt dead and sterile. We descended into its depths at great speed with the use of the anti-gravity platforms. Plummeting, apparently controlled, in mid-air would have disturbed me not so long ago, yet I had experienced much recently and was not the man I once was.

However, I still could not shake the feeling that there was something I had missed and that I was still being manipulated and out-manoeuvred. It all seemed to be going too smoothly and I felt sure Garianne was planning something from the shadows. I had to figure out what that was.

"We have a specially allocated terminal room where you can access the archive, Jonas," said Sevine as we reached the end of an extremely high, narrow chamber. We entered the terminal room via an unusually thick door, causing me to wonder what other defences they had. The room reminded me of the simulation room aboard Lom, except here there was a large machine in the middle, the nearest part of which housed a seat.

"If you would take the seat, Jonas, I will show you the most efficient way of accessing the archive's records," said Sevine.

We both knew I had a more direct means of interfacing with the archive, yet we still needed to keep this from the watchful eyes of Garianne.

While paying attention to Sevine's instructions I readied myself to plunge my consciousness into the Phalinon archive system directly. I felt my mind link up to it and could feel the terminal before me come to life, as I started to familiarise myself with its structure, at the same time getting a feel for the archive system which lay beneath the interface.

I could sense Garianne's gaze upon me and wondered if she could tell what I was about to do. Much depended on this. The path ahead of me seemed dark and unknown. I knew there was an element of risk but I would gain nothing if I did not proceed. The only way was forward.

I jumped into the archive's system.

As soon as I committed myself, I realised I had made a fatal error.

The Phalinon system was ready and waiting. Instead of only just a part, I felt the entirety of my mind being sucked inexorably into the system. Forced against my will, my consciousness was like an iron filing, brutally slammed and held fast against an immense magnet. Escape was impossible from this trap, which had been apparently designed and waiting for me all this time. Mentally I screamed with animal ferocity and outrage, though in the terminal room there was no physical sign of my distress. The smallest part of me could sense Garianne standing there, her arms folded, unmoving.

Sevine, what is happening? I shouted with my mind, hoping this was some kind of terrible mistake. Deep down though I knew the truth.

I am sorry, Jonas, but this is the way it must be, Sevine said through the archive system.

You have decided to turn traitor now, why?

We've been working with the Nacuerians for some time, making sure all our communications with them looked like they came from Garianne, in case the Nacuerian network was compromised, however unlikely that seemed.

For what end?

The same reasons I gave for Garianne's apparent betrayal – immortality. The Galacien, including the Phalinon, are used to the idea of living forever. We come into this world believing our individual existence is eternal. Safely stored we never believed that truth would ever be threatened. That was until the Nacuerians came. Now it appears the destiny of all species in the galaxy is extinction. You know of what I speak, it is the reason for the Nacuerians' existence, their true purpose; it is why they are here.

I did indeed, though I had not spoken to anyone of it, even thinking of it was such a terrifying concept.

Garianne, I am sorry I doubted you.

But she stood there, completely oblivious to what was happening.

Garianne, the Phalinon have betrayed the Galacien to the Nacuerians, Garianne! I shouted as hard as I could with my mind.

Again a part of my consciousness left my physical body, yet it was inconsequential for that which was truly me was still trapped; I could only observe. I looked down on the three of us in the terminal room.

Garianne unfolded her arms. "Sevine, is Jonas alright? I sense something out of the ordinary."

Being trapped in the system, I could see perfectly what it was about to do.

Garianne, the archives defences are about to attack you, I screamed at her.

"No, he is not alright, none of you are," replied Sevine.

From hidden openings in the ceiling sprang lethal looking metallic tentacles, heading for Garianne, threatening to tear her apart. Her reaction was instantaneous, her leg whipping out in a blur of motion that beggared belief, connecting hard against Sevine's midsection and sending him flying across the room. The tentacles were upon her like a frenzied pack of animals, taking her up into the hidden darkness of the room's ceiling. It was over in seconds and she had not made a sound.

I became aware that the archive's exterior sensors were now picking up numerous excessive gravity distortions surrounding the complex. This could only mean one thing.

I looked on in horror through the archive's visual sensors, as all around emerged hundreds of Nacuerian ships into hyperspace, closing in slowly around the archive.

I saw Sevine walking back towards where my physical body remained subdued, any damage received from Garianne's brutal kick seemed to be repairing itself quickly.

"Interesting. Garianne was quicker than we had anticipated; only one slight miscalculation from so many is acceptable though." Sevine regarded me, held there unmoving by the terminal interface, before leaving.

I looked helplessly down upon my body trapped by the Phalinon. I could not move and the system seemed to sap the very essence of my will. I had no way to help the others who could be dead already. Despair took me and I gave it no resistance, for I knew there was no hope of escape.

PART 3. Chapter 23. States of Being

At the thought of my comrades suffering at the hands of the Phalinon or Nacuerians, my despair deepened. Were they even still alive? I struggled with all my will against the system's trap that held me so effortlessly, yet it was to no avail. As the seconds slipped by, I felt that any chance I had of saving them had now come and gone.

To never see Min again was yet another loss I was going to suffer. It was my fault they were here and it would cost them their lives.

Sevine must have given our location in the Amelerian system to the Nacuerians when we were ambushed. I was so careful on the Nacuerian ship not to make the super-system aware of my presence or my ability, only to return to Lom and report everything to the traitor. What a fool I had been! I should have scrutinised the data more meticulously. I never questioned that the data was fabricated to appear to be from Garianne rather than Sevine. Perhaps then I would have discovered the real traitor sooner. With this in mind I fell further into the well of guilt.

That's quite enough of that, said a familiar voice in my head.

Garianne is that really you or am I imagining it?

It's really me.

You are not dead?

No.

I thought you were the traitor. I brought you all here and they were ready for us.

It appears so.

I am sorry.

I said that's quite enough, her firmness bringing me back to alertness.

Garianne, I did not tell you or the others when returning to the ship, but we only have three standard days until the Nacuerians and the Phalinon attack the Galacien home system.

Stay calm, despair is completely unproductive and it makes us inadequate to cope with the tasks we must face. Don't you agree?

I wanted to shout at her, tell her how totally and utterly finished we were. The Nacuerian ships were out there; it was over. However, she expected an answer to the question. She was waiting. She was Garianne.

Yes

Look at me, Jonas, she commanded.

Where? I began, but I could see her. She too had somehow left her physical body, her metaphysical self resembled her physical body, except that it seemed to be made entirely of light; it was beautiful.

I did as I was told and looked at her.

That poise, those eyes.

How can you remain so calm and confident in the face of what has happened? I exclaimed.

It is easy to be calm when you are in control, the trick is to be calm and confident when things aren't going so well, don't you think? she continued without giving me the opportunity to answer. *Or to ensure you are always in control. Wouldn't that make life incredibly boring, to have every conceivable outcome and factor accounted for?*

Garianne looked at me smiling. I was not sure what to say.

Do you remember what I said when we met for the second time on Earth?

197

You said, "Sometimes something can be lost when taking the quick and easy way: appreciation, learning, understanding. Many take the quick approach, though their view of the world would always be a basic perception of what is really there, they would miss the finer details." Why is that so significant?

Yes. Jonas, You have moved so quickly in such a short space of time. You have missed a great deal. You have not noticed that which many of your kind before you have, because they had the luxury of time.

Her metaphysical form moved away from the terminal room, passing through walls and floors, until she came to a stop outside the archive in the depths of hyperspace. I drifted up beside her, curious as to why she felt it necessary to be out here. In all other aspects I was still trapped by the Phalinon, yet being out here gave me perspective on our current plight.

Garianne gazed about looking magnificent and awe-inspiring, like a goddess. She looked at the stars, hanging there beyond the depths of hyperspace, the Nacuerian ships, which were barely perceptible points of light, the Phalinon archive and finally at me.

It was then that I realised.

You knew this was going to happen?

She nodded in affirmation. No pride or arrogance, just a simple nod.

How could you have foreseen this?

I needed to know all the players and their roles before we could continue. There can be no unknown factors, except you, and I need you ready as soon as possible.

I need more time.

But we do not have it. Unfortunately, this was the only way. Despite the strategy I have been planning for so long, I had to make sure the enemies plans were fully revealed, that any traitors felt secure enough to make themselves known, and to play it so that they believed they were in control, that they have us beaten. With nothing standing between them and their goals.

What happens now, according to your plan? I asked.

Why, you save us all of course, replied Garianne frankly.

I do not think that is going to happen. I cannot break free.

You obviously don't see what I see. Look about you, Jonas. This is the third time your metaphysical form has left your physical one; what do you see? asked Garianne.

Light. Everything seems to emanate light especially that which is alive. You, more than anything else. Why is that?

What you are seeing is, will, vitality, intelligence. All those things that give us strength to do what we can, or must do. You may see more light emanating from a smaller, even weaker man compared with someone twice his size and strength, if his will is strong and his intellect keen. Sentient creatures can accomplish what may seem impossible with the use of such qualities, as well as many others in the appropriate manner. You asked me how I can remain so calm and confident through all of this. In the form you currently inhabit, you have seen what sentient beings look like, a living spaceship or a being like me who has lived a very long time. Yet you have never seen yourself, Jonas. You have never seen a super-sentient. I am looking at one now.

It occurred to me that she was right. I seemed to have no physical representation.

I cannot see myself, I admitted.

Let me help, she replied.

The oddest sensation came over me. I was already away from my physical body, yet I felt my point of view shifted again from my metaphysical self to Garianne's perspective, as if I were now inhabiting her body.

For a moment I thought I was looking into a sun, the light was so intense, although I found I did not need to turn away from it.

Is that really me? I asked.

Yes, and now do you understand why I have such confidence in you. Believe in yourself, Jonas, the rest will come.

I returned to my own metaphysical self and seemed to have gathered a feeling of how to create a visual representation of a form. All I had to do was imagine it. Even now I could see light coalescing into limbs which closely resembled my physical form.

Garianne looked at me and nodded her approval.

Now what? I asked.

Follow my lead.

We returned to our bodies, to the prison the Phalinon had prepared so well for me, though I could see now that no prison could hold me. I had perceived myself as a tiny sliver of iron held upon an immense magnet, immovable. Now I knew the potential will I possessed and the deep well of power I could draw upon. I reached for them both and like the building of an immense storm shook the foundations of my prison until they shattered to dust before me. As the pieces fell the Phalinon's defence programs gathered frantically to surround me, preparing to defend the archive and dispose of me.

Garianne my mind is free, should I return to my physical self?

No. Do what you came here to do. You'll have to take over their system to accomplish that, but be quick about it. We don't have a lot of time.

She said these things as if they were easy, though we both knew it was not. Nevertheless I would not let her down.

I'll be quick. What are you going to do? I asked.

I sensed a great commotion from the darkened ceiling. Then numerous objects fell with a loud clatter onto the terminal room's floor, followed by Garianne. She fell far, however she landed perfectly, as if she had only fallen only a few feet.

Protect you. Now get going.

Whatever she had done, the terminal room was now devoid of all internal defences but we both knew, though, that the archive's mobile defence units would arrive soon.

Chapter 24. Gambit

Garianne stood beside my physical body, ready and waiting. Phalinon warriors would be transported to the terminal room in seconds and I was sure Garianne could not hold them off for long. A lot could happen in the system in a relatively short amount of time. I had an awful lot to accomplish and the Phalinon's was a type of system I'd never encountered before.

I could not help but feel a little intimidated by the archive's defences, yet there was more to gain here using subterfuge rather than brute force. There was no point in destroying the very same system I wished to take control of.

The last vestiges of my prison were falling away now and I disguised a significant part of myself as fragments of the prison, to fall away with them into apparent dust. The only purpose that could be built into those particles was that they combine again in a safe, less observed part of the system.

Meanwhile, the part of me that stayed behind made to move and I was immediately attacked. The battle began in earnest.

To deceive and out-manoeuvre like Garianne, I attempted to be several steps ahead of my enemies. While a part of me fought on against the archive's formidable system defences, another part of me coalesced unseen in a quiet corner of the Archive's system. I felt awareness and conscious thought return. It was a curious experience being in two places at once.

I secured the immediate area while the final of my consciousness fell into place in this unseen area of the system I then reached out carefully with my senses. The

Phalinon system was very different from the Nacuerians which I perceived to be akin to the intricacies of biological form; organic patterns, seemingly chaotic, though able to perform and carry out the task required of any complex system.

In comparison, the Phalinon system was built in a very orderly fashion like the workings of a complex clock, in application for the most part, yet it did involve a small amount of unknown factors in its workings.

The archive's system worked on many different levels simultaneously, at its most fundamental level subtly manipulating the very nature of alternate realities like a master craftsman, to achieve mind-boggling calculations. It was this incredible degree of intricate complexity which I found myself up against. I sensed the system around me, working with frightening speed and efficiency. I would have to be very quick and clever to overcome such refined technology. To do this I would have to alter myself and my mind to operate in a similar manner. Instantaneous multi-thinking would have to become child's play. I did what I do best – I observed and I learned.

Within the system many tasks had been performed, yet only mere seconds had passed outside. Long enough for the archive's mobile defences, its warriors, to teleport outside the terminal room and break open the door. The only thing that stood between them and me was Garianne.

I saw what happened next through the archive's sensors, seemingly in slow motion due to the speed of my thought processes. Eight of them exploded through the door and I immediately knew Garianne was in serious trouble.

The archive's warriors were humanoid, over nine feet tall, with long, powerful arms and legs. They had a multitude of very lethal, retractable, metamorphic, kinetic and energy weapons, adaptable armour, shielding and cloaking abilities as well as flight. Garianne was about to be slaughtered by these Phalinon super-soldiers. The Galacien had no record of these things being created; they were even superior to the SIBATs.

It did not matter anymore that I was not ready; I could not take my time and watch her be killed. I concentrated on completing my task far faster than I previously dared, though I knew I would never be able to prevent their first strike.

Lethal energy beams sprang forth focused onto Garianne, igniting bright flares inches from her body; she had her own personal shield. I had never sensed it before and, seemingly, neither had the Phalinon. How could it have passed by undetected by their advanced sensors? It seemed impossible. Nevertheless she had one and it protected her from their initial assault.

The warriors covered almost half the distance, Then they split up and cloaked. They could not be detected by heat or electromagnetism yet the archive was informed of their positions and so, in turn, was I. She wouldn't stand a chance if I didn't alert her to their positions even at the risk of focusing the system's attention onto myself.

I begun to move from the shadows of the system.

Now they knew.

The part of me in the system, where my former prison had been, faded away losing itself in the archive.

There was no need for secrecy or subversion anymore; they knew exactly where I was – in their control system which closely resembled a sentient mind.

Though what could I do in a fraction of a second? That was the only time I had now until they were upon her.

Garianne herself had not moved.

I hit the Phalinon control system with the sheer force of my will. I had to help her. The defences of the system were resistant to my attack and it could sense my desperation. As well as defending their control system, they initiated an attack of their own and were upon me like a plague of locusts. The attack was brutal but I held fast against the storm of their assault.

Time was running out.

Inside the archive control system or ACS, programs went skittering about like busy insects, quickly performing their pre-consigned tasks, to help protect it. One such program's task was to check and quickly analyse how the other programs were performing. It didn't hamper the ACS's defences but went about its menial task as quickly as possible with an almost imperceptible, vigorous determination. It had almost performed its first sweep, when the archive realised something was wrong with it; it had been corrupted.

It was too late. I initiated the signal and instantly all the programs within the ACS, which had been touched by my other self, were subverted. The archive's control system was now mine. The part of me left outside, fighting the larger system was no longer attacked by the ACS and I was let in. The two parts of me joined together and I was whole again.

Now I had the ACS but how long would it be until I could subvert the entire system to accept any order I issued? The closest Phalinon warrior was about to land its first blow and there was nothing I could do but watch.

The warrior's huge arm, which had formed into a lethal, curved-edged weapon, came down in a death stroke. It crackled with an energy specially generated to cut cleanly through Garianne's personal force-field. As the edge of the Phalinon's arm came into contact with Garianne's force-shield, she moved. With a crackling of energies the weapon slid slowly down and was pushed away from Garianne, while she stepped aside and twisted. The Phalinon had its side to her and was in the middle of its own perfectly executed follow-up move. But Garianne was too fast and had already out-manoeuvred the creature, her face now a mask of impassive death. Her own arm came down, her force-shield cleanly and swiftly cutting the Phalinon from head to crotch in a clean, ruthless stroke.

I could see the broken warrior immediately attempting to use its amazingly efficient repair system, to make itself whole again, yet residual energy left by Garianne's blow overcame this, eating away at the Phalinon faster than it could repair itself. It was all over in two seconds.

Garianne continued to move as if in a dance, flipping and spinning into the air, efficiently dodging the invisible killing machines, anticipating their every move to perfection. Her arms and legs struck out leaving them all dying, one after another, fallen to the floor in her wake. Finally, it was only she who was left standing.

I felt a quick pulse of emotion from her, which basically was her way of telling me to stop wasting time staring and pay attention to the task at hand.

The system was now completely mine and, as Garianne had so firmly suggested, I wasted no more time in getting what I had come for. I had not forgotten that the Nacuerian ships were still closing in on the archive and would make contact at any moment.

I still had a little time.

Before I did anything else I quickly checked on Min, Lom, and the crew. In the world of the system I breathed the equivalent of a sigh of relief. They were unharmed, although the crew were unconscious. It seemed that the Phalinon had taken over Lom's system, in much the same way I had taken over theirs.

I evaluated the situation in a nanosecond. It was possible to purge the Phalinon infestation from Lom, but it would take considerable time if I was to cause Lom no permanent damage. However, multi-tasking had become second nature and a part of my mind began working through the arduous process of curing Lom, while another part began to sift through the enormous amount of information contained within the archive in search of the Kinsmen.

Despite the incredible speed at which I could search the archive, the sheer volume of data was astounding.

Taking on a third task I applied my mind to the problem of the Nacuerians.

Garianne, I am downloading information to your implant concerning our current situation. Do you have any thoughts as to how we can escape the Nacuerians surrounding the archive?

She considered the question. *Not yet. You?*

No.

Of course I had already been working on the problem, with no forthcoming solution. Lom was in no fit state to run against a blockade of Nacuerian ships and the archive's propulsion system was not adequate enough for an escape.

The archive was receiving a signal from one of the Nacuerian capital ships. It slowly filtered through the Phalinon system, requesting to be granted access to the communications network. It couldn't be allowed and I had only seconds before they became suspicious – a considerable amount of time in the system. I used it to further ponder our predicament, surprised at how calm I remained. The signal repeated and I knew they were becoming suspicious.

There was a way, though it had one major personal drawback. I spared a fraction of a second considering whether there was an alternative, and another on whether to attack the Nacuerians first or to play for time, comparing scenarios in my mind given current variables.

I decided surprise would give us the best chance of survival. I dispatched the archive's entire complement of Phalinon warriors out into hyperspace to attack the Nacuerians and then brought up the archive's shields. Finally I fired on the approaching Nacuerian ships hitting them hard and fast. As anticipated, I caught them completely off guard. In the short moments before they knew what was happening, I was able to disable an appreciable percentage of their capital ships.

I struck to wound and rather than waste precious seconds destroying any one vessel. I only needed enough time for my plan to come to fruition and that depended on slowing them down as much as possible. I could not hope to stop them permanently without destroying us all.

Although the Nacuerians had no idea what had happened on the archive, they knew how to respond. Many Nacuerian fighters were immediately dispatched and engaged my Phalinon warriors. Others sped about the archive like angry wasps, their energy weapons striking out against the archive shields, looking for weak points. The Phalinon warriors, who had not so long ago threatened our lives, now readily threw down their existence to buy us the time we needed.

With a hiss of its smooth metal encasement, I disengaged myself from the archive terminal. After what seemed like a lifetime, I finally stepped away from it, and back onto my own two feet.

I touched my nose and my fingers came away covered in blood. "I am bleeding," I said in disbelief. I looked incredulously around me as if expecting an answer from someone.

"You have limitations, like everyone else. You can't push yourself and not expect consequences. You can die, I expect. Not easily, but it is possible," said Garianne.

I continued to stare at the blood on my fingers. My body had never shown any sign of weakness or fragility before. My experience on that world of illusions had seemed real to me at the time, yet it was not. This was *my* blood.

"Are you still linked?" asked Garianne.

"Through my implant, though I have made some slight modifications. I am managing to maintain the same speed of thought process but it is very strange having your mind in two such different worlds simultaneously, and working at vastly different speeds," I said, whilst sending and receiving a great number of instructions into and from the archive. "We have only one chance and it is you who must follow my lead now."

"Very well," she said, seemingly content.

Using the archive I quickly teleported us to a small ante-chamber with a large door in front of us.

The archive shook; a vast low rumble which permeated the entire structure in every direction.

"The archive's shields are weakening. We do not have long," I said. "We are just outside the blast radius."

"You mean to destroy the interior of the archive then, creating enough room to jump through hyperspace from within?" said Garianne.

"Yes," I said, surprised she understood my intentions.

"Can Lom do it?"

"It is the only thing he will be able to do, all other systems will still be infected. Lom has no defences or weapons, and can't move. I am using some of the archive's anti-gravity units (AGUs) for that."

The explosive device was already configured. I teleported it to its destination at the archive's core and brought up a force-shield at the edge of the blast radius, completely encompassing it. I sighed. I could not risk leaving it any longer.

In that last fraction of a second my mind raced frantically about the Phalinon system for any trace of the Kinsmen, a little longer, just a little longer, until...

"Jonas!" exclaimed Garianne.

I detonated the device before she finished the word. There was no noise, the force-shield I'd erected protected the outer structure from harm and dissipated the sound, though the shockwave was unmistakable. The archive's structure shook more violently and abruptly before calming to a gentle rumble.

"Were you able to find anything?" said Garianne.

"For a moment I thought I sensed something, but..." I shook my head in disappointment.

The shockwave had caused a momentary lapse in my link to the archive's system and disrupted the shields for a fraction of a second, long enough for some of the Nacuerians to teleport on board.

"Some of them have managed to get in. We need to go," I said to Garianne. We made for the door, which I commanded to open while simultaneously bringing down the force-shield.

The hatch opened and we looked out over a precipice, a sudden gust of wind rising against us. We overlooked the vast spherical emptiness of what had been the archive's core, the piercing noise of metal tearing apart, sliding and crashing to the bottom of what was the ground in this devastated part of the archive. For a moment we took in the spectacle. Garianne as always was quite calm; I wish I could say the same for myself. I was receiving no telemetry from the Phalinon warriors, they had obviously all been destroyed and I could sense the entire force of the Nacuerian fire power trying to batter down the shields. The archive's systems were becoming more and more useless by the second, mostly due to the devastating explosion I'd unleashed in its core. I could sense that those Nacuerians within were doing their utmost to destroy the archive and, although I could not track them, I knew they would be here soon.

As far as the fight outside was concerned, all I could do now was hold out for as long as possible using the archive's surface defences. I could only hope that we had time enough for the anti-gravity units to push Lom through the path I had laid out for him, into the middle of the enormous empty space. Below my feet I could feel the vibrations as Lom made his way excruciatingly slowly out into the newly created inner space of the archive and then I could see him. It was a welcoming sight, except now I could see a vile, dirty yellow stain like hellish rust, on his surface, an outward sign of the Phalinon infection that still incapacitated his systems. It was quite some distance down to the ship's surface, yet I knew Garianne could make it.

I looked behind me "Damn, the shield has gone. They are coming. We are going to have to jump."

Before either of us could make a move, the Nacuerians appeared behind us. Garianne was faster than I was, her force-shield activated instantly as she gracefully brought down the first couple of attackers with a quick succession of blows. I, on the other hand, tumbled like a brawler to the floor wrestling with my foes, their tentacles wrapped around my arms, my legs, even around my mouth and eyes. I had faced far more than these in the past, and soon enough had torn them from my person.

Garianne was making quick work of them, moving with perfect balance and precision, anticipating their moves. None of the Nacuerians could lay a tentacle on her, anything that came near her was instantly dismembered. It was like throwing meat into a carving machine – a macabre sight to behold. They soon got the message and began shooting at us instead, which did them no good either.

They are just trying to delay us. We will soon be up to our necks in them and we will no longer be able to reach Lom. Come on, I communicated to Garianne through the implant.

I sprinted for the open door. One of the Nacuerians stood in my way, but I could not delay any longer. As the creature made to grab me, I simply picked it up and jumped over the edge, plummeting to the ship below.

We landed hard and for a moment I was dazed and apparently alone. Perhaps the Nacuerian had fallen off the edge of the ship. The devastating explosion had cooked up some strange and unpredictable air currents, which had blown me almost completely away from Lom. I now appreciated how large Lom was, his form spread out before me into the distance, yet he was a mote inside the archive such was its size and the space I had created. Still Lom was too large to teleport, the anti-gravity units had been the only way.

I ordered the Anti Gravity Units to move us to the centre of the archive as quickly as possible. The wind blew up against me and pieces of metal fell like rain from far above. Some of the pieces were as small as pebbles, others were far larger. It would only take one a fraction of Lom's size and it would be over for all of us. Some pieces had already damaged or embedded themselves in Lom's hull and I felt an enormous wave of guilt for putting us all in this predicament in the first place.

I picked myself up from Lom's surface and looked around. The Nacuerian I thought had fallen to its death, was now limping towards me, firing its built-in weapons. I was lifted from Lom's hull and fell on my back as the Nacuerian's fire hit me. Before either of us had made another move, Garianne landed next to the Nacuerian and delivered a quick blow, which resulted in it stumbling about like a demented animal as it eventually wandered over the edge of Lom to the emptiness below. I felt no pity in my heart for them but I was a little unnerved by Garianne's efficient ruthlessness – almost as if it was personal. Perhaps, like all of us, she was simply angered by the vast number of sentients whose deaths they were responsible for.

She approached me and death faded from her eyes. "One day we'll have to teach you how to fight," she said.

"I know how to fight," I responded

"No, you don't," she said pointedly. "Though one day you will," she affirmed. "There is an airlock over there. We need to go."

We ran along Lom's surface to the airlock, avoiding some of the larger pieces of debris that fell around us.

"They must still want us alive, otherwise they would have destroyed us by now," I said.

"It's you, Jonas, only you they're interested in. Even after all this, they still want you alive. You're different to everything else in the galaxy. Once they have you, though, it would only be a matter of time before they'd decide to dispose of you, too," said Garianne.

We heard a deafening noise all around us, tearing metal and its dreadful echo reverberating off the walls of the cavern. I could see huge shapes, like giant creatures breaking into the shell of an egg. The Nacuerian capital ships had rammed themselves through the archive; its hull integrity broken, exposing us to hyperspace. The archive was almost entirely dead, no defences, no force-shields. In fact, there was nothing left of use at all, except for the AGUs pushing Lom.

The wind picked up immediately, so strong that Garianne and I were lifted from our feet, as the air rushed out through the Archive's hull breaches into hyperspace. With her shield Garianne's hand instantly punched through Lom's hull, and configured itself to anchor her. Her other hand had seized mine preventing me from being blown from the ship. There was an almighty explosion not fifty metres from us. It was too late, they had fired on us. We were finished.

I was wrong.

Shapes suddenly emerged from the debris. They were Galacien SIBATs spreading out in a defensive position around Lom.

We'll buy you the time you need to get through the airlock, said Min's voice in my head. The crew had obviously regained consciousness, and although Lom was no longer operational they had somehow made it to the SIBATs which, being separate from Lom's system, had not been affected by the infection.

You blew open Lom's docking bay, I stated.

It was the only way, now move!

With a thud, two SIBATs landed next to us and erected a two-layered force-shield just in time. My implant informed me that the Nacuerian's had just attempted to teleport me aboard one of their ships as well as unleashing focused energy weapons to dispose of Garianne. The SIBATs' shields protected us from this together and with the effect of being sucked out into hyperspace nullified, we fell back to the surface, and manually started opening the airlock. The Nacuerian ships were firing on Lom, but the SIBATs used interceptor weapons to prevent any damage to the defenceless vessel. Our force-shield was taking a severe battering, as Garianne finally opened the airlock and pushed me through; she quickly followed and shut it behind us.

"Do it," she ordered.

"What about the SIBATs?"

"There's no time."

"Wait, I have to…"

Lom's engine's came to life and created the portal enveloping the ship; we finally jumped out of hyperspace.

I sat with my back against the wall of the airlock chamber, a wry smile spreading across my face.

"What is it?" enquired Garianne.

"Just thinking of the surprise I left behind for the Nacuerians," I said.

Garianne returned my smile guessing what I meant.

As I imagined the fate awaiting those mass murderers, my smile broadened. In a moment, everything within a light-minute radius of the archive would be consumed by fire and boil away into the hyperspace abyss.

Chapter 25. Adrift

Garianne and I sat in the airlock chamber, in silence for some time, when, with a piercing tear, the inner door was opened.

Min stepped through. "Are you alright?"

"Fine," I said picking myself from the floor.

Garianne rose up in one fluid movement. We looked briefly at one another. There were things we inevitably would have to discuss, for now though there were more pressing matters to attend to.

"Did it work? We figured out your plan eventually," said Min.

"It worked perfectly," replied Garianne. "Thanks to you and the crew."

Min shook her head. "It was terrible for the Amelerians; they had to cut through Lom to get the SIBATs out."

"It is fine, Min. He is unaware of anything, the Phalinon infection made sure of that" I said.

I saw a flicker of confusion on Min's face.

We left the airlock and made our way to the command deck.

"Most of Lom's systems are out. We can't seem to get them online no matter what we try," explained Min.

"I am working on it. Permanent hyperdrive and propulsion systems should be ready in a few hours," I said.

Min's look of puzzlement deepened.

"Jonas has learnt a great deal about intelligent systems recently," said Garianne. "It was he that overtook the Phalinon system and made it possible to initiate Lom's hyperdrive."

Min stopped in her tracks looking at us both in disbelief. "What? We presumed it was *your* doing!" she said gesturing towards Garianne.

"Then you were wrong. Jonas is the reason we are still alive," said Garianne.

"That does not make up for the grave error I made in trusting the Phalinon so blindly, putting all our lives in danger in the first place. I…"

Garianne raised her hand, stopping me abruptly as if I had been struck dumb. "Let's not concern ourselves with the past. I think there's enough in the future that requires our undivided attention. Now it's time you told us everything you know."

It took us nearly half an hour to work our way through the ship. All of the automated doors were inoperative, and so we either had to manually open them or re-route.

On the command deck Garianne opened our implant communication links to everyone on board the ship.

"Lytpniuph, how are the crew?" she asked.

"Good, considering the circumstances," said Lytpniuph. "Lom, controlled by the Phalinon infection, introduced something into the ship's environment that rendered us all unconscious. When we woke there was much confusion. We had no idea what had happened, only that Lom's entire system had been brought down. Our implants were unaffected, though. Min managed to get to a SIBAT and use its scanners to find out more about the situation. After the explosion in the archive's core, we realised your plan."

"As I explained to Min, it wasn't my plan or actions that saved us today; it was Jonas." Their reaction was similar to Min's; there was a lot of commotion amongst the Amelerians.

Garianne raised her hand, and everyone instantly was quiet again. "We have three days until the Nacuerian attack the Galacien home system."

"Assuming they don't change their plans," said Lytpniuph.

"They won't. This is the minimum timeframe for their forces to reach Galacien Prime," said Garianne.

"Including the Phalinon forces," I added.

Once again the Amelerians broke out in mutterings of shock and disbelief.

"I'm afraid it's true. The Phalinon have betrayed the Galacien. Unlike the Nacuerians, this enemy is a part of the GCW infrastructure; they are already in the home system. We can only imagine what kind of damage they have been planning all this time," said Garianne.

"We must warn them, but we risk being detected," said Lytpniuph.

"Yes, we are almost defenceless. Are there any SIBATs left, Lytpniuph?" asked Garianne.

"Yes, three," replied Lytpniuph.

"Dispatch them in a perimeter around the ship. We can use them to send a signal to Galacien Prime. You realise though that any signal we send may not get through and could give away our position to our enemies."

"We have to try and warn them," I pressed.

Garianne nodded. "Do it."

"Sending the signal," said Lytpniuph.

"Let us see what happens," Garianne said.

We were adrift in the vast depths of space like a lost leaf on the ocean. The SIBATs informed us we were seventeen light years from the nearest star. I was glad to have them as our eyes and ears, protecting us from stray pieces of debris, natural and sentient made. With Lom in his present condition, he was completely defenceless. Something no larger than a pebble could cause serious damage to the vessel for it would be travelling at great speed and could puncture through us before we knew it was even close. Fortunately the SIBATs were incredibly sensitive to their environment and could detect anything as small as a grain of sand from a million miles away; we were quite safe from any possible debris while they were out there.

I sat on the command deck, my fingers cradled, thinking of possible ways to cleanse the infection from Lom. Two more hours until I could get the hyperdrive operational for another jump through hyperspace, then there was almost two days to Galacien Prime. I knew that the Nacuerians must have sent word before the archive was destroyed. Would the Phalinon strike before the planned time? Garianne seemed sure they would not, yet I wasn't convinced.

I soon came to the conclusion there was no way to speed up the process of purging the infection. I would have to be patient and hope we were lucky.

We were not.

Nearly an hour before I could get Lom ready, the command deck was suddenly awash with purple light.

A ship coming out of hyperspace, Min's SIBAT informed through our implants.

I stood up abruptly.

Garianne was already up, her eyes keen, ready to calmly analyse the situation.

"Configuration?" ordered Lytpniuph.

"Nacuerian, one capital ship, launching a complement of… thirty-two fighter-class ships. Optimum firing time at maximum velocity – three minutes, nine seconds."

Everyone looked at Garianne.

She did not hesitate. "Engage the fighters as soon as possible. Only the fighters mind, ignore the capital. Min, is that clear?"

"Yes mistress," replied Min obediently.

"What about that capital ship?" I said.

"The capital ship is slower. We have a little longer before it reaches optimum firing distance," said Garianne.

"Not long enough. We both know that those SIBATs won't be able to stop those fighters quickly enough, if at all."

"Then you're going to have to stop it," said Garianne simply.

"On my own. How?"

"After everything you've accomplished, all that you have seen and learned, in such a short space of time, you still don't believe in yourself. You remote-controlled the archive."

"But I had already established a link and was inside. Have you seen how far away that ship is? An implant can't help me get through their defences at this distance."

"You do not need the implant."

"What?"

Everyone on the command deck looked at Garianne in disbelief.

"Even if that's possible, they know what I can do now. They will be prepared."

"It is easy if you know you have an edge, if you know something your enemy isn't aware of. Fighting a battle like that doesn't require bravery. This does. I believe you can do it, Jonas. Believe it yourself."

She spoke with such conviction, her eyes full of unwavering confidence. She knew something I was sure of it, something that made her so certain. I was determined to know what it was.

"If I do nothing, we have no chance. At least this way we have some chance."

Many of the crew were still looking at me; I could not let such noble souls down. I forgot the implant and reached my naked mind out as gently as possible towards the system of the capital ship.

"They are waiting for me," I said to the others, "though they have not detected me. Their system is aware of my abilities and my past strategies. I will have to try something new."

"It must be soon," said Garianne.

I shook my head. What could I do? Dare I attempt a frontal assault? There had to be another way. I continued to observe the system from the outside as it buzzed away at an accelerated rate. Precious seconds slipped by all too eagerly.

"Jonas. Time is passing," said Garianne.

That was it!

I concentrated hard, focusing my mind, bringing up the speed of my thought processes to be on an even footing with that of the Nacuerian system. I perceived the events in the ship's system slowing down, while those around my physical self became significantly slower. Yet this was not my ultimate goal. As my mind came into synchronisation with the Nacuerian ship's system, I submitted my will, pushing my thoughts even faster, to that of the superior speed of the Phalinon system and beyond. Now the former lightning buzz of the Nacuerian system was slowing down substantially, and everything in the outside world had slowed so much, that to all intents and purposes it had stopped entirely.

I now felt apart from the rest of the universe, distanced, for I could no longer communicate with anyone or anything in either world.

My meta-physical self moved.

And in an instant I was falling to the floor on Lom's command deck.

My mind was a maelstrom of confusing images and sounds, and through it Garianne's voice, sluggish in my mind.

Jonas come back to us, Jonas can you hear me?

I used her voice to try and synchronise my thoughts back to their normal speed. I could not move and found I was in severe discomfort. I could see the others as blurred shapes moving frantically around. I could not hear what they were saying, however, I knew I was in bad shape. Had I pushed myself too hard? What damage had I done? I tried to speak my words coming out as a slur. I coughed hard and could taste blood in my mouth. Eventually the world came back into focus and I could hear again.

"Min, report," said Lytpniuph.

"The Nacuerian ships, they just stopped, all of them."

"Stopped?" said Lytpniuph.

"They're not doing anything, just floating out of control, inert," said Min.

"Severed from their network. Useless," I croaked.

"How?" asked Lytpniuph.

"Outpaced their computational speed," I said, assuring Garianne I was able to stand on my own, yet it took all my strength and will. "Severed their link myself, before they knew I was even there, messed their system up rather well."

"Messed them up? Is that a technical term?" mused Garianne.

"It worked," I said managing an unconvincing smile.

The others looked concerned at my weakened state. Did their history exaggerate the abilities and invulnerability of those such as I?

"Will other ships notice this sever in the link and come to investigate?" said Lytpniuph.

"That will not be a problem," I replied. "I sent out a false set of signals from their vessel, marking their position some distance from here. We should be safe while I finish purging the Phalinon infection from Lom's drive systems."

"Meanwhile, Min, destroy those ships. I want nothing left by the time we make the jump to hyperspace," said Garianne.

Thirty minutes later we made the jump and were on course for Galacien Prime.

Chapter 26. Galacien Prime

I wondered how long the crew had been awake for, although I required no sleep and minimal rest, the Amelerians relied on nano-technology to keep their minds and bodies going.

We had another day until we reached the edge of the Galacien home system, and then who knew what would happen? In comparison to Galacien ships ten thousand years ago, these living ships were completely self-sufficient; an order would be given and the ship would be duty bound to take all necessary steps to fulfil it. To all intents and purposes though, they were sentient, anticipating and reacting to new situations, making decisions far quicker than any crew-ship symbiosis. For the most part the ship was in control of its own destiny, as much as any sentient within the Galacien.

I understood that there were other ships out there which had chosen a different path, preferring a solitary life exploring the stars all alone with little or no crew. This life did not sound too bad to me.

As Lom's automated systems were still inactive, we had to find ways to access them through our implants; otherwise we would be completely defenceless when entering the Galacien home system.

I stood apart from the rest of the crew, a sense of unease growing in me, until finally I caught Garianne's attention. She excused herself from her conversation with Lytpniuph and Min and came over to join me.

"Yes, Jonas, what is it?" she asked.

I switched to the secure implant method of communication.

We are running blind with no idea of the situation in the home system. We are going to get caught out again. We need information.

I've come to the same conclusion, she replied, knowing I was referring to the archive. *You've got something in mind haven't you?*

My metaphysical self could travel to the home system, and find out what is going on.

Jonas it's over eight thousand light years away. I'm not sure you can make it.

How far away were you when I did it the first time from Earth?

Less than a quarter of that distance.

I think I can make it. I don't feel that distance matters.

She looked thoughtful. *There are those who share that view, yet others find the further the distance the harder it is, so there is no general consensus concerning your theory.*

Exactly how many others in the GCW have the ability to do this?

Very few. Only those like myself who are the longest-lived amongst us. Most are not even aware of this ability.

Am I likely to encounter them?

Do you mean in their metaphysical state? Not unless they happen to be roaming about in that form in your immediate vicinity, otherwise they won't be able to see you; it is highly unlikely. Those of us who possess this ability are quite private about it.

I do not know who to contact. Who do I warn if I make it?

Don't worry, I'll still be able to communicate with you.

Garianne I do not want the others to know of this, let us just do this quietly without…

I understand, she said, seeming to accept that I had my reasons, yet I still felt obliged to explain.

The less people know of my full potential... I began.

... the less likely they'll be able to take your measure, she continued. She nodded at me, an understanding passing between us.

If you could use fire instead of your fists against your enemies, then eventually they would take your measure and overcome you. Yet if you only fight with your fists, forge your body into a perfect living weapon, then you could keep your fire a secret and your enemies would never know of it. It would only be used as a last resort. You would be a formidable enemy, especially if using fire were not your only talent.

There was a palatable silence.

Who told you that? I asked eventually.

She smiled. *A super-sentient like yourself, long ago in my past. It is a strategy that will serve you well, and one I have lived by all my life. There are things about me, abilities and knowledge that few know of. They have great advantages when used correctly, at the right time, and especially when you're the Galacien's supreme strategist. I have surprised the GCW on more than one occasion, which has earned me yet another useful tool.*

What?

Faith. It was this and this alone which allowed me to leave the war effort for a time and make personal contact with you. I insisted on it.

I remember. The old woman, I nodded to myself. *That fateful night you taught me to read and write; my path was forever changed.*

It was an honour, Jonas.

I knew there was still so much she was not telling me.

Are we still working to that grand scheme of yours?

In a manner of speaking. I'm sorry but it's still down to you. You're still the unknown factor, the one they haven't accounted for. The Galacien have been observed and infiltrated so there's nothing we can do, except fight and die. I realised that a long time ago, Jonas.

I understand, though I don't think even I have the potential to stop all this. Still... if the supreme strategist for the Galacien Conglomerate of Worlds wishes me to put a stop to the joint Nacuerian-Phalinon invasion, then I would do well to obey. I bowed my head and raised an eyebrow.

She beamed at me and my world lit up, for it was like a force of nature. I felt more sure than ever that there was something uninterpretable between us. I could not possibly let her down. I could not let her die.

You'd better, she replied almost playfully, ironic considering the gravity of our situation.

Her face returned to its usual calm composure. *You have no idea what you are capable of; I know one day you will understand. If you survive.*

Min approached and was about to speak when Garianne held up her hand. "Min, we don't wish to be disturbed until further notice."

Min's face tightened becoming like stone.

"No, she can stay," I said.

"Are you sure?" asked Garianne.

"Yes, it is fine," I assured her.

I could tell Min was angry from Garianne's rebuke. She merely waited patiently rather than ask what was going on, yet her eyes asked the question anyway.

"Jonas is going to 'remote view' the home system for us."

"He can do that?"

Anger flared in me, but it was controlled. I was tired of this. "Do not answer Garianne. Speak to me, Min, if you wish to know something about me."

It was time she treated me with a little more respect. Respect I felt I had earned.

"Can you do that?" she repeated chillingly slowly.

"Yes, do not worry, Min. I will be back before you have time to miss me."

She merely raised an eyebrow at that.

We walked into an adjoining room where I made myself comfortable in a chair with Garianne and Min standing either side of me.

"Remember what it felt like Jonas, the state of your mind, your consciousness. Simply try and repeat that process."

It was not hard. Again, my viewpoint shifted until I was looking down upon the three of us from behind. It almost made me chuckle, for I felt like a child up to mischief. Garianne gave the briefest of looks back and I knew she had sensed me. How? I did not know. I was sure that I could not be detected. Was this what she had meant by abilities that others knew nothing of?

"Good, now take yourself outside the ship and keep alongside us," said Garianne.

I drifted up until I passed like a gust of wind through the exterior shell of the ship. I was now moving through hyperspace with Lom below me.

I heard Garianne's voice. "Now you need to sense Lom's course until it reaches the star that does not shine. You know the one."

I was already on my way and in moments I was there. If only there was a way to travel this quickly physically. Lom was many light years behind and would take hours to reach me.

The star that does not shine. That was not quite true but I knew Garianne was just being poetic. It shone alright, yet from outside the magnificent artificial shell, which encompassed the Galacien home system's sun, it could not really be seen. This super-sentient made construct was Galacien Prime.

I truly envied those who had witnessed its creation all those thousands of years ago. At the very height of the Golden Age the Galacien had stretched their potential to their wildest imaginations. Though only with the help of almost every known super-sentient in the galaxy, were they able to create something that would go far beyond even their advanced technology, allowing them to achieve what any similar civilization would deem to be impossible. Here was enough space for the Galacien to accommodate the entire population of the GCW, or conduct experiments on a truly epic scale. On Galacien Prime dreams could be made real.

I allowed myself a moment to stare in wonder and awe at the simple majesty of its existence in our universe, and I felt blessed at having had the opportunity to see such an artefact. I knew I would have to consult my implant regarding the construction of this artificial shell which harnessed the power of a star. Many questions remained unanswered as to how they had managed such a feat. I wondered, for instance, where they got all the stellar material with which to build it from, as I calculated there would not even be enough material in the home system to create a shell thick enough. I suspected that the answer lay in the abilities of those long-lost super-sentients.

Dim points of light and dark shades of colour were its only features from this distance. The lights I surmised must be openings, though pin-pricks from here, were probably large enough to accommodate entire moons. It hung there as large as my fist even though I was still almost a light-hour away from its surface. Its habitable interior surface was millions of times the size of Earth's, and could easily fit the entire galaxy's population, into a mere fraction of its area.

The Galacien home world itself orbited further out around the star. Since the creation of Galacien Prime, the Galacien's planet of origin had become a holy place. Not dedicated to any deity of course, it was now a quiet, natural and spiritual world. Some of its ancient past was cleverly preserved – like pieces in a giant museum spread across the planet. Archaic cities were unoccupied but maintained so they never fell into disrepair, purely so that they could be experienced by those visiting from Galacien Prime. The Galacien visited this place to remind themselves who they were and where they had come from, what they were now, and what they could become. It was a place for answers and sometimes a place to search for questions.

I moved back towards Galacien Prime now, it began to spread out before me, filling my view. Even though I was still over a million miles from its surface, it was like some unimaginable wall without end in every direction. I looked away and out again to the stars. There I could see ships, everywhere. Not only those which I sensed were part of everyday life, but the massing of many thousands of Galacien warships, some coming into dock with the immense stations that sat in orbit above Galacien Prime. Many were moving away, coalescing, and organising themselves into fleets. I considered them a moment, so much power, yet I knew it would not be enough to stop what was coming – the Nacuerians, their numbers without limit, a tireless unrelenting force, and the

Phalinon traitors, who were already here in the home system. There was no fighting yet, but the Nacuerians were close now and the Phalinon had decided to wait here for them, undoubtedly with their devices of chaos all prepared, unseen and undetected.

Garianne's voice was gone now, though I could still sense her intent. I knew that back on the ship she was telling me that there was someone here that I could trust, someone who could get a message to the right people without the Phalinon finding out.

I began moving above the surface of Galacien Prime searching for the station where I would find Garianne's confidant. Again I had that euphoric feeling that was almost intoxicating whenever I broke free from my physical self. I swam through space like a fish swimming through water, over and under the ships around me, awash with a total sense of freedom. Was this how Lom felt every day of his life? What a life.

Now I could clearly understand why some citizens of the Galacien chose to integrate their minds into the systems of such ships and become one themselves, choosing never to return to their previous forms. The Galacien, the Amelerians, Garianne, Lom, Min, and even Davern, whose memories resided here waiting to live again. I could not let them die, I could not let this catastrophe come to pass.

Chapter 27. Nemulous

Eventually I found the station I was looking for; its scale was staggering. It was larger and newer than most of the others I had seen on my journey. Despite being half the size of Earth's moon, it was a grain of sand in the desert when compared to Galacien Prime.

I paused. Unsure where to enter. Although I could pass through any part of the object, I still needed a starting point, some kind of orientation. I could not hear Garianne, but rather felt her instructions guiding me. I passed through the hull of the station and through several floors and walls into what I took to be the one called Nemulous' vast living space. It amused me to find myself moving purposefully through an unknown environment. This was his private space, yet it was larger than any town or city on Earth, with its multitude of large open spaces and staircases which seemed to sit unsupported in mid-air.

After a quick search, I sensed that Garianne wished me to move on having surmised that he was not here. Once again I followed her unseen guiding hand, moving quickly in a straight line through walls, corridors and rooms of varying sizes, inhabited by a multitude of creatures I had only seen previously through my implant. So much strangeness and unfamiliarity it was almost too much to take in.

I stopped, realising I was close now, and that I needed to move directly down. I dropped through several hundred floors and came to rest outside a large concourse leading to an elaborate, ornate arch. I sensed that this was a place where only beings of high authority were allowed to tread.

Despite being undetectable I could not help but move cautiously toward the archway, where I heard voices within. I passed the guards with more than a hint of trepidation; the irony that I was actually light years away aboard Lom, was not lost on me.

Inside, a few hundred sentient creatures sat or stood in circular rows, each row higher than the one in front. They sat in silence in the vast, dimly lit chamber, while holographic figures in the centre moved about and talked like actors on a stage. I noticed that one of the figures was Nemulous, yet in reality he sat several paces away from his holographic self. Using their implants they had created doppelgangers, and held debate with one another. Somewhere here was the system, which organised this communication system; otherwise the room could be full of copies arguing with and over each other. As I moved slowly towards Garianne's confidant I listened to what they said.

"The third wave has just made the jump to hyperspace and are 'sitting dark'," said a bulky grey creature, its features were tiny and hard to discern against its heavily patterned dark brown hide. It looked similar to one of Earth's crustaceans and its voice was a throaty whisper, yet its communication was clear.

The holographic representation of the one I had come for nodded. He was a tall, long-limbed, bipedal, blue-skinned being with a small mouth and eyes.

"We don't anticipate a problem," he remarked. "Although there will be casualties; the simulations we have from the Phalinon defence platforms (PDPs) are quite manageable for our forces."

I shook my head knowing that the simulations were wrong and the PDPs, would be turned against their own ships.

I saw the presence of the Phalinon, making sure everything went exactly to plan, keeping the Galacien painfully unaware of what was really happening, while they themselves gained every invaluable insight on strategy and contingency the Galacien had worked hard on.

I winced inwardly, wanting to break the maddening formality of the room and shout my accusation at the betrayers of all sentient life, but I could only watch and suffer.

You are the wild card in all of this, the unknown factor – I recollected Garianne's words. How could it be enough? How could I stop the combined Nacuerian-Phalinon force?

I calmed myself, and regained my composure.

The meeting was over; it seemed that everyone knew what they were doing. Despite not noticing the traitors amongst them, the Galacien worked together with admirable efficiency.

I waited until the one called Nemulous left and followed him silently through many corridors until finally he was alone in his home. I felt him give his implant a subtle command and a faint green glow drifted down his body from head to foot. He sighed and stretched his limbs, still seemingly wary as he walked to a large window which looked out into space, and below to Galacien Prime.

I shared his moment of contemplation looking out at the grand spectacle, at the treasure that could not be lost.

I attempted to communicate with him, a mere suggestion in his subconscious that he should shut down certain protocols in his implant, where it may be possible for the Phalinon to listen in.

It was done. Now I was confident we would not be heard.

Nemulous, if you can hear me, make no sign of it for the Galacien have been betrayed, and they may be monitoring you very closely. I projected my thoughts to him. *Do not use your implant to communicate, for I believe it is not safe; just think and I will hear you.*

And who might you be but a figment of a tired mind? thought Nemulous with the barest twitch of his head, as he continued gazing out amongst the stars.

I am Jonas. Garianne sent me.

You – we've been waiting for you, for so long... so very long. She's still alive then?

Yes.

You will never meet anyone quite like Cieshella in the entire galaxy, you know.

I can easily believe that.

It was curious he referred to Garianne by her first name; I could never recall anyone else having done so.

I can think of only two ways you might be doing this, might I ask which one you are using?

My metaphysical essence is standing not ten feet away from you, I said.

Ah, he replied in understanding, still showing no outward sign of the discussion taking place.

The Phalinon have betrayed you. Garianne and I have witnessed it first-hand.

Quickly recounting the events on the Phalinon archive. I sensed Nemulous being hit by each and every ramification. I waited while he moved over to his work area, where a drink materialised in his hand. He took a long, slow sip.

What can we do? Our strategy is already in motion. Any change now will surely make the Phalinon suspicious.

Nemulous fell into his chair. Deep in his eyes I could see that he had the look of someone who had already seen all his worst fears come to pass. He knew what the Phalinon betrayal meant; they were the creators of the defence platforms that encompassed the Galacien home system as well as supplying the apparent number of forces and other logistics pertaining to the Nacuerian invasion. They knew the Galacien strategy and had completely infiltrated its infrastructure; it was too late.

Nemulous again looked outside. *They even know our survival plans. In the event of the home system falling there are a number of contingency strategies to ensure the sentient species of this galaxy do not become extinct. I could think of nothing more despairing than that. If the Galacien system fell, there would be no respectable defensive force left to stop the Nacuerians. Every sentient being in known space would be hunted down until there would be nothing left.*

I know, I said, sharing his despair.

Does Garianne believe we have any chance?

Only one, I replied reluctantly. *That somehow I can save you.*

How?

I wish I knew. I have seen your records of the super-sentients of the past. None of them could have handled anything like this alone, even with their centuries of experience. How am I supposed to?

Nemulous gave a heavy sigh, the first external sign of what he was hearing, but not enough to give the enemy cause for concern.

If only we had more time. We could have prepared. It has been so long since we have encountered any new sentient species, not to mention a hostile one. The Galacien have become complacent. They have forgotten that the universe is in a constant state of flux and that everything changes. Now it seems we will pay the ultimate price for underestimating the unpredictable nature of existence. It seems that it is truly the end for the Galacien Conglomerate of Worlds.

Do not give in to despair. Garianne needs you to do something for her, I said. Her name seemed to bring him back from his melancholy state. *She needs you to secure as many ships as you can, ones not compromised by the Phalinon. There won't be many that have evaded their touch utterly so be careful. A few more will not make a difference, better that you are not discovered, than we have a few more extra ships. Have these ships ready and under your command on our arrival at the edge of the system.*

She does have a plan then?

I do not know. Perhaps. She just needs you to do this.

It will be done and you will have what you need.

I knew the Galacien were made of sterner, nobler stuff than humans. I both envied and admired them, yet I had uttered those words of encouragement more for my own benefit than for his.

And what of you? asked Nemulous, *Are you prepared for what lies ahead?*

I sensed something in him and, even in my slightly euphoric state, I felt my emotions boiling. *Do you find something amusing?*

I'm sorry. Only that you seek to lecture me about despair when I've seen things that would give you nightmares for the rest of your life – if you had nightmares that is.

Again I felt there was something not quite right here, something I was missing. *What kinds of things?*

Believe me, you wouldn't want to know. Suffice to say when the end came I was distraught, yet in some ways I was glad to be rid of it.

To be rid of what?

You mean Cieshella didn't tell you? She does have a bad habit of not volunteering information. I used to be just like you, Jonas, I used to be super-sentient.

He waited for a reply, yet there was none; I was stunned. After a moment he decided to continue.

Cieshella must have told you that you are the only known super-sentient being to exist for nearly two thousand years, yes?

Yes.

Those of us that came before systematically had ourselves copied over the centuries, so that when we eventually died, and we all did, we became, in every sense, ordinary Galacien citizens. Super-sentients live and die like everyone else, we just have extraordinarily long lifespans. When there were no more of us being born it was just a matter of time before the last of us died naturally and we would become extinct. Ever since then we live amongst the Galacien. We live for so long, moving to a new body like the Galacien do. We possess some interesting memories, yet none of our abilities.

I sensed great sadness in him as he appeared to go into a quiet reverence. As the moments went by, I decided to break the silence.

What could you do?

Still maintaining his outer demeanour, Nemulous suddenly changed, as if a magical fire had been ignited within him.

Like all of our kind I had many abilities. Quite often one particular talent is more prominent than the rest, and so it was with me. I was what they used to call a

239

multiversal teleporter – one of the best of my time. I could teleport mass and energy from one part of the multiverse to another almost instantaneously.

I considered the staggering implications of his statement for a moment.

What was it like? I whispered.

The Galacien call that period of history the 'Golden Age' and we were the reason. The things we accomplished, would normally be deemed impossible, but that was what it meant to be super-sentient – to achieve the impossible.

Nemulous was silent and I gave him time to remember. *Of course you've seen Galacien Prime, but there are many other things we created during that time. Some still exist to this day, others have been lost through... circumstance,* he continued.

Circumstance? What does that mean? The Galacien cannot simply forget where they leave their treasures.

Oh we know where they are. Unfortunately, we don't have access to them all anymore. You see some exist on worlds in very distant galaxies, while others exist in parallel universes. Without one who possesses abilities such as I used to have, we can no longer reach these places. It is a great pity there are certain artefacts which would have been very useful for our current predicament; artefacts wondrous and terrifying.

What are those other universes like? I asked, remembering briefly Lom's simulation room and its representation of the multiverse.

You don't have to look to other universes to experience a multitude of worlds, if that's what you're looking for.

I am aware of what is out there, I stated simply.

I'm sure your implant has informed you, although it is an altogether different matter to experience it for yourself. However, we digress. The multiverse: imagine, if you can, an infinite number of universes, each one barely insignificantly different to the next. In this room now is an infinite number of Jonas's having infinite variant conversations with myself.

It's hard to imagine being able to travel freely to any and all of these places.

Well, it's true, Nemulous said. *I have travelled and taken many others to such places.*

It seemed unbelievable that the being before me had had the ability to do such things, yet something told me that he spoke the truth. It was then that I felt Garianne tugging at my mind wishing me to return.

I would like to hear more, unfortunately I must go now. Be ready when we enter the system and good luck.

I think I'll need it, hopefully we'll survive this, Jonas, and we can talk some more.

Perhaps. I said.

I moved towards the wall making to leave, and suddenly stopped as a thought occurred. I slowly turned back.

How do you know that I don't have nightmares?

Excuse me?

I never told you that I do not dream. How did you know? I was becoming suspicious.

Nemulous smiled inwardly. *It's alright, Jonas. The answer is simple. You are super-sentient, you don't dream; none of us ever did.*

But I have, I thought.

He seemed surprised

In all your travels, all of your experiences, did you ever hear of the Kinsmen?

Nemulous paused for a moment, my fate hanging on his next word.

No, he replied eventually.

Hope abandoned me and once again I felt the full weight of the galaxy upon my shoulders. I made to leave, yet for the briefest of moments, I felt a connection with him, a part of something akin to family, lost in time.

Chapter 28. Conflict

As we drew closer to the Galacien home system I became ever more anxious. Garianne was running through scenarios with Lom's now working holographics, puzzling over anything that did not involve a one hundred per cent loss on our part. Had it really come to this? Was there no way to save even a fraction of the system's population? Was she considering the possibility of how to save billions, millions, or mere thousands now? I shuddered to think what was going through her mind?

On the command deck Garianne called everyone together, and opened up the ships communicator, to talk to the rest of Lom's crew.

"I'm very pleased to inform you all that Lom is back with us and is eager for battle. Jonas tells me he will now be able to have the last of his systems, including communications, fully operational by the time we hit the edge of the home system. You have all been looking to me, for it is my unenviable task to form a strategy to stop the invading Nacuerian-Phalinon force. I still believe that our only hope lies with Jonas."

Anger rose in me again, yet I kept my composure and spoke calmly.

"How do you think I can stop all of them?" I said, gesturing at the holographic of the approaching enemy fleet.

"I'm not saying you can… " she replied.

"Then you admit it?" I challenged in an icy tone, tone, matching her calmness and holding her gaze.

Min and the Amelerians looked at one another, not because of Garianne's admission as I initially thought but, as I looked at them, it dawned on me that no one ever challenged her in this manner.

"Every possible scenario we've simulated, ends with our annihilation. Only you as an outside force represent a possible exception to that outcome, no matter how small," she continued.

"What about the Kinsmen as an unknown external factor?"

"Do you really believe that they exist? Do you think they will appear and vanquish the enemy as if by magic?"

"They are out there, I know it."

"You are trusting in gods that do not exist. Trust in yourself instead. It's a terrifying thing to realise that your fate, not to mention that of so many others, is wholly in your hands and yours alone. However it can also be an empowering thing to know that it is you who controls your own destiny."

I felt trapped by the cold harsh truth of her words. All I could think was that if there truly was nothing else out there, then we were all going to die.

The time had come.

We were minutes from the edge of the Galacien home system when we heard the first incoming transmission. A representation of a Galacien appeared on the command deck.

"Amelerian ship, you are 'running dark' and are about to enter Galacien home system," said the Galacien suspiciously. "I'm sure you realise that we are on a status of highest alert here. State your identification and purpose immediately."

Even using Lom's cloaking field we could not hide from the Phalinon defence net.

"I identify myself as Lom of the Amelerians. My purpose is to help defend the Galacien home system."

I could see Lytpniuph and the other Amelerians were glad to hear their ship once more. Lytpniuph looked over to me and gave me a short nod of gratitude. An unexpected wave of emotion flowed over me and I respectfully returned the gesture, finally feeling an intellectual and emotional equal to these beings I respected so much.

"Captain Lytpniuph you know there is a vast invading Nacuerian force not far behind you?"

The Galacien was unaware of Garianne standing away to Lytpniuph's left, inconspicuously back and out of his field of view. She listened intently.

The Galacien looked away for a moment to something unseen to those of us here on the command deck.

"You have been requested to decelerate. Why haven't you?"

Lytpniuph looked to Garianne, who shook her head.

"I'm sorry I can't do that," he said.

"Drop out of hyperspace immediately or we will be forced to fire upon you."

It was then that I heard Garianne give the order over the private com. *Now Lom.* I felt something vibrate through the ship and a moment later something screamed. On the holographic representation a Phalinon fell into view lying immobile on the floor next to the stunned Galacien, who seemed now at a complete loss for words at this sudden dramatisation.

Lytpniuph stepped aside as Garianne now walked into the Galacien's view beckoning me to join her. I could not believe he could have looked any more stunned than he did at that moment.

"Garianne, we thought you were dead!" whispered the Galacien. He seemed unable to do anything but stare at her.

"We've got your priority-coded signal transmitting throughout the home system. Everyone should be able to hear you," said Lytpniuph.

I knew that when Lytpniuph said everyone, he meant it! All those billions of sentients stopping what they were doing as she appeared, through holographic projection, in cities, on ships, or superimposed on their vision. Even those asleep were suddenly woken from the slumber. They all saw or heard her, every last one of them. She had the undivided attention of hundreds of billions.

"This is Cieshella Garianne Phulum, supreme strategist for the Galacien Conglomerate of Worlds. The Phalinons have betrayed us all to the Nacuerians. We have just initiated a paraneurolamadan pulse resulting in the temporary incapacitation of every Phalinon in the home system. However, in a few moments they will have recovered and adapted from this unique form of attack, making it impossible for us to try anything like this again. When this happens they will attack us with all the resources at their disposal. Considering the fact that the enemy has been working amongst us for so long, assume the very worst. If you are in close proximity to any Phalinon, kill or incapacitate them now, by any means necessary. If this is not possible, remove yourselves from harm's way." The Galacien stood there in shock and everything seemed to stop for a moment "Move!"

Her last word seemed to be unnaturally loud it reverberated around the command deck. My heart quickened and I could feel adrenaline exploding through my body. I knew that those too stunned to move before had done so now.

"You have perhaps a few more minutes before the home system plunges into complete chaos. Be under no illusion this was the only option – this way, perhaps, there is still hope."

Garianne made a point of looking at me and I suddenly felt billions of eyes upon me, reminding me of my first experience in the simulation room. I held fast next to Garianne, attempting to convey an unbreakable resolve.

The com to the home system was off and Garianne signalled Lytpniuph to switch it over.

"Nemulous?" said Garianne.

"Cieshella," said Nemulous, appearing before us.

"Show me what you have."

Nemulous made a gesture and data sprang into the air before us.

"All awaiting your command," Nemulous stated.

With lightning speed Garianne used her implant to manipulate the holographics. "Those are your orders, go."

And just like that it was done.

I saw that Davern's name was on the manifest of one of those ships. Strange, I knew the man, yet he possessed no memories of me. He would be informed of our encounter before dying in the Amelerian system. But as far as he was concerned we had never met. The Galacien thought of themselves as immortal, yet parts of them died all the time; significant parts.

I saw that Nemulous's force was made up of capital ships, protector class SIBATs such as ours, as well as guardian-class SIBATs. These were relatively new for the Galacien and not derived from Phalinon technology. They had been around for a couple of hundred years and were basically similar to the standard SIBATs, yet almost ten times larger, and far more powerful. Like the standard SIBATs they housed only the sentient mind and could morph their shape into anything imaginable. I wondered how they would fare in a battle against the Nacuerians. Garianne had selected specific ships to join us while the rest attacked the Phalinon defence platforms having been made vulnerable by the paraneurolamadan pulse.

The command deck changed and we could see a vastly reduced representation of the entire home system. Using her implant, Garianne reviewed the battle, pulling up different views and analysing the attacks of thousands of Galacien vessels on a similar number of Phalinon defence platforms or PDPs. The Galacien struck from a distance, some using focused energy beams to quickly slice up the PDPs and others firing their smaller-yield world-destroyers.

In hyperspace we flickered passed the boundary where the PDPs were being wiped from existence in bright flares of light, like hundreds of dying suns. Then a moment later we felt something, a rumbling that echoed from normal space into hyperspace, shaking Lom.

The Phalinon were awake and were retaliating. Now we could see from the home system representation that the PDPs were doing what they were designed for and doing it very effectively. Both forces had weapons, destructive on a planetary scale; it was just a matter of who could survive the vicious onslaught.

As far as individual short-lived battles were concerned, the outcome depended on initial circumstances. Those PDPs that recuperated to find a Galacien world-destroyer moments from their hull, could do nothing but be obliterated. Others had more of a chance to defend themselves by desperately firing interceptor nullifier weapons and were only partly destroyed or incapacitated in the initial volley.

Almost half, though, were destroyed in the initial assault. The other PDPs were adequately able to defend themselves by the time any of Garianne's forces had a chance to reach them. It was then that the real battle began.

"Be ready to intercept their targets," ordered Garianne to her forces.

The PDPs were now firing projectiles through hyperspace at planets, moons, and habitats in an attempt to bombard the Galacien home system. Their targets encompassed the entire system. Their smart projectiles traversing through hyperspace, making it a matter of seconds rather than minutes or hours it would take in normal space, it would be extremely difficult for the Galacien interceptor weapons to destroy the Phalinon projectiles safely.

Any one of them could destroy a world or even threaten the existence of Galacien Prime. I could see how precariously fragile the situation was.

The ship shook again.

"They are going to get through soon; you cannot contain it," I said, staring at the trajectories of the projectiles through the home system, in normal and hyperspace.

"I know," Garianne whispered so only I could hear, the rest of the room being too busy to notice the exchange. I looked into her eyes and sensed the anguish "As I said before, I've always known it would come to this."

The ship's alarm sounded.

"Reports of rogue ships attacking our defences throughout the system," said Lytpniuph.

"We knew this would happen. Let's deal with this as best we can," said Garianne to Lytpniuph. Again without hesitation she adapted her strategy and moved her forces to accommodate the new threat.

I shook my head in frustration. I saw the Phalinon were getting through the Galacien defences to the planets and habitats. How much longer until they fell?

"They are getting through!" I repeated.

"Calm yourself, Jonas," said Garianne abruptly, glaring at me. I noticed that she was still giving orders through her implant while she advanced on me. "Are you now giving way to despair, after what you said to Nemulous? Practice what you preach, or are you still no better than all you despise, and nothing you aspire to." She quickly turned her back on me, committing her attention fully to the battle.

My mouth hung open.

I had come so far. After all I had learned, all she had taught me, when it mattered most, I panicked.

Was I fooling myself? When the darkness came I reacted like an animal, like those I left behind on Earth. I looked at the noble souls around me, the Amelerians, at Min and Garianne, not to mention Lom.

They would fight on for all they held dear, never to give in to despair or madness. I looked at the battle being played out on the command deck; the ships sacrificing themselves to protect the population of their comrades, home world, or Galacien Prime; to prevent yet another devastating weapon from getting through. A stunned awe came over me.

Could I do any less?

"They've hit crucial memory store facilities on Galacien Prime." said Lom.

The Amelerians looked at one another.

"The effect will be devastating," said Garianne

"What do you mean?" I asked.

"Can't you see it? We're vulnerable. Our apparent fearless warriors are now overcome. Do you see how they hesitate, how they fight so defensively? They're overwhelmed with the terrifying thought that this moment may be their last. "

"Humans are mortal, yet they are not numbed by fear like this."

"We are not used to being mortal. The Galacien don't know what it is to be truly reckless, to ultimately put their life on the line, with no hope of coming back. This change to mortality is too sudden," said Garianne shaking her head.

The ship shook violently.

"Shockwave from a Phalinon weapon," announced Lom. "I've dropped out of hyperspace. There was nothing I could do."

"Position," said Lytpniuph looking above the battle; another image was superimposed.

We all looked at the information scrolling down through the air.

"Three light seconds from home world," said Lom.

"Take us there Lom, best speed," commanded Garianne.

Galacien ships controlled by the Phalinon began jumping into normal space ahead of us so we had no choice but to turn away and avoid them. After a few moments allied ships joined us and were able to make a safe path for us to fly through.

Another abrupt jolt to the ship.

"A Phalinon weapon was able to get passed our ship's defences and detonate in relative close proximity," said Lom anticipating the obvious question and showing us on the holographics. Lom then switched to layouts of its own design "As you can see, it has destroyed many of my functions, and even though I have been able to compensate, this solution will only last a short time. I'm sorry but my crew life support functions will be gone in a matter of minutes."

"In that case our only option is to teleport to home world's surface. Can you make it, Lom?" said Garianne.

"I will make it," said Lom.

"Then start with the bulk of the crew and leave the command deck until last. I need to finish off here." Garianne turned her full attention to the holographics and her internal dialogue with her implant to appraise the Galacien of our situation and give them their final orders.

Garianne's eyes caught mine. "I'll be with you shortly."

Chapter 29. Dark Discovery

I felt a brief sensation of falling, although I could not be sure in which direction, before finding myself outside. It was dusk and I quickly lost my footing on top of the large sand dune on which I had suddenly materialised. Scrabbling to my feet I spat out sand from my mouth and looked up. The stars were not the only lights in the sky. It was obvious that there was a desperate battle being fought across the heavens but from down here I could hear nothing but the sound of nearby waves crashing to the shore.

As I stared impassively at the sky I felt something unnerving and definitely profound had changed. A new kind of dread filled me as I saw the backdrop of stars blinking out of existence.

The Nacuerians had finally arrived.

All of them.

Their numbers so staggeringly vast they were like black dust blotting out the starlight.

"Admiring the view?" asked a familiar voice behind me.

Garianne approached with an almost total lack of expression on her face.

I quickly looked at the still disappearing stars, and then back as she casually regarded the spectacle.

"Where are they?" I said quietly to myself, looking up at the battle being savagely played out.

"Where are who?"

"The Kinsmen. They exist, I know it. They can help us."

The seconds passed, the crashing waves seemingly indifferent to the end of it all.

"Where are they?" I repeated.

Garianne clutched my arm. "Jonas. It's up to us. It's up to you."

I looked at her and knew the sobering reality.

"They're dying out there, waiting for you to at least try and save them."

"How can I stop it?" I whispered.

"How could you manipulate a Nacuerian system or take control of a Phalinon archive? You had no idea you could do those things until you tried. You need to try now. Do something, for their sakes, for all of us, while there's still time. There is no alternative?"

"I am afraid," I admitted.

"Of course you are."

"I know you have been hiding something from me. What is it?"

"There is not enough time to tell you what I know. Like the house that must be built stone by stone your education on certain matters must be done slowly or not at all. If you truly wish to attain the knowledge that I possess, to know what I know, then you must stop them," she said, looking skyward as the last of the stars disappeared.

I followed her gaze. "The Kinsmen have not come." I said. "Perhaps they don't exist anymore, only that which they left behind long ago, a shadow, a memory. Is that what is to become of me, is that what we are all about to become? Perhaps not even that."

The Galacien and all its worlds were now on the brink of annihilation and only I had the smallest hope of stopping them.

I stood upon the beach where the waves broke calmly upon the sand and reached out my senses into the heavens. I could sense Lom above us, other Galacien ships trying desperately to help protect him, yet they were outnumbered.

In a blink of an eye I was there.

I witnessed a Galacien vessel destroyed as it moved itself in harm's way to protect Lom from a rogue ship's attack. Two other ships, too close to use world-destroyers on, moved in for the kill, when a Guardian SIBAT moved between them and abruptly destroyed itself, taking the two ships with it in a shockwave of energy.

Another rogue ship jumped in from hyperspace, right on top of Lom, immediately unleashing a focused energy beam against his shields.

In his weakened state, they held for only a moment.

I froze as I saw what happened to my friend as the shields were cut down; as my father was cut down. Another beam mercilessly sliced Lom clean in half – I could not help but see the image of my mother's throat being sliced open.

My metaphysical being stared, stunned, at the two halves of Lom floating apart from one another, dead in space. A raging fury within me built with such alien strength, I was not sure it was my own. I now beckoned all my inner demons to come and face me in my mind, but this time it was they that were blown to nothing, for they dare not face the fury which engulfed me.

Pure rage was not enough. I needed control. I had been trying to discipline my mind since leaving Earth. Mind was the key. I focused my will until it became stronger than steel, diamond, even the very forces that held matter together, and again I moved.

The universe around me slowed as I moved faster than light into the rogue ship which had killed Lom, even its stunningly quick systems seeming sluggish. I moved about making adjustments, leaving my lethal legacy. Seconds later it would be vaporised by its own energy source, but I would be long gone having entered many other enemy ships, making the same deadly adjustments. Their fates were sealed. I split off a small part of myself to try and save what was left of Lom, while the rest of me carried out the destruction of the thousands of rogue ships throughout the Galacien system.

I gradually became aware that I was being monitored. Though I exceeded their operational capacity, enough time had passed for the Phalinon to notice that something unusual was occurring in the Galacien home system. They had obviously been looking out for signs of me and now I could sense their awareness. Although they were now suspicious of my activities, they could not stop me or that which I had put in motion.

I intercepted and tracked the Phalinon monitoring device back to its origin – Galacien Prime. By the time they were aware, I was already in.

Yet inside this Phalinon system all seemed different. Everything was dead and empty, except, I sensed, something further inside. As I drew closer I sensed a giant globe of intricate gold light floating against an endless black void of deadness. It was a system unlike any other I had previously encountered. Its operational speed matched my own and was all too ready to out-pace me.

Jonas, as you may have guessed we have sacrificed many to become something far greater so that we may exceed even your accomplished abilities. In moments we will surpass you and disrupt your thought processes faster than you can repair them. We would have liked to have studied you further for your unique nature. Unfortunately, you have shown us that you are far too unpredictable for us to take such a risk. Goodbye Jonas.

It was upon me with a speed I feared would overwhelm me immediately, yet with all my conscious fury I fought against it and focused my will. This was only the beginning, however, the pace of its attack soon increased tenfold, then a hundredfold. Nothing in the Galacien's long history had speculated that thought at such a level was possible. I did not know myself how this was possible I only knew I had to match it.

I desperately pushed myself to keep up, finding I had to let go of all conscious thought and slip into a state of pure instinct.

I defended my mind from their attacks, knowing that to give even an inch, would mean a significant loss of my faculties and from there, the systematic deconstruction of my mind.

I had to forget everything: Garianne, Lom, Min, the Earth, the Galacien that I fought to protect, even my mother and father, everything that I was. I fought for only one thing, survival – to surpass that which sought to end my existence.

I became so immersed, that I lost my sense of self, falling faster and faster. I feared that this still would not be enough, that the Phalinon super-mind would soon destroy me.

It seemed inevitable.

I could not defeat this enemy; it was impossible, yet something echoed in my mind, from what now seemed another life – that to be super-sentient was to achieve the impossible.

The Phalinon continued to accelerate its attack yet I still kept pace with it.

Faculties which were not needed to defend my mind fell upon the Phalinon super-mind. At first they were of no consequence to it, like the first drops of rain, yet as less and less was needed for protection they soon began to build until they became a downpour and finally a deluge. The Phalinon super-mind's own attack had now stopped as it deftly used all its resources to halt its own demise.

It sensed it had reached the limits of its design and I had surpassed it. It could not keep up and with brutal efficiency, I first dismembered its major faculties and then ground its thought processes to dust. Had I any sense of emotion at that time, I might have felt something akin to pity for it, for I could fully sense its end. Only after, would I appreciate the dread it must have felt as its mind was stripped away until finally there was nothing left.

Actual seconds passed in that void, while I regained that sense of self and memory which I had temporarily lost. My mind still worked at a capacity I had never experienced before, as I contemplated many things, while the universe outside appeared frozen.

I knew I could not maintain this state for much longer and even for me time was short. In an instant I had left the dead Phalinon system behind and was heading out from Galacien Prime, straight towards the Nacuerians and into their systems. I passed their defences as if they were ethereal, and surveyed their systems landscape, recalling the first time I had experienced their world. I smiled; all that had seemed challenging then was now child's play. I forgot about any one system and focused on the Nacuerian super-system, noticing something different, something hidden, that I would not have noticed had I not been operating at this level.

I discovered something that gave me pause, information about the Nacuerians themselves, hidden in a way that no one would ever find.

Why?

I even felt that the Nacuerians themselves were not aware of this, but could that be?

I looked into the archaic evidence and discovered that the Nacuerians had once been a peaceful species, far more than humanity at this specific stage of their evolution. They began to explore space and spread out throughout a galaxy different to our own. One day they apparently discovered something terrible. The translation was difficult, yet my best interpretation was 'the adversary'. Those that first discovered it suffered torment in the most hideous ways imaginable, the others had their minds and bodies twisted and transformed beyond all recognition. Like blood-thirsty animals they existed now only to serve and wipe away life for their master. They brought this thing back to their colonies and finally to their home world, until, their entire species had been changed. For thousands of years they had brought genocide to all sentient life throughout their own galaxy. Nothing existed there except the Nacuerian species, their numbers vastly exceeding the GCW. This adversary had apparently instilled in them an unquenchable lust to destroy all sentient life and, after a time they decided to search it out in other galaxies, including ours.

I was filled with anger for what had been done to them, to their entire species. What if it had been the Galacien or my own species. Nobody deserved that.

They had been so peaceful, I had seen it. So much potential, what they could have been. What it had done to them was like a constant raping of their eternal souls… I could feel it, yet they had forgotten. All that was left was this memory lost in their system, here, for someone like me to find, to know the truth of what happened to them. I could not bear it – every second of their existence was like torture to who they were and what they had been.

I tried to think of a way to undo what had been done. They were hapless victims of that which was behind all of this; *it* had made them into its tools.

They had been such a noble species, taking pleasure and pride in everything they created and did. They took their time and enjoyed every moment of their lives, for they felt it to the core of their being, to be the most precious thing in the universe. Until the day of that fateful encounter.

Then it all changed.

What could I do? They were on the cusp of wiping out all life in the Galacien home system. I continued to think of a way out for all of us.

I was only delaying the inevitable. There was only one way to save them, to release them from their curse. I knew that if they were aware of what they had become, it would be what they wanted.

That made it a little easier. As I neared the end of my unenviable task, I became conscious that something in the super-system had changed. Like a billion faces slowly turning my way I could see they had become aware of me, their killer instinct coming to the fore. Like a force of nature they began to set themselves against me. Though slow-moving it was still a terrifying force to behold.

Yet they were too late, I already had their destruction in the palm of my hand. Sorrow threatened to overwhelm and paralyze me as I surveyed all that was before, remembering who they had been.

I am sorry, I whispered to their memory, and left.

Chapter 30. Turning Point

I awoke in my physical form lying on the sand, looking up at the black sky, the sound of the beating waves. Garianne stood there with all the patience of a statue. For a long time neither of us said a word until, as the light reached the Galacien home world, the stars came out again.

"I am alive," I whispered.

"For a moment you weren't. I'm surprised there's no physical trauma to your system, all things considered," said Garianne.

"You brought me back, thank you."

As I stood-up slowly on shaky legs, tears streaked silently down my face, falling upon the sand.

"It was necessary, Jonas," said Garianne "They would have been the end of us all."

She knew.

I could not reply, I merely looked across the ocean.

"No species should meet its end the way they did," I said.

"Didn't you make it as quick and painless as possible?"

"I did. The end I refer to was the one long ago, when that 'thing'," I said, spitting out the word in a snarl, "twisted and broke them from what they were, into what I had to destroy."

"Are there others?"

Still looking out across the waves I shook my head. "Not here, not in this galaxy. They've invaded others though."

I found it unbelievable that there were other galaxies out there which, right now, could be going through what we had. Would they be able to resist and claim a victory? I found it intriguing to think that the higher powers I sought, may still exist in other galaxies, and perhaps found the Nacuerians no more than a nuisance. I had looked for similar beings here to no avail; again, was this just wishful thinking on my part, looking for a higher power out there when I still had not learnt that I was looking in the wrong direction and always had been?

Or were these galaxies populated by species not as advanced as the Galacien. In which case, their sentient species could at this very moment face extinction. It may have already happened, for the adversary had set forth its minions many thousands of years ago. Who could tell what could have happened when considering such time scales?

"The 'thing' you spoke of…?" Enquired Garianne.

"The Adversary. If it truly exists, then it is out there somewhere."

"What do you know of it?"

It was Garianne asking the questions now and I could not deny a slight feeling of satisfaction at this turn of events.

"Not very much, for the Nacuerians themselves knew very little of it. However, it is a being possessing power seemingly without limit and it is only a matter of time until it realises it has failed in exterminating sentient life here."

"What do you think it will do?" asked Garianne.

"Perhaps create something far worse than the Nacuerians – to do what they could not…"

"…Or?"

"Come here itself and find out what happened. Finish what its creations began. We would not stand a chance." I said assuredly.

At last I looked straight into her eyes. This time I did not look away.

"How long have we got?" said Garianne her eyes narrowing slightly. Her mind already set to the impossible task at hand.

"A guess? Two thousand years, perhaps longer. I may be wrong, though."

Garianne looked thoughtful.

"Not long considering the forces at play here," I continued. "I do not believe even with two thousand years of progression and planning that the Galacien can match whatever a god can release upon us. I am sure it will take all possibilities into account and make sure that the next time is our last."

Garianne's keen eyes pierced mine, her mind already furiously at work. "Two thousand years you say. Let's see what we can come up with shall we?"

Of course the people of the GCW wanted to honour me in the greatest way possible. The word had spread quickly throughout the Galacien system and then, the rest of the galaxy of what had happened that day.

It was no secret that there was a super-sentient amongst them now, and their lives were never going to be quite the same knowing I was there. I think in a society where most of the universe's mysteries have been solved and it seems there are apparently no gods, a being such as myself must bring something a little magical to their lives.

Voices demanded rewards for me that ranged from the humble to the downright ridiculous, for it was I alone, they said, that had stood between them and extinction.

Rarely have I seen the citizens of the GCW bicker so much. Not as much as those they refer to as immature species, though some came close.

They discussed for days the matter of finding a super-sentient after so long, and the obvious debt they owed me. All the while I noticed Garianne unusually quiet in the background. When I caught her eye she would just smile knowingly.

After no unanimous decision could be reached, they finally asked me what I wanted.

I explained that I only wanted two things.

Chapter 31. Beginnings

Garianne, Min, and I stood upon the land of a new world, my world, previously uninhabited by sentient life until the moment we teleported to the surface. The sun dropping in the sky was bright, and the orange rocky ground still gave off plenty of heat from the day.

"I think this will suffice, don't you?" said Garianne.

I looked around slowly and bent down, plunging my hand into the ground, lifting out the dirt and rubbing it between my fingers, breathing in the air around me deeply.

"So much like Earth," I said looking around.

"Though with a population of only three of us at the moment," Garianne stated, "and with a surface area equal to that of Earth's. Is a whole world enough space for you?"

"I believe that will be more than enough, even for me." I could not help but smile a little. "And I will not be disturbed?"

"I will make sure of it personally. No one will be allowed near this planet. You will be contacted passively only if deemed absolutely necessary, and, of course, you may contact anyone in the GCW should you happen to become lonely."

"I will not."

It was Garianne's turn to smile.

"The Galacien do not like it of course. It is extravagant. Also they believe as the only super-sentient in existence you should devote yourself to the betterment of GCW. However they cannot deny you this one thing, they owe you too much. In fact they owe you everything."

"You knew this would happen," I said.

"Yes. I knew what you wanted. The Galacien, however, want you to work for them. You could be the key to a new golden age. But for what you have done there's no option but to provide you with that which you have always desired. Otherwise they risk becoming that which they deplore most."

"An immature species for trying to restrict my freedom, you mean?"

I considered Garianne a moment. Did I dare do what I felt had to be done? What had to be said? Even after everything I'd been through, how far I'd come, she still gave me pause.

Garianne and Min made as if to leave.

I wasn't finished with her yet though.

"Like metal upon the forge, the body and mind can be made stronger," I quoted like a challenge. Garianne stopped in her tracks and Min looked puzzled at the expectant look upon the other woman's face.

"That is what you said to me just before we left Earth," I said. My heart began to beat strong in my chest, feeling like it was rising up to my throat and into my head.

"What of it?" she replied approaching me slowly, like a dangerous predator closing on its prey. I wondered if I had made a terrible mistake, yet I had to hear what I suspected from her lips.

"Perhaps it would be better if we were alone," I said glancing at Min.

"Min can stay," said Garianne, not taking her eyes from mine, calm and controlled as ever. She seemed to make it look so easy, while my control was a nervous energy, held in check by my will alone. An extreme gulf of experience separated us.

Could she really mean that? Did she know what I was about to say?

"What is this about?" asked Min standing firm next to her mistress. She looked as beautiful and dutiful as ever, and had a slightly suspicious look in her eyes.

I nodded my head, in agreement. Min would hear it too then, but if any harm should come to her...

"They are calling me a saviour and a hero, something you have made me into. Though unfortunately for you, Garianne, I think you made me a little too well. For I have learned things about you too, things that no one else seems to have noticed."

"Such as?" said Garianne.

"I believe almost everything that has happened from our first meeting was planned to happen that way by you, including my intervention at the battle of the Amelerian system, the betrayal by the Phalinon, as well as our discovery by the Nacuerians while adrift in space."

"Jonas!" exclaimed Min. "How can you believe that Garianne would do such a thing, after everything she has done for you, for us. She has served the Galacien for thousands of years. She has proved yet again during this crisis both her loyalty and her abilities. Despite what you have done, who are you to accuse her of such things?"

"I do not question Garianne's abilities, Min. On the contrary, I believe she has superseded those around her." I focused my attention on Garianne. "I know what she has done. I want to know, why?"

"You know nothing," said Min, her human face flushing red. I could see the verbal assault about to erupt, when the gentlest touch to her shoulder tamed it to silence.

Garianne's eyes looked into Min's and confirmed the truth. "He knows enough. It is true my dear."

Min did not seem to comprehend what she had heard.

Garianne looked up into the sky and sighed. "I always knew there would be a danger you would discover my deeper strategies, Jonas, although given your nature it would only be a matter of time before you realised the truth."

"Garianne," interrupted Min carefully, "we're not being observed are we?"

"No."

Min knew that Garianne was divulging information she had kept from the rest of the Galacien and was not sure where it was going. She was unsure as to what Garianne had done exactly but was reassured to know no one else was listening.

Garianne continued. "As I've said before, I assessed the war and come to the conclusion long ago that in all possible scenarios the Galacien and then all sentient species throughout the galaxy would be wiped out by the Nacuerians. That is until we discovered a super-sentient on the immature, pre-spacefaring planet Earth. I told you before Jonas, that you were the new element in this war, a possible way out for us." Garianne's tone changed as she put her hand on Min's shoulder. "The thing was that Min was right as well when she said there is no way a single super-sentient could bring down the entire Nacuerian force, especially one with no experience and no training. During the Golden Age it took decades for a super-sentient to master their abilities. I knew for you to stand a chance I would have to push you hard and fast. There was no time for training. I had to throw you in at the deep end and hope that you would survive the experience."

"Fortunately, I learn very quickly."

"Unfortunately, with the Galacien's original plan, not quickly enough. So I decided to take things into my own hands and in a direction where others would not dare to go. Unknown to them, I was able to bring the Nacuerian ship down to Earth, to give you first contact experience. Even before we left Earth, you'd had your first encounter with them, all the time your conscious and more importantly your subconscious mind gathering information, learning. You remember the orientation lesson I gave you on the nature of reality?"

"How could I forget?" I replied.

"Any other being at your stage of evolution, even a super-sentient, would have gone mad from such an experience. I was testing you. That day I knew I could push your mind beyond what the Galacien would deem normal circumstances. These were not normal circumstances and so required very unorthodox tactics."

"So you manipulated events putting me in situations to push me to breaking point?" I said.

"Yes," said Garianne. "I was aware of the Nacuerian ambush, and made sure you would be cornered into taking personal action against them. You were quite predictable then. I'm glad to say, less so now. The traitor Sevine Anoor was always known to me and was another situation I manipulated where I made sure our only hope was you and your resources."

"This is madness," said Min. "We could have all died and you let that happen."

"I made sure it happened, Min, because it had to. It was the only way."

Min shook her head, her wide eyes staring at Garianne. "I don't believe it."

"Nevertheless, it is true. Jonas needed experience of outwitting Phalinon systems. We had no time for setting up simulations. He needed to believe his life and ours were at stake; it was these conditions that pushed his abilities beyond a capacity we have never seen before. It was what I had hoped for."

Min said nothing.

"Go on," I said.

I saw sadness in her eyes briefly, yet she masked it quickly as she continued. "I was growing confident that victory was a possibility. However, after seeing what you were capable of, they would never allow you to knowingly touch them again. I had to create a situation where you would be forced to break your limitations – transcend or die."

"Whilst we were adrift you arranged for us to be found," I said.

"Yes. A subtle signal in one of the SIBATs, unknown to the wearer, gave away our position to the nearest enemy ship."

Min looked up at the sky her teeth clenched, a very human gesture. "How could you? You could have told us."

"Everything depended on keeping the players unaware, especially Jonas. Anyone I told could have been a weak link in the strategy and my plan would not allow for that. The stakes were too high."

"And what if ten ships had turned up instead of only one?" said Min.

"Then Jonas would have had to stop ten ships instead of the one and he would have a better chance in the end because he had been pushed even harder."

"If he survived," said Min.

"If he survived," confirmed Garianne. "Min, it was the hard way for Jonas, or death for us all. What lay at the end wasn't going to give him a second chance, there wasn't anyone else to back him up when he felt the weight of the galaxy upon his splintered back, when death was trying to take the last gasps of his breath from him, he needed to not break, not him Min, anyone but him."

"There must have been a better way, yet you chose not to discuss this with anyone else. In your arrogance you chose a path which could have killed us all a hundred times over."

Garianne's eyes narrowed slightly.

"No, Min," I said. I faced them both now. "It was perfect, and though the galaxy shouts my name in gratitude, it should truly be hers."

"Stop there please," replied Garianne. "Don't praise me. When I think of the things I have done to you, even though we both know they were necessary, it still grieves me deeply for the harm they have caused you."

I was momentarily caught off guard by this insight into her emotional state.

"As you said it was necessary. Min, Garianne's plan is the only reason we are still able to have this conversation."

"My deepest apologies, Min. I hope that if you cannot forgive me today, then perhaps you will one day," said Garianne.

"Perhaps," Min said impassively. "But not today. If it's all the same with you, I'll be going now." She gave Garianne the briefest of glances, then myself one that seemed to last an age as her expression softened. I thought she was about to ask Garianne to leave us alone a moment. I almost said it myself, but I had made my choice. The path which lay before me wasn't the one I wanted, but the one I must walk. Min's expression hardened and she disappeared. All too suddenly I felt some small part of me gone too and the land seemed very large and empty around me as I looked at the spot where Min had stood.

"She was also a part of it, wasn't she?" I said.

"As you have realised, weakness of the mind would have been fatal. I needed to plant that idea as early as possible that your species is particularly irrational when it comes to emotional attachment. Min's presence in your life gave rise to this necessary insight sooner than any other approach."

"And yet, despite this insight, I still feel something for her," I admitted.

"However, despite this insight you can remain objective."

Garianne and I still had much to do and a great deal to discuss, but now was not the time.

This was the time for deception, patience, and preparation for what was to come. We both had our parts to play now. Like actors on the stage we would always seem to be something we were not. And though deep down it pained me, I would diligently act out my role, whilst all the while planning for what was coming.

"I think I will set up residence over there." I declared pointing to the top of a nearby hill.

"You could live in a palace of regal splendour beyond imagination," speculated Garianne.

"I could," I replied, a smile spreading across my face, "though I think something smaller will suffice."

"What do you need?" asked Garianne.

"The raw materials which my mother and father had to build their own home." I considered the site again. "It will take time, yet if I build it myself one step at a time, I think I will learn more that way. Don't you agree?"

She nodded slowly with a knowing look, of understanding passing between us.

Then she too, was gone.

I strode towards the hill knowing what I needed would be there waiting for me – to build, to begin again, to learn. Content for now, I was home.

Epilogue

It is over two thousand years since the Nacuerian-Galacien War, and I find myself growing ever restless knowing what is to come. I feel like an old man waiting for death to knock on his door, though to look at me you would think that I have only aged a decade, as far as a typical human is concerned. The Galacien are as immortal as ever, their citizens have died and recuperated many times over. I have become more and more alienated from them; a situation of my own making, for it is still my most ardent wish to be alone.

I watch them. I watch them all; the Galacien and those from whence I came, during those times when normal sentient creatures sleep and dream. That is when I watch, in my own special way, where the laws of space and time do not matter, where I cannot be seen or heard or detected by anything or anyone.

Well almost anyone.

More recently I do not like what I see, though I knew it would eventually come to this. The feeling that I have missed something permeates my being; I cannot shake it. We are not ready. I am not ready for what is coming. She said there would be time to plan, and at first I believed her, though now the time seems to have gone all too quickly and again I find that my only hope now lies in finding that which I believed for a long time doesnot exist – the Kinsmen.